The German pitched forward, falling across Indy's legs and continuing to stab at him with the knife. The blade grazed Indy's raised arm and slammed into the earth near his head. Indy dragged himself backward up the slope of the shell hole, his fingers raking the ground. The German was still sprawled across him, his left arm hugging Indy's legs. Indy unsheathed his knife and plunged it between the German's shoulder blades. The German arched his back like a swimmer performing a swan dive, his arms flailing at the knife buried in his back. Indy kicked at him, and the man rolled to the bottom of the crater, driving the knife through his back to emerge at his chest.

Indy fought for breath, shaking where he lay.

THE YOUNG INDIANA JONES CHRONICLES

Book One

The Mata Hari Affair

James Luceno

BALLANTINE BOOKS • NEW YORK

TM & Copyright © 1992 by Lucasfilm Ltd. All rights reserved.

All rights reserved under International and Pan-American Copyright Conventions. Published in the United States of America by Ballantine Books, a division of Random House, Inc., New York, and simultaneously in Canada by Random House of Canada Limited, Toronto.

This is a work of fiction. While Young Indiana Jones is portrayed as taking part in historical events and meeting real figures from history, many of the characters in the book as well as the situations and scenes described are inventions of the author's imagination. In addition, where real historical figures and events are described, the author has in some cases altered the chronology and historical facts for dramatic effect.

ISBN 0-345-38009-6

Manufactured in the United States of America

First Edition: July 1992

For "Jake," along for the ride

Acknowledgments

Thanks to Richard Ives for showing me the ropes of the Paris Métro; and to Richard, Christina, Ben, and my true love KA, for enduring a miserable winter day at Verdun. Thanks also to Owen Lock for thinking of me; Ellen Key Harris for her editorial savvy; George Lucas and Lucy Wilson, of LucasArts, for granting me the leeway to expand on the original teleplays; and Steve Massey, who eased me over several beginner's hurdles in WordPerfect 5.1.

Of the dozens of books consulted for period detail, I have leaned heavily on two: Georges Blond's *Verdun*, a compelling account of that horrific nine-month siege and countersiege; and Russell Warren Howe's *Mata Hari—The True Story*, which seems to be just that—especially in light of a plethora of discrepancies that plague the countless other biographies of the famed dancer and alleged spy. The point should be made, however, that Howe stakes no claim to his work being the last word on the remarkable Margaretha Geertruida Zelle.

PART I

Verdun

"One night in Paris will make up for all of this."
　　　　—remark attributed to
　　　　Napoleon upon his seeing
　　　　the dead at the Battle of
　　　　Wagram

1

His first mistake was in thinking there was some way around the madness; that by pursuing an oblique course he could escape the chaos along the Road, where every animate and inanimate thing was a potential target. His second mistake was in believing in shortcuts; that by pursuing that same oblique course he could arrive safely and with all dispatch at some fortified resting place. But there was danger in confusing the map with the reality. And now he had to find a way out of the hopeless mess he had gotten himself into.

The map—the oilskin rectangle he'd studied before leaving Second Army headquarters at the commandeered town hall in Souilly—had shown an alternate route to Fort Souville: a dirt track veering northeast from the perpetually clogged artery that fed the Verdun military zone from the south. What one had to do was make straight for Troyon, crossing the Meuse River there, then turn north, paralleling the French trench line until one arrived at Fort St. Michel. From Michel it was scarcely two kilometers to the forward command bunker at Souville, where he was to report to Colonel Barc, the battalion commander.

The alternate road wasn't suitable for the chain-driven Berliet trucks which twenty-four hours a day plied the Road, as the resupply link between Verdun and Bar-le-Duc was known. But the overland route had seemed made to order for a lone young courier on a sleek new French-made motorcycle.

Of course, one couldn't expect to encounter a flat stretch of land; nothing but lifeless terrain deformed by six months

3

of continual enemy artillery bombardment. Then there
would be the mud: a week of rain had left the yellow clay
as slick as ice and the shell holes filled a yard deep with
green-white water. But he had been prepared for all that.
What he hadn't counted on was the German aviator who had
spotted him and was even now closing at a low altitude from
the southwest . . .

The young courier's name was Indy Jones, born Henry
Jones in Princeton, New Jersey, the U.S. of A., on July 1,
1889. Henry, Junior, that was; or more often just plain Junior. A well-built seventeen-year-old with pensive good
looks, a thick thatch of light brown hair, and an inch-long
scar under his lower lip accidentally left there by the errant
crack of a lion tamer's whip. The sobriquet was short for Indiana and not, as some wanted to believe, independence.
Nor, as others thought, had he named himself for the 500-
mile auto race that was celebrating its fifth-year anniversary
back home. It was simply a case of Junior reinventing himself at an early age. His father had nothing but disdain for the
choice; he had always thought it more fit for the family dog.

Home had been much in Indiana's thoughts of late. But
home might as well have been a distant planet this rainy summer morning in northeastern France, with a German biplane
swooping in for the kill, and where a different sort of contest
was under way—one whose outcome would have grave im-
plications throughout the European theater of the Great War.

Indy thumbed the spark advance and gave the cycle's
throttle a full twist, urging the most from its 225-cc single-
cylinder engine. The bike bounded up out of a shallow shell
hole and down into the tenacious mud of a second, Indy's
legs outstretched for stabilizing effect. The rear end slid
precariously to the left and nearly out from underneath him,
but the drive wheel dug in at last and shot him forward. The
angry drone of the aeroplane's engine was loud in his ears,
and he wished he were wearing a tin hat instead of the
leather aviators' cap he thought looked so smart on him.

As the motorcycle slogged its way to the rim of the hole,
the German pilot loosed the fury of his cowl-mounted ma-

chine gun. Rounds zipped into the thick mud at Indy's back, stitching a geysering path up the side of the crater.

He cursed his luck and propelled the machine down into the muck of another pit and up the opposite slope, the cycle momentarily airborne as it topped the rim. As soon as the rear wheel touched the ground, he threw the machine to the left and began to weave a sinuous course through earthen mounds cut by water-filled furrows.

The dull clacking of the machine gun ceased as the biplane raced overhead and banked into a sweeping turn to the east, toward the German front. Indy craned his neck to track its flight, the fingers of his left hand wiping dollops of mud from his goggles. His upper lip curled in anger. This war would get him yet.

The aeroplane was a Fokker, a streamlined, dun-colored crate with black crosses painted on the tail section and the undersides of the wings, probably returning from a hunt for French planes. But that the pilot was alone, separated from his *jasta*, his hunting squadron, was an ill omen. For all Indy knew, it could be Fantomas in the cockpit—the name the French at Verdun had given to a particular German aviator with a reckless disregard for antiaircraft fire and a penchant for searching out solitary targets behind the Allied lines. Only a week earlier, Fantomas had gone after General Mangin's red Opel coupe as it was traveling between Souilly and the Verdun Citadel.

Some identified Fantomas with Manfred von Richthofen; others held that he was either Oswald Boelcke or Max Immelmann. But all agreed that the black-helmeted flier always appeared in the same machine: a biplane just like the one Indy's wide eyes were fixed on, equipped with twin Spandau machine guns and a powerful Le Rhone rotary engine salvaged from a downed French Voisin. Indy had seen photos of the trio of German aces in a British magazine. He especially remembered the Prussian, Boelcke, with his shaved head, thin lips, sculpted cheekbones—

And forty confirmed kills.

The Fokker was coming around, approaching from the

southeast this time, not more than one hundred feet above the hellish terrain of the Meuse's right bank. Here was what remained of pasture, field, and once-wooded hillside: the ruins of a bombed and fire-gutted château, its innards spilled across the land; the blackened mud-plastered trunks of savaged poplars and alders; the riddled earth turned inside out.

North, beyond the *chemin-de-fer* to Fort Tavannes, the land rose steeply, and crowning those misty heights—almost within spitting distance now—were the redoubts of St. Michel and Souville.

Shelter.

If Indy could only make it.

"Attaboy," he told the motorcycle, patting its petrol tank. "Show 'im what you can do. Beat him across the finish line. Just this once."

Indy could sense the Fokker over his shoulder even if he could no longer see it. The biplane was riding his tail, and it wouldn't be long before that Spandau was chewing up the ground once more. Without waiting for the inevitable, Indy turned his straight run into a slalom, leaning the cycle to one side then the other as an Alpine skier might wind his way down a mountainside. He threaded the cycle between shell holes whose rims touched each other in a succession of yawning indentations, accelerating at every opportunity. Shortly, he heard the distant thud of the machine gun, and right and left the tortured land spouted fragments of wet earth and shattered stone. Fantomas, whoever he was, veteran of countless aerial scuffles, was no stranger to a lone rider's evasive tactics.

Indy decided he had one card left to play: he could do the unexpected and stand on the bike's rear brake. If there was one thing the cycle could do, it was stop dead—something important for a machine capable of doing fifty-five miles per hour. The brake was actually a grooved drum attached to the spokes of the rear wheel, rotating in sync with it; when the brake pedal was depressed, a hard rubber pad pressed into the groove and brought the cycle to a speedy and efficient halt.

When that groove wasn't slathered in mud.

Indy put the weight of his left leg on the pedal, already

picturing how he was going to open the throttle, spin the cycle through a rooster-tailing semicircle, and send it accelerating straight under the German's nose. But instead of slowing, the cycle merely hurtled forward, entering into an uncontrollable slide when the brake pad finally found purchase in the groove.

Indy went down into the mud along with the bike, riding it for twenty yards, a plowing wedge of human and machine. When at last he managed to scramble to his feet, breeches torn and thigh-length leather jacket torqued, it was just in time to watch the first of the aviator's eighteen-pound bombs hit not fifty yards away. The shock wave rolled under him, knocking him off his feet. Dirt and mud and bits of rotten tree stump rained on him. The concussion from the second explosion left his ears ringing.

The Fokker lazed overhead and dipped into another turn. Indy lifted his face from the mud, pushed himself up on arms and knees, and crawled for the safety of a nearby rock overhang. The earth tugged at him as though desperate to enfold him. His arms plunged elbow-deep into the waterlogged ground; his legs felt absurdly heavy, like bolsters filled with lead shot. Halfway to the overhang he stopped to catch his breath and risk a look at the sky. Surely the German pilot had better things to do than waste his time on . . .

"Sonuva*bitch*!" Indy said to the low ceiling of clouds. The plane had completed its eastward turn and was commencing yet another run in his direction.

His eyes searched the blasted horizon. When you needed him, where was Archie? as the British tommies at the Somme had called antiaircraft fire—Archie being a clamorous character from a famed music hall song. Or if not AA, Indy thought, how about a dawn patrol Stork out of nearby Nancy?

Somebody.

Something!

Then he saw it, the answer to a prayer: a smudge of gray in the southern sky that gradually took shape as a solitary French biplane, a Nieuport Bébé. And the German must have seen it as well, because he was suddenly climbing out of his attack run. The Nieuport changed course and gave pursuit as a cautiously hopeful Indy scampered out from under his rock to raise a muddy fist in the air.

"That's it," he told the Fokker, "turn tail before you get yourself in a fair fight!"

Only the German wasn't fleeing for his own lines; the plane was describing a long arc to the west, signaling that it had accepted the Nieuport's challenge. Pushing the goggles up onto his forehead, Indy moved farther away from the outcropping for a clearer view of the sky, heedless of any danger now, a spectator in this war to end war. The same thing would happen even in the front-line trenches when two aeroplanes engaged: the machine guns would quiet, the snipers would put aside their scoped rifles, and for a moment, everyone would tip back their casques and gaze at the heavens.

Fantomas was the first to open fire; with one thousand rounds to the Frenchman's forty-seven, the German could well afford to. But at three hundred yards there wasn't much chance of hitting his target, and the pilot in the Nieuport had designs of his own. Seeking to make the most of the German's brief fixation on aiming the Spandau, the French flier powered gracefully through a loop and successfully positioned himself at the plywood tail of the heavier craft.

And all at once the dance of death had begun, the two planes each attempting to outmaneuver the other, climbing and diving, passing to one side then the other in elongated S-turns, continually searching for an opening, a crucial target—the gas tank or the pilot himself.

Watching, you could understand why the engagements were called dogfights.

Only two years earlier pilots had been exchanging shots with revolvers or rifles held to their shoulders while their legs gripped the joystick. À l'américaine, those one-on-one duels had been called, because they were considered to be the aerial equivalent of cowboy contests, Main Street shootouts. It wasn't thought sporting to engage an opponent who wasn't armed or to take him from the rear by surprise. Now, though, with the advent of propeller interrupts and machine guns synchronized to fire between the whirling blades of the airscrews, dogfights boiled down to aerobatic skill and pure guts.

Indy's jaw dropped in awe as the planes rolled and vied for superior position, guns chattering, engines misfiring—both in danger of stalling at the crest of poorly executed loops. And his mouth fell even wider when he realized that the pilot who'd come to his aid wasn't a member of de Rose's Storks—*Les Cigognes*—after all, but a volunteer flier with the Escadrille Américaine. The evidence was as clear as the insignia on the Nieuport's fuselage: the facial profile of a snarling Indian brave—a Sioux, Indy had been told—wearing a full war bonnet.

As if that wasn't enough, the pilot looked to be wearing a cowboy hat.

Indy doffed his leather cap and waved it over his head in a rousing show of support. As the Nieuport dropped beneath the Fokker, then accelerated into a sudden steep climb that left it upside down and firing from the German's overhead. The German was caught unawares and hit. His craft wobbled in flight, and yellow flames erupted from the cowling. It peeled away from the fight and banked east toward the trench line, trailing oily black smoke.

Indy threw the cap in the air and cheered. In response, or so it seemed, the Nieuport dove straight for the ground, pulling out only at the last minute to execute a series of triumphal rolls and loops. As he flew by, the pilot waved his cowboy hat at Indy; then he set off after his defeated opponent, perhaps to confirm the kill, perhaps to drop a wreath over the crash site in a show of respect.

On wobbly legs, Indy returned to the motorcycle to inspect it for damage. It was lying on its side near a steaming shell hole dug by one of the German's bombs; except for the twisted handlebars and a crumpled rear fender, the thing was intact. Indy swung a leg over the seat and stroked the petrol tank. "Good show."

He thumbed the compression release lever, pounced on the kick starter, and the engine thumped to life.

Another near miss.

But the machine, at least, would live to do another day's service.

2

The road into Fort Souville consisted of rough-hewn planks running side by side for almost a mile. Off to both sides of this wooden lane sat broken-down supply trucks and high-wheeled wagons sunk to their naves in the mud, their huge water barrels burst. The horses that had hauled some of the wagons had been left to rot where they fell, victim of strafing runs, shells, toxic gas, God knew what. The decomposing corpses had been bloated by the summer heat.

The stench of the front, of the war and the stinking evil that fueled it, had begun as far back as St. Michel. When the wind was wrong, the smell would hang like a pall over the woods and ravines of the river valley. Indy, motoring slowly along the planks on his bruised machine, had tied a kerchief around his lower face to keep out the smell of death and putrefaction, but he was sick to his stomach by the time he reached the moat that encircled the old concrete fort.

A constant barrage of artillery rounds had flattened the surrounding terrain, and even now the high land to the east was blossoming in orange-and-black explosions. The air roared, shrieked, and whistled with projectiles. There were no shell holes here, no rain-filled furrows; simply a treeless, gritty plateau of densely compacted earth from which the remains of the embattled redoubt rose like a jumble of stones.

Indy left the motorcycle to cool in the west tunnel entrance and followed a sublieutenant along a long corridor to Colonel Barc's bunker. Gaslight brightened the interior, but the place was cold and dank. Water dripped from cracked ceilings, puddling on the cement floors, and the reports of the artillery barrage reverberated from the mold-encrusted walls.

Indy had left the leather jacket and aviator cap behind with the bike and was now stripped down to English-made khakis, lace-up boots, and brown leather gaiters that buckled at the instep and below the knee. Green-and-yellow patches adorned the stand-up collar of his tunic, while two diagonal red lace bars on the cuffs indicated his corporal's rank in the Belgian army. Over his right shoulder was a leather message cylinder. Following his guide, Indy put on and straightened his peaked military side cap. From his waistband hung ammunition pouches and a holstered 7.65-caliber revolver.

The sublieutenant led Indy up a rampart and through a series of arched doorways to Barc's observation post, where the colonel himself had a field phone pressed to one ear.

"That's correct, Major," Barc was saying in French, loud enough to be heard over the explosions outside. "Not in a week, not in two days, but *tonight*. Tomorrow morning at the latest. And make no mistake about it, Major: If I have to send my men over the top without grenades, I will hold you personally responsible for each and every casualty we sustain."

The bunker was no more than twelve feet square, and yet it accommodated four bunks, a map table, two desks, a field kitchen, and several chairs. Narrow openings high along one wall overlooked the ruins of Fleury and other devastated sites to the north. A portion of the cement ceiling sagged and seemed to be in danger of collapsing entirely.

Barc handed the headset to his radioman, muttering, "Maybe if those idiots at Tavannes came out here and saw for themselves the condition we're in . . ." He turned and stormed away from the pedestal table that supported the boxy field telephone, noticing Indy for the first time.

Indy snapped his heels together and saluted. "Message, sir." He produced the sealed envelope from the message cylinder. "From staff command at Souilly."

Barc took the envelope but made no immediate move to open it. "Corporal, I expect you to disregard the comment I made about Tavannes."

Indy remained at full attention, eyes forward. "What comment was that, sir?"

Barc allowed a snort. "At ease, Corporal." He looked Indy up and down. "You're Belgian."

"Yes, sir."

Barc arched an eyebrow. "No French couriers back at Souilly?"

"All dead, sir."

As Indy had heard it, the French courier teams had been infiltrated by German double agents, and General Nivelle had put in a request for Belgians. In light of that, dead might have meant executed as opposed to killed in action.

The colonel's eyes had wandered away for a moment. "Ran into some mud on your way here, did you."

"I came by motorcycle, sir."

Barc snorted again. "Well, aren't we getting fancy."

The colonel was in his late thirties, Indy guessed—a veteran front-line rifle-battalion commander, with a weathered face and clipped mustachio. He wore an officers' *vareuse* with waistband and cross strap, pantaloons with yellow piping along the seam, and an 8-mm revolver in a black leather holster that dangled from a worn Sam Brown. A Burberry trench coat that had to be Barc's was hanging from a wooden coat rack.

"What's your name, Corporal?" he asked.

"Defense, sir," Indy told him. "Henri Defense."

His *nom de guerre*, or his alias at least—the one he had used when he and Remy Baudouin had enlisted in the Belgian army in London. Indy and Remy met in Mexico, where the Belgian had been serving in Pancho Villa's ragtag rebel army. Remy was somewhere in the Verdun trenches, though Indy had yet to locate him.

As to why Belgians were in France—the rumor about the couriers notwithstanding—one had only to comprehend that those in control of such things had deemed it essential that shoulder-to-shoulder comradeship be demonstrated up and down the Allied front. Consequently, one encountered French forces at the Ypres Salient in Belgium; English tommies, Australians, and Canadians at the Somme; Algerians, Moroccans, and Senegalese spread out along the line.

But as to why an American *posing* as a Belgian was at Verdun, one had to dig somewhat deeper. Not that Indy was the only American about, in any case. There were the volunteer fliers, the ambulance drivers, the Foreign Legionnaires . . .

"Well, Henri Defense," Barc was saying, "you can put away that well-creased side cap of yours." The colonel tossed him an Adrian helmet. "You're at the front now, soldier, and men have been known to get hurt out here."

Indy let the comment pass. He slid the side cap under the epaulet of his tunic and regarded the battle bowler. He had little taste for the things—they were heavy and uncomfortable, and they made it all the more difficult to scratch at the lice in what was left of your hair. Most front-line soldiers used them for anything but the dubious head protection they offered; as washbasins, bowls, chamber pots. Below the riveted reinforcing band of the helmet was the French "RF" insignia rather than the Belgian lion's head.

Barc saw him take note of the detailing and smiled in a patronizing way. "You'll excuse us if we're fresh out of Belgian helmets, Corporal."

Indy slipped into the tin hat and snugged the chin strap. "I'm proud to be wearing a French helmet, sir."

Barc muttered something unintelligible and turned his attention to the message. As he did, the artillery bombardment intensified; the fort shuddered on its fifty-year-old foundations, and earthen debris began to sift down through the ceiling joints, creating a brown haze in the room.

"Good God," Barc said after a brief coughing fit. His jaw was tensed and his face had lost color. "Not again." He swung to his radioman, instructing him to raise a Major Gaston on the set. The radioman, whose outsized helmet drooped low over his eyes, bent to the task, turning the radio's crank and shouting position requests into the headset.

"Hurry, damn it," Barc said, pacing like a cat.

But the radioman only shook his head. "It's no use, Colonel. Lines to the entire sector are down."

Barc looked imploringly at the ceiling and whirled on Indy. "God grant that you are as agile a runner as you are a motor courier, Corporal."

Indy motioned to himself all too casually. "Me, sir? Actually, I'm not. A runner, I mean. I'm not familiar with—"

"Don't trifle with me, Corporal Defense!"

Indy snapped to, flashing a grin that had opened many a door for him. "Begging the colonel's pardon, sir, but I've only been here a week, and I don't know the lay of the trenches. May the corporal suggest the use of a carrier pigeon?"

"A carr—" Barc regarded him in astonishment, then laughed madly. "A pigeon, Corporal?" He stepped to within two inches of Indy and pointed to the ceiling, as though to call his attention to the ferocity of the man-made storm outside. "Do you honestly believe that a pigeon could fly through *that*? Heavens, man, even the sparrows are boggled. They're nesting in the goddamned ground, do you understand?"

"The corporal understands, sir," Indy managed. "Perhaps a messenger dog."

Barc's bloodshot eyes glared at him. "All dead. *You* are my animal, Corporal."

"And proud to be one. *Sir!*"

Barc snatched a pad from the radio table and employed a newfangled fountain pen to scribble out a message. "The current salvo is ours," he told Indy at the same time. "Major Gaston's grenadiers have been ordered to advance on Fleury, and that advance must commence the moment our cannonade ceases." He sealed the message and straightened, turning to Indy with an inquisitive glance. "Have you been to the front before, Corporal?"

"In Flanders, sir. And at the Somme."

"Then you need have no concern about the lay of the trenches. One is like any other, Defense. From Belgium to Switzerland, they are all alike. You run forward until the

next step will place you in no-man's-land. Then you ask for
Major Gaston's *abri*." He shoved the message into Indy's
right hand. "Now, tuck that under your wing, boy, and you
fly like the wind."

Like any soldier sane enough to know his arse from his
elbow, Indy loathed the trenches. The trenches made you
feel that much closer to burial.

Better to think of them as roofless mine tunnels, he told
himself as he set off from Fort Souville. Yes, that was what
they were, mere tunnels six feet deep, with duckboard floor-
ing and sumps that were meant to manage the rains but
never did. All you had to do was disregard the fact that their
sides were heightened by parapets of sandbags, in which
machine gunners nested like deadly insects waiting for prey.
That, and the fact that outside the crumbling walls, rein-
forced here and there with timber, bundles of rushes, and
sheets of corrugated iron, snipers were waiting to put a
bullet between your eyes.

No one—whether at the Somme or Verdun—dug the
trenches in straight lines, for to do so would be to invite catastrophe: an easy enfilade of artillery fire that could wipe out
an entire company in minutes. But the French had a veritable
fascination for angles; even their *boyaux*, the communication
trenches that intersected the front line at right angles, zigged
and zagged every few yards, creating a crenelated line of
shallow bays. Verdun wasn't so much an overworked mine
as it was a labyrinth out of the Greek myths.

Except that the fabled minotaur was on the outside.

Hurrying Barc's message forward, dodging soldiers every few feet, Indy observed that the French favored station-
ing two sentries in each bay, where the Brits up north had
kept only one. Someone had once told him that there were
national styles to the trench lines; that where Germany's
were clean and efficient and England's were amateurish and
vague, France's were nasty and cynical—but you would
often catch a whiff of good cooking.

At intervals along the unfriendly side of the trench were

excavations that served as billets for company commanders and other officers. These dugouts—*abris*, as the French called them—were linked to the surface by short flights of earthen stairs. To the British they were simply funk holes, which said it better.

Elsewhere Indy hastened past delousing stations, casualty clearing stations, dressing stations; weather vanes and gas-alarm warning bells; soup carriers, bent double from the weight of the cans strapped to their backs; signposted bays that told him he had reached "Shrapnel Corner" or "Flamethrower Junction"; and latrines, marked with the French word for "toilet paper," as if anyone's nose needed to be reminded.

The trenches smelled of mud and waste and years of human misery. Here, at Verdun, most of them had been scooped out of the earth long before 1916, long before the mobilization. But it was the trenches that had kept Verdun from falling to the Germans in 1914, when their lightning-quick advance had brought them to within twenty-five miles of Paris.

Now the permanent trench line ran from Nieuport on the Belgian coast, four hundred miles south-southeast to Beuenevisin on the Swiss border; the upper forty held by Belgians, the next ninety by the British, and the remainder by the French. One mathematically minded tommy whom Indy had met in Ypres calculated the total trench miles—on both sides, German and Allies, including communication, approach, and departure trenches—at something close to twenty-five thousand miles.

Enough to circle the earth.

Which seemed incredible by itself—that mankind could master such a feat of engineering—until you remembered what the trenches were there for. And then you had to accept that human progress and creative evolution had suffered a terrible defeat since the turn of the century. That instead of looking to the skies as H. G. Wells, Henri Bergson, and other great thinkers would have had everyone do, mankind had been driven into the ground. Returned to savagery. That after thirty years of wondrous advances in science and technology, mankind had been reduced to huddling in the muck and formulating plans for global catastrophe. To subsisting at an insectile level. To eating, sleeping, drinking with the dead.

That same mathematically minded British soldier—one night when seemingly all the stars in the universe had conspired to show themselves—had wondered aloud to Indy if it wouldn't be possible to walk all the way from Belgium to Switzerland *without once ever setting foot above ground*. Or to launch a verbal message at one end of the front line and decipher it at the other.

And the one he had wanted to launch was: *When will it end?*

3

The communications trench debouched into a wider, front-line traverse that was stepped along its eastern wall to a height of five feet to facilitate rifle firing through narrow openings built into the sandbag parapets. Of the perhaps six hundred soldiers Indy sped past, only a handful manned the fire step, the daily dawn stand-to-arms come and gone. Save, of course, for the machine gunners in their sheltered perches, adding clatter to overall cacophony with their gas-operated Vickers and Lewis machines. Otherwise, the majority of the men sat with their backs to the fire step or lay sprawled about at the edge of the duckboards, wherever a parcel of dry ground was to be had.

The integrity of the trench had been violated in places by German heavy-artillery shells, but teams of sappers were busy repairing the damage.

In his haste, Indy careened through a jag in the trench and collided head-on with a pair of *brancardiers* who were carting a dead soldier from the scene of a recent shell strike. He apologized profusely, and then made use of the momentary lapse in momentum to inquire after Major Gaston's quarters. One of the stretcher-bearers pointed to a nearby funk hole.

Indy announced himself through the canvas drape that hung in the opening, and stepped down into a recess gouged out of the hillside's chalky substratum. The small room was roofed with a slab of rusted iron, and the walls were shored up with timber. The French sometimes leveled acres of woods to fortify their dugouts, though they were known to charge their British allies heavily for the privilege of doing likewise.

18

The *abri* was poorly lit and filled with eye-smarting smoke. There was just enough headroom to stand. Six sullen men were grouped around a glowing brazier, trying to dry out boots, socks, and unwound puttees—strips of cloth that were worn around the lower leg in lieu of actual gaiters. The dugout reeked of old socks and wet leather. Renderings of naked women had been charcoaled along the rear wall. Elsewhere, scattered about, were Linnemann entrenching tools, picks, spools of barbed wire, mauls, petrol tins of chlorinated water, haversacks, sniper panoplies, water bottles, enameled mugs, and tin pannikers.

Gaston, young but already hardened by experience, was easily identified by his uniform. Indy went over to him, saluting and displaying the written communiqué.

"Urgent from Colonel Barc, sir," he said, still winded from the run.

The major accepted the message with obvious reluctance and moved to a table littered with whiskey flasks, wine bottles, and empty Goldflake packets. In the scant light provided by a stub of candle, he read Barc's note. Indy heard him utter a sardonic laugh.

While his comrades regarded him with wary concern, Gaston buried his face in his hands and shook his head.

"It falls to us," Gaston said, coming to his feet. He crushed the message and hurled it toward the brazier. Then he turned to Indy as the men began struggling into boots and binding their calves. "Wait for me in the fire bay, Corporal. I may have need of you later."

Indy saluted and backed out of the dugout. The temperature had fallen, and the rain had returned. Several soldiers manning the fire step had trench coats thrown over their pack-laden shoulders. Everyone else seemed as immune to the rain as they were to the stink and the ceaseless screaming of the sky.

"Two-fifty," one veteran commented as a projectile roared overhead in the direction of the rear. The German batteries were concentrating on the supply lines just then, and no one in the trench seemed overly dismayed.

"Sounded more like an eighty-eight to me," a second soldier countered.

The first waved a filthy hand. "A mere cannon. The eighty-eights make a whirring sound. That one was more a roar."

A sudden chorus of hurrying shrieks culminated in a series of greenish yellow bursts north of the fire bay. Clots of earth and debris settled into the bay along with the rain. "One-oh-five shrapnel round," someone said. "You can bet your gold francs on that one."

Everyone agreed, even Indy.

The 105s had a definite shriek; unlike, say, the whistling sounds made by the *minnenwerfer*—the weapon that had come to be called the trench mortar. Both the British and the French had their own versions—the Stokes and the *crapouillots*.

Then there were the various cannons—the French quickfire Krupp 75s, the short-range Rimailhos, the old Banges. As well as the booming 150s and 210s, the ones the tommies called Jack Johnson, in honor of the American heavyweight prizefighter. And of course there were the whizzbangs, which you hardly heard at all, oftentimes until it was too late.

Indy's eyes scanned the soldiers in the fire bay. Some were old enough to have marched into battle to the sound of drums rather than cannons; others were fresh-faced kids no older than himself, with the look of shell shock in their eyes.

Just as Colonel Barc had said that one trench was much like any other, so too were frontline fighters, no matter their nationality. Bedraggled, disillusioned, hollowed by their experiences . . . The French regulars called themselves the *poilu*; no different than the British calling themselves tommies. Except that *poilu* apparently meant "the hairy ones," the whiskered manservants of war. They wore greatcoats, field khakis, puttees, and tin hats, and each carried a combat pack called a *barda*—a combination cartridge belt and harness, weighed down by a knapsack, canteen, ammo pouch, and Tissot gas mask in a metal container. When they talked about the *barda*, they called it a "bazaar" or a "bordello";

and they called the knapsack "Fido" because it had once been made of dog skin. Their ankle boots were clodhoppers, and each strip of the chevrons they displayed on the left sleeves of their blue shirts indicated six months of service in the army of France.

They used their bayonets to open tins of beef or as skewers for grilling sausages, and they scrawled the names of their girlfriends on their helmets. They shot at the Germans with 86.93 Lebels or Lee-Enfields or old breech-loading needle-fire rifles; and they mopped up in the trenches with the sabers that hung from their belts.

They slept when they could, fitfully at best, and they gradually adapted to the smell of death and decay. They grudgingly shared their space with lice and fat red slugs and the ever-present gray rats. They accepted the maggots and the swarms of blackflies and the mosquitoes and the sicknesses—the diarrhea, trench foot, influenza, cesspool jaundice. And they lived in mortal terror of snipers, mustard gas attacks, and orders to go over the top.

But most of all, they simply endured—for days, sometimes weeks at a stretch when there was nothing to do but sit and wait. They would stare in near disbelief at their reflections in the water that pooled in the trenches, and they would whisper lovingly to photos of their loved ones back home. They fashioned jewelry from scraps of exploded shell casing, and walking sticks from bits of ravaged tree. Anything to puncture a tedium relieved only by the dawn and dusk stand-tos, the fleeting glimpses of eerie sunrises and sunsets, the luxury of a "morning hate"—a quarter hour of undirected small-arms fire that could sometimes ease the tension stirred by days of foul weather.

Indy lapsed into despair as he contemplated the attack orders he had just delivered to Major Gaston. The strategy was all too familiar: days of artillery bombardment directed against a section of frontline trench would have driven the enemy deep into his bunkers. At the moment of cease-fire, the French would charge across no-man's-land in an effort to reach the abandoned trenches before the Germans could scramble from their holes and resume their firing positions. At the Somme, the contest had been dubbed "the race for the parapet." But who was Indy to break the news to everyone that things were about to change for the worse . . .

"I'll take mustard gas over shrapnel any day," one of the younger soldiers said during a pause in the shelling. The rain had slowed to a cold drizzle now. "It's the best way to go: quick and clean."

"You cackle like a rooster and your mouth foams pink," another argued.

"Don't tell me about gas," said a third, the projectile expert again. "I remember back when all we had were nose clips. We'd piss onto our hankies and hold them to our noses to cut the effect of the Germans' chlorine."

There were murmurs of amazement.

"I was at Ypres when the *boche* rolled five thousand gas cylinders across no-man's-land, and the wind blew it right back in their faces." He was an older soldier with a gray mustachio and a long scar on his face, and his recollection drew a short burst of laughter.

Boche meant German, but not when you heard a *poilu* say it; then the meaning was closer to criminal or monster. *Le boche . . . Le bon dieu boche.* The goddamned German.

Hans, to a Tommy. Hans or Jerry or Fritz—

All at once an alien voice rang out in the stillness. The laughter had somehow found its way across no-man's-land to a German listening post, and a *jäger* had emerged from his hole and responded to it.

"What did he say?" someone asked.

" 'Laugh now,' " Indy said without thinking. Two dozen faces turned to him, but no one seemed to question that a Belgian could understand the language of the enemy. "He said, 'Laugh now, there will be no tomorrow.' "

The shell expert cursed. "Five francs says that's the same *boche* who was singing the other day. The one who speaks French. He has some kind of megaphone." The soldier climbed onto the fire step and cupped his hands to his mouth. "No tomorrow for you, *boche*!" he shouted in

French. "We're going to send you and your *kronprinz* packing back to Berlin."

"Tell him we have a nice juicy pineapple for him," someone squatting at the base of the step suggested, flourishing one of his grenades.

"We have some nice juicy pineapples for you, *boche*!"

Everyone looked to Indy when the reply came in German.

"Uh, he says pineapple will go nicely with all their fresh sausage and sauerkraut."

At the mention of food, everyone became glum.

"Tell him that all that sauerkraut is what makes their gas so deadly."

The veteran smiled and relayed the comment. Then, before the artillery barrage began anew, laughter erupted in the German trench and rolled across no-man's-land.

"Do you think they really have fresh sausage over there?" a kid Indy's age asked in what amounted to a shout. You could practically see the young soldier's mouth watering.

"Fresh sausage and a lot more," a rifleman told him from his position on the step. "Their *stollen* are forty feet deep from what I hear. There are separate messes for officers and the *sturmtruppen*. And even the regulars have recessed bunk beds and water tanks with working taps. The rooms have writing tables and door bells, wallpaper and rugs, mirrors and furniture . . ."

Indy too had heard the rumors. But then it was also accepted in some quarters that the Germans could make it rain on demand and that they could direct the water straight into the allied trenches. More, that the enemy, all but invisible in his field gray uniform, wasn't entirely, well, *human*. His helmet was spiked like the head of a unicorn; his sandbags and barbed wire were "different," and his weapons—even his *bread*—were black.

"Stop your bellyaching about how the *boches* live and what they have to eat," a machine gunner yelled down from his fortified nest. They're on French land, that's all that matters. And it's French women who are selling themselves to them for a stinking loaf of their black bread.''

The gunner's rejoinder set everyone in the vicinity of Gaston's dugout on edge. Still embittered by the Prussian victories of 1870, many *poilu* viewed the battlefield as a kind of duelists' field of honor: a place to test one's hand, to prove oneself a man.

''We'll be coming for you, *boche*!'' a wiry grenadier screamed, although it was doubtful, given the fury of the artillery volleys from both camps, that he could be heard twenty yards away, let alone two hundred.

And a moment later one could have almost believed that some of those shells had pierced the low-hanging clouds, for the rain began to fall in sheets. Indy hunched his shoulders and hugged himself for warmth as the rain danced a maddening tattoo on the tin hat and instantly soaked him to his skin.

''If it keeps up like this, it'll be the navy who finishes this war!'' someone called out.

''Better the navy than us,'' the soldier next to Indy answered. ''I'm not spilling any more of my claret for them. Not for Joffre, not for Pétain, and sure as hell not for Nivelle!''

''You're all fools if you think this war is meant to be won by *anyone*!'' the shell expert said. ''You think the munitions makers and profiteers want to see it end? Or their wives and mistresses who shop in the Faubourg St-Honoré? You think the conscription dodgers want to see us return to threaten their soft jobs in the factories? You think the Ministry of War officials care about us? Or the newspapermen?''

He raised his face to the sky for a mouthful of rain and spewed it toward the now submerged duckboard floor of the fire trench. ''War is a *machine*, you stupid sons of bitches! And machines don't break down when they're being tended to night and day by trained hands. We're the oil, comrades. It's our blood that keeps the moving parts lubricated.''

Indy thought of a British soldier he had met at the Somme, a soldier-poet named Siegfried Sassoon, whose sense of the Great War was no different from the Frenchman's. *The makers of arms*, Indy could almost hear the dark-haired Sassoon saying. *They have every desire to keep this war going. Their profits have tripled since the damn conflict began.*

Would it never end? he asked himself. Was it possible the war could drag on and on, encompassing the whole world in the end, like something out of an H. G. Wells novel? More and more, as the war entered its third year, he had been hearing the same question posed: "When will it end?"

And more and more the soldiers at the front line had begun to draw a distinction between friend and enemy that had less to do with France and Germany, *poilu et boche*, than between "us and them": front and rear, soldier and profiteer, friend and foe, man and machine.

Indy was growing uncomfortably conscious of his clean-shaven face and longish louse-free hair, the comparative neatness of his uniform, though soaked and muddied. Just now he was one of *them*.

And, indeed, several of the soldiers were regarding him in an unsettling way.

He was about to say something to dispel whatever misgivings they might be harboring—to describe in part the horrors he had witnessed firsthand in the north, and again behind enemy lines—when Major Gaston suddenly appeared from his dugout, his sidearm holster unsnapped and a whistle vised in his teeth.

He blew long and hard on the whistle and gestured to the eastern parapet of the trench. "Stand-to, men," he shouted above the diminishing tumult of the French cannonade. "We're going to retake Fleury. Prepare to go over the top!"

4

The French artillery salvo was abating, but in the fire trench
soldiers were scurrying about like ants in a frenzy. Some of
Gaston's platoon commanders were marching to and fro,
slapping sheathed sabers against thighs, shouting orders to
fix bayonets and stand-to on the fire step. Others were taking head counts to ascertain that everyone had emerged
from their holes in the ground.

Gaston himself had ascended a wooden ladder to the top
of the sandbag parapet and was exclaiming into the rain:
"We can do it, men. We can beat the *boche* back and take
what was taken from us. Our foes will be vanquished by the
gallantry of our charge, and our valor will ensure the spir-
itual peace of our fallen comrades."

Indy found that despite what he had experienced in the
north, he could still be stirred by the rhetoric of the Cause.
His heart pounded in his chest, his limbs trembled, and his
mouth went bone dry—even though Major Gaston had ordered him to remain behind and await a report from the field,
which he was then to run back to Barc at the Souville fortress.

"Remember your training, men," Gaston continued.
"Those of you who are going out for the first time, keep
low, bend as close as you can to the ground and move
forward. This isn't a march, so don't treat it like one by
presenting the *boche* with an easy target. Follow my example, and listen for the whistle. We move on one trill, we
stop on two." He paused to gaze down in both directions on
his rain-soaked line of grenadiers. "To the rest of you,
privates and noncoms, render what assistance you can, but

keep everyone moving. Our guns have given the Germans a good pounding, and we have the added blessing of the rain. With God's help, we'll drive them out of Fleury, drive them out of Douaumont, drive them out of France!''

While some of the regulars were raising rifles and bayonets in a cheer, a black-haired soldier of nineteen or so snaked through the throng to Indy's side. He was pale and gaunt, surely ill with influenza or trench fever. "Take this, please," he said, forcing a small wooden box into Indy's hands.

Indy stared at it in bafflement. "What is it?"

The soldier's quivering fingers went to the brass clasp that secured the lid, and the box sprang open. "Personal things, you see. Some photographs and some letters. And a ring I bought in Vittel untouched by the fighting." Vittel was a resort seventy-five miles south of Verdun. "My wife's name is Nicole. She lives in Paris on the rue Jacob near Saint Germain des-Prés. The address is there, on the top letter. Take it to her. Please."

Once more, he urged the box on Indy.

"I'll keep it for you," Indy told him, summoning a weak smile from his depths. "You'll be back."

The young soldier shook his head. "I won't be back. I'm a dead man." His dark eyes were filled with terror as he hurried off.

The shrill sound of Gaston's whistle cut the air. *"Vive la nation!"* the major shouted from the parapet. *"Vive la République!"*

The soldiers rallied to the call and charged over the top like sportsmen rushing onto a playing field. And for several moments Indy heard the sound of their call and only that: the crazed shout of nearly one thousand men, loud enough to silence the unrelenting bombardment of the rain.

Then the enemy fusillade began.

First the steady clack and chatter of the German Maxim machine guns; then the snap and crack of individual rifles. The French machine gunners responded with all they could muster, fingers wedded to triggers, free fists tapping at the butts of the weapons to lay down continuous arcs of cover fire for the advancing grenadiers. Sure hands were quick to replace the expended drum-type magazines. Spent shell casings fountained into the air. The gun barrels sizzled and smoked in the rain.

German rounds thudded into the sandbags and streaked overhead in sibilant passing. Indy heard the echoing reports of hand-tossed grenades, the booming detonations of dynamite at the wire. He didn't have to witness the charge to know its sights and sounds and smells. The explosions, the cordite, the flashes of orange light brought the Somme back to life for him. And yet far from sending him racing for shelter, it was all he could do to keep himself planted in the trench. Not fifty feet from him men were risking their lives for the Grand Cause, and here he was, a mere messenger boy for generals who rarely forsook the comforts of the rear.

Unable to contain his mounting anguish, Indy leaped the channel of water that now flowed through the trench and scrambled up onto the fire step near the spot where Major Gaston had gone over the top. There was a field periscope there, an aged device, rusty but still serviceable.

When he peered into the twin eyepieces, however, Indy saw nothing but diffuse light, and he assumed for a moment that the lenses were hopelessly fogged. Then he understood that the terrain into which the soldiers were advancing was blanketed in smoke, lying in striations of red, black, and yellow across the battered ground.

Indy swiveled the scope left and right, searching for signs of movement, some indication of how the charge was progressing. Where the battle shroud had thinned he could see clear to the thickets of barbed wire, past mounds of upheaved earth, and here and there an arm or a leg protruding from over the rim of a smoking shell hole.

Beyond the wire, he could hear concussive sounds and the animal cries of wounded men.

Disregarding Gaston's orders, he abandoned the periscope and clambered up the parapet, placing the young soldier's ornate box of photographs and letters in a protected spot. Keeping his head low, he drew his Browning revolver and eased himself over the top, down into the malodorous sludge of no-man's-land. Ahead of him the comingling of mist and smoke was a howling translucent ether, illuminated from behind by bursts of intense yellow and silver white. But he hadn't bellied more than ten yards from the trench when he detected a change in the timbre of the battle; and when he looked, squinting into the veil, he was finally able to discern the shapes of running men.

But those shapes were running *toward* him.

Emerging rifleless from the mist. Emerging with helmeted heads lowered and hands clawing at the earth. Emerging on two legs, on all fours, crawling, screaming, stumbling, limping. Slowed by the rain and the mud and their bulky clothes and the cumbersome loads hitched to their backs. Slowed by the glue ten thousand footfalls had made of the ground. And greatly reduced in numbers—by half at least, Indy calculated.

The charge had disintegrated short of the German wire. But the horror was far from over. Men were still dropping by the half dozen, cut down from behind by enemy fire. Indy spied the young soldier fall not fifty feet from him. Shot in both legs, the soldier tried in vain to stand, only to be shot again and sent tumbling into a crater.

"Come on, fella, you can make it!" Indy shouted.

A second soldier went to the aid of the downed one, laying aside his weapon and heaving the young man up onto broad shoulders. But he, too, was quickly brought down, collapsing in a heap into the same crater.

And suddenly Indy was up and running, bent at the waist and conscious of little more than the need to arrive at the shell hole the two had disappeared into. He rolled down into a furrow choked with corpses; rolled down into another where the water pooled at the bottom swirled red with blood. Then at last he reached the hole where the two had fallen.

The soldiers were bound together in a macabre interlocking of limbs, the younger one obviously dead from a round that had torn a gaping hole in his neck. But the other man was alive—bleeding profusely from both thighs, but alive.

"I'll carry you back," Indy told him.

But the soldier only looked through him and tightened his hold on his comrade.

Indy pried at the man's muddy fingers. "Let go of him. He's dead. I can carry you in."

The soldier shook him off. "Carry yourself in. I'm not going back without him."

"Did you hear what I said? He's dead. You can't do anything but get yourself killed. Now, give me your arm."

And the soldier did, but not quite as Indy expected. The wounded man swung a blockish fist that caught him square on the chin, sending him sprawling to the opposite wall of the crater. He hit the slope backward and slid down into two feet of brown water. When he next looked, shaking his head and spitting water, the soldier had tugged his comrade into a sitting position and was supporting his lolling head with a hand.

"You see, he's not dead," the grenadier told Indy. "Go ahead, Emile, tell him you're not dead. Tell him, Emile."

The soldier withdrew his support, and Emile pitched forward, somersaulting like a rag doll down into the pool. Seeing this, the grenadier lifted his face and railed at the sky; then he fell backward against the crater wall, crying.

"Help me," he implored Indy. "God, help me."

Indy made use of the incline to maneuver the man over his shoulders in a fireman's carry. Then he struggled to his feet and staggered toward the French trench line.

5

Lunch was just ending at staff headquarters in the town hall of Souilly when word was received of the failure to retake Fleury. The news did not sit well with General Robert Nivelle, recently appointed commander of the Second Army. In fact, Nivelle was so distressed to learn of the rout of Gaston's grenadiers that he ate scarcely a mouthful of his creamy dessert.

"Leave it to a Belgian to deliver bad news," Nivelle's adjutant had said. Indy had ridden the message in from the front.

"Three hundred dead, twice that number wounded," Nivelle was saying now, pacing the length of a plush Oriental carpet. "And for all their losses they didn't retake a foot of ground." At sixty, Nivelle was rheumy-eyed and balding, but he had the energy and tensile cunning of a much younger man.

"The Germans are deeply entrenched along that front, Robert," General Charles Mangin thought to point out. "That's why I suggested concentrating our attack on Froideterre."

Mangin was seated at the Louis Quinze table on which lunch had been served. The napkins were fine cloth, and the utensils were silver. He was a small man, four years Nivelle's junior, with a broad face and large ears. A dark mustachio curled around the edges of his mouth.

The two generals were similarly attired in horizon blue service dress and leather knee boots. The uniforms were not as glamourous as those favored during the Boer War at the turn of the century, or even as gallantly cut as those worn two years earlier when the French troops had marched into combat in blue hammer-tail coats and red trousers. Even so, the command tunics were adorned with the requisite oak-leaf clusters and stylish braid—and Mangin was affecting a wristwatch.

Nivelle's face had contorted perceptibly at the Fifth Infantry Division commander's comment about Froideterre. "Fleury is the gateway to Fort Douaumont, Charles. And Douaumont is the key to Verdun."

The centerpiece of Verdun's defensive fortifications, the once-thought-unassailable Douaumont, boasted concrete walls eight feet thick, a moat twenty-four feet deep, barbed-wire fields ninety feet wide. The fort had become Nivelle's bailiwick since his promotion. A mere four hundred yards in places from the French line, Douaumont had become the focal point of the Verdun counteroffensive. Its recapture would be the crowning achievement of a military career that had begun in the Ecole Polytechnique and the War College and had seen earlier peaks in Alsace, at Soissons, and at Quennevières.

Mangin nodded sagely. "*D'accord.* But General Pétain may take issue with our methods. And we will never gain his support by continuing to hurl men against a formidable line."

"If General Pétain had spent less time brooding over casualty lists and more time securing results, we could have pushed the Germans to the Rhine by now." Nivelle had ceased his pacing and was standing arms akimbo in the center of the rug. "This setback at Fleury is a prime example of not hurling *enough* men at the line."

Nivelle might have gone on had his adjutant not appeared at the door to announce the arrival of General Philippe Pétain himself. Pétain was expected, but his sudden presence in the building was more a cause for concern than celebration.

"The general requests that you meet with him in the briefing room," the adjutant added.

Nivelle and Mangin exchanged looks of surprise. "Doesn't he even wish to share a cognac beforehand?"

"The general submits that he has no interest in food or drink. He wishes the generals to be advised that the Grand Quartier Général is impatient for intelligence on the Verdun counteroffensive."

Mangin's thick fingers smoothed the ends of his black moustachio. "Well, I suppose we know where we stand."

He gestured graciously to the doorway, and Nivelle preceded him from the luxuriously appointed room. They hastened down the cold corridor leading to the stairway to the second floor, where a single gas lamp was burning on the landing.

General Pétain stood at one of the tall windows that overlooked the supply road to Verdun—the "conveyor belt," as it had been dubbed by G.H.Q. The mud had brought the traffic to a standstill, and just now hundreds of canvas-topped trucks sat idling in the rain. Pétain heard Nivelle and Mangin enter and turned from the view, acknowledging their salutes and accepting handshakes. He, too, wore the dress blue uniform, in addition to a heavily braided brimmed cap, the kepi. At his left breast hung the Legion of Honor and the Military Medal, and at his left shoulder the Fouragere of the Croix de Guerre.

He was tall and trim, with light blue eyes and a long gray mustachio that retained a trace of red. Born at Cauchy-a-la-Tour, Pas de Calais, in 1856, Pétain had been a pupil of the Dominican fathers of Arcueil, a graduate of the War College, and a lieutenant in the Chasseurs à Pied. He was unanimously regarded as a brilliant field officer, but his frankness had cost him many a promotion until the outbreak of the war. "Pétain is not enough of an intriguer," people were wont to say behind his back. By which they meant that he had a limited tolerance for politics and politicians.

His sturdy legs were encased not in leather boots but in knee socks such as a cyclist might wear. The socks bore a diagonal pattern that made them look almost like puttees. Eyeing the wool socks, Nivelle understood why Pétain had emerged as a kind of father figure for the frontline troops.

"I'm sorry you couldn't join us in a brandy, General," he said now. "It's an 1856 vintage."

"And what is it we would drink to?" Pétain asked.

"Why, war, of course. War raises a career soldier's spirits, does it not?"

Pétain swung briefly to the view of the Road with its myriad stalled vehicles. "The only thing that could raise my spirits is an end to this madness." He took a deep breath and removed his cap. "Today a group of new arrivals paraded past me on their way to the military zone. Green troops—our class of '16. Confident, filled with optimism, completely ignorant of what awaits them in the trenches. And as they offered their brisk salutes, I began to feel as though their eyes were raking me. Because I know that in three months those courageous smiles will have given way to terror. And I thought: If there is only some way to keep them out of it. If there is only some way to have them emerge from this war without having been robbed of their innocence, without having been returned to their home villages discouraged, hopeless, physically and spiritually exhausted by their ordeals."

Mangin and Nivelle regarded one another in pointed silence. Mangin's expression said, *I warned you, Robert.*

"Chief of Staff Joffre is anxious to learn of your plans," Pétain said suddenly. "So let us get on with it."

The three men gathered around a table piled high with situation reports and aerial photographs. Few would have guessed that the terrain revealed by the enlargements corresponded to anywhere on earth. The land appeared infected with smallpox; the trenches resembled threadlike scars.

Nivelle unrolled a large oilskin map and laid it over the litter of papers. He drew a pointer from the slash pocket of his tunic and indicated a red icon on the map.

"We are finalizing plans to coordinate an attack on Douaumont from the west. Thus far we have been busy clearing a path through Fleury and positions to the north and west. Once that has been achieved, our troops can storm the fort, breeching the counterscarps here and here, and chase the Germans from the casements along the west side."

Pétain looked at him askance. " 'Clear a path . . . chase the Germans from the casements' . . . You make it sound as though you are planting a garden and ridding the ground of bugs."

Nivelle nodded. "I find the analogy most appropriate."

"Save that these 'bugs,' General, bear deadly stingers." Pétain motioned to the area surrounding Nivelle's objective. "This entire sector is fortified with machine guns and within easy range of German artillery positions in the Hardaumont woods. Your own reports state as much."

"We've taken that into account," Mangin said. "We have recently moved twenty thousand support troops into the area."

Pétain looked from face to face. "What about our batteries? What do you have them doing?"

Nivelle answered. "Well, naturally we've been bombarding all positions around Fleury."

"Along with providing the infantry with rolling barrages," Mangin contributed.

Pétain shook his head vigorously. "You have to concentrate on the fort—on Douaumont itself." He jabbed a forefinger at the map. "These rolling barrages are accomplishing nothing. You must *saturate* the area. Pound it night and day."

"I disagree, General," Nivelle said. "Artillery fire can work to the opposite effect. It apprises the enemy of our intentions. They secrete themselves in their bunkers lying in wait, and surface unharmed. No, there is danger in planning too carefully. An attack requires surprise. *Punch*, one might call it."

"It's primarily a matter of having sufficient troops to accomplish the job," Mangin said.

Pétain glowered at him. "Solely when you insist on defining warfare in terms of trenches and infantry assaults. But, my God, don't you understand that you're fighting this war the way Julius Caesar or Napoleon would?"

Nivelle cleared his throat meaningfully. "Empires were built on the results of such tactics."

"Yes—but three men with a machine gun can stop a full battalion of foot troops. And you know this to be true."

Nivelle made a motion of dismissal. "You're talking like von Falkenhayn, General."

"Perhaps I am. But the Crown Prince's general is no fool. And we agree on one thing: the art of war is *movement*. Not trenches, and certainly not ill-considered charges into the face of roaring guns. Artillery is the solution."

The room fell silent for a moment; then Mangin spoke. "In the case of Fort Douaumont, our batteries must be content with a supportive role. The individual soldier is the key to success. However, one must know how to handle an army of men, General. That is, with *audacity*."

Pétain understood that the remark was aimed at him, and he studied Mangin for a long moment without comment. Mangin had fought the Sudanese on the Niger, the white burnuses at Nzala Adem in Morocco. He had been present at the evacuation of Fashoda and at the capture of Marrakesh. He was robust, courageous, a brilliant cavalryman—even at the Somme, where the Fifth Infantry Division had sustained heavy losses. And yet he refused to accept the truth about modern warfare: that mechanization was paramount.

Mangin thrived on the glamour of warfare. The man was a dandy, with his custom-tailored uniforms and his entourage of adjutants and aides—including the devoted Negro who had followed him from North Africa. He had more cars at his disposal than Joffre himself. Pétain thought about the posh decor of the room downstairs.

How he wished de Gaulle were still at Verdun; that he hadn't been captured during the seizure of Douaumont, where most of the Thirty-third Regiment of the First Battalion had fallen. Intelligence reports had it that de Gaulle was still imprisoned at Dusterstadt, in Bavaria, after numerous escape attempts—the latest of which was said to have involved a young Belgian corporal. De Gaulle and Mangin had been cut from the same mold in that both men were mavericks, full of bravado, sporting their numerous wounds like medals. But Charles would have grasped the need for artillery in the retaking of Douaumont.

Pétain had first gotten to know de Gaulle at Arras. He and Charles hadn't seen eye to eye on everything then—certainly not Philippe's womanizing or his love of gambling. But Charles had been as outspoken about Joffre as Pétain had, always confronting "Papa," as Joffre was known, on the importance of mechanization. Pétain missed him greatly, and had awarded him the *Croix de Chevalier de la Legion d'Honneur* in absentia.

"If batteries are your concern," Nivelle said, breaking the silence, "then at least secure us some that are capable of matching the Germans' howitzers. Even one thousand seventy-fives won't deliver the firepower you have in mind."

His tone was more patronizing than conciliatory. Nivelle knew what Pétain's response must be, and Pétain understood that he was being drawn into a trap.

"If the decision was mine, you'd have two four-hundred-millimeter mortars rolling this way tomorrow. But Joffre is procrastinating. Consequently, my hands are tied."

Nivelle shrugged his eyebrows. "Then so are mine. Hence, the need for troop reinforcements."

"If you could convince Joffre to accede to our request for four additional divisions—" Mangin started to say.

"Impossible," Pétain cut him off. "You'll receive two at best."

Nivelle blew out his breath. "We'll need one division of engineers to dig the departure trenches alone."

Pétain worked his jaw and held Nivelle's icy gaze. "You know that every available regiment is being sent to the Somme."

"Well, naturally," Nivelle said with calm assurance.

Only his eyes revealed how he relished his small victory.

Chief of Staff Joffre had chosen the Somme to be the site of France's major counteroffense, even though Verdun was taking the brunt of the German push. The writing had been on the wall six months earlier, but no one had paid attention.

The Germans pronounced it "Verdoon," and the town had long held a special fascination for them. Charlemagne, whom Germany regarded as one of its own, had decided on the symbol of his power—the two-headed eagle—at Verdun. Germany had actually held the city in 1792 and again in 1870. So Verdun basked in the prestigious glow of historical importance. There was a magic to the place, and by overrunning it a third time, Germany hoped to boost the morale of its war-weary troops while simultaneously undermining the confidence of the equally overtaxed French.

With its numerous outlying forts, Verdun had long been thought impregnable. Few saw cause for apprehension in the massing of German troops and materiel on the Meuse's eastern bank. So no new trenches were dug; no barbed wire was installed; no reinforcements or heavy cannons were sent in. Meanwhile, the Germans were digging in for a long stay. Walther Rathenau was keeping the railroads working and the ammunition flowing. Verdun was where Germany would "bleed France white," as von Falkenhayn had said. Where, as another German statesman had it, a suction pump would be applied to the body of France that would "gradually but steadily drain the strength from its half-open veins."

When the attack was finally launched on February 21, 1916, five German armies were thrown against the area's then meager defenses. The railroads were cut off, and one by one the forts fell: Hardaumont, Vaux, Douaumont. Hundreds of thousands of men had died in the months since, and half-a-dozen villages had been wiped from the face of the earth.

When Pétain had come to Verdun the previous March, a sense of defeatism was already creeping in. There were grumblings about the never-ending war, the soft life of the rear; and there were desertions and mutinies, looting and pillaging of villages.

But rather than move for a counterstrike, the French High Command at Chantilly instead classified Verdun as a holding operation, a local objective. *Ils ne passeront pas* became the rallying cry: They shall not pass. Pétain had been ordered to wear the Germans down; it was a strategy that was costing France the lives of three thousand men every day.

And now suddenly President Poincaré wanted Verdun "resolved." For the morale of France. He wanted results from Joffre, and Joffre in turn was demanding them of Pétain, whom he had accused of equivocating. The remark had struck Pétain as a blow, and it had strongly influenced his decision to assume command of the Central Armies Group and hand over command of the Second to Nivelle. Nivelle, whose aggressive approach had won him such favor among the High Command.

"Speaking of mechanization, General," Mangin said from the window, "is it true that the British plan to debut a land battleship at the Somme?"

Pétain nodded, plainly distracted. "They're calling it a 'tank.' Its introduction will change the face of the war."

Nivelle scoffed at the idea. He had moved away from the map and was sitting stiffly in a one-hundred-year-old armchair on the far side of the briefing room. "As much was said about the machine gun, and look at the stalemate we've been facing for two years."

"That stalemate could be broken if you would reconsider the priorities," Pétain told him. "I urge you, both of you, to rely on the guns you have at your disposal. Pin the Germans in their bunkers. Drive them mad with cannonade. Flatten their trench lines. Then send in our infantry."

Nivelle made a fatigued sound. "I'm sorry to disagree, General. I would have liked to have had your support on this. But we are going ahead with the counteroffensive as planned."

"If you could hear me out, General," Mangin said, returning to the map. "Here, poised to strike against Thiaumont, are two battalions of the Sixty-third, supported on the north by the One hundred sixth Light Infantry. Here, the Nineteenth Chasseurs, in the Fontaines Ravine and the Vaux-Chapitre woods. At La Voux-Réginer, the One hundred seventy-first Infantry. And massed against the whole of the Fleury-Douaumont front—a mile of trench line—the

One hundred twenty-ninth and Three hundred fortieth Infantry Divisions.''

Pétain snorted derisively. ''A battle plan is easy to concoct in the comfort of this building, with its carpets and draperies and paintings worthy of the Louvre. But it is quite another thing for the men in trenches to carry it out.''

''Not if they follow orders and resist the urge to flee at the first show of resistance,'' Nivelle said.

''They flee,'' Pétain countered, ''because they see no glory in being used as cannon fodder. They flee because they know they can't count on us to reinforce their positions. They flee, General, because men will always flee from sure death—even when sure death is backed by words of high moral purpose.'' He shook his head. ''An attack of such magnitude must be planned down to the last detail.'' He looked to Mangin. ''You know this, Robert. And I insist upon it.''

''*You* insist?'' Nivelle rose out of the chair and approached the table.

Pétain held his ground. ''As commander of the Central Armies, I insist, yes.''

Nivelle narrowed his eyes. ''Need I remind you why command of the Second was turned over to me?''

''There's no need of that.''

''Then let me say this much,'' Nivelle said with an air of finality. ''We appreciate this unprecedented visit, General. And we will certainly take your concerns under advisement.''

6

Klaxons were sounding an all-clear as Indy piloted the motorcycle into Verdun, the sun—out these past few minutes—setting on a horrific day. The ride from Souilly had air dried his uniform, which was now stiff with caked mud.

The town sprawled in near medieval splendor along the left bank of the Meuse at the confluence of several branches and tributaries. Under steady bombardment since the previous February, Verdun's civilian population had been evacuated to Normandy and Brittany, and the place was currently a garrison for the troops of the Second Army. Soldiers filled the cobblestone streets below the heights of Notre Dame and the Bishop's Palace. The bridges spanning the Meuse were mined with long strips of guncotton, primed for ignition at word of a German offensive against the town.

After a week at the trenches, a frontline regular could generally count on passing a week at the St. Paul barracks, close to one of the town's ancient, fortresslike gates. One week of drilling, training, filling sandbags; perhaps a few minutes with a local prostitute if one had a sou left after splurging on smokes or drinks and sending money home to the family.

Officers and members of the Quartermaster Corps or the military police were billeted at the so-called Citadel at the western edge of town, a vast subterranean fort built at the turn of the century. One hundred feet deep, immune to even the largest of artillery shells, the star-shaped complex was replete with stores, officers' bars, and dormitories, and often mentioned by men at the front in the same breath as paradise.

Bound there with a dispatch from General Nivelle, Indy was having trouble believing that the Citadel and the trenches he had run only that morning coexisted in the same war. Even the broad gallery leading down into the Citadel was paved and strung with electric bulbs. Angling off the main tunnel were side galleries with faintly pink stone walls and fine sand floors. The air at the core of the complex was warm and dry, but the pace was frenetic. Indy felt as though he'd ridden into a beehive, where the pollen gathered by countless drones was being processed into a kind of intelligence honey.

As instructed, he reported to a Captain Renaud, who had his own telephone and a desk piled high with sheafs of pink telegraph forms. An ambulance corps volunteer dressed in baggy khakis, in his early twenties with a prominent nose and black curly hair, was slouching in a chair alongside the desk, leafing through a French magazine. The kid eyed Indy up and down and smiled to himself.

Renaud stamped the message, set it aside, and waved Indy away. A buttoned-down, gray-haired bureaucrat, he had sharp features and nervous eyes.

"Sir, General Nivelle's adjutant, Major Marat, said I should billet here for the night," Indy told him.

"You look like you could use a soft cot, Corporal. Have you eaten?"

"Not since yesterday, sir."

"Then go to the scullery first and fill your belly. Take corridor B, then sixteen to seventy-five."

"Corridor B to sixteen to . . . Thank you, sir." Indy started to leave, then stopped. "Excuse me, sir, but I was wondering if you could tell me where the One-oh-six Light Infantry are positioned."

Renaud's gray eyes appraised him for a moment. "Does this have something to do with your courier duties, Corporal?"

"No, sir. I'm looking for a friend. His name is Remy Baudouin. A Belgian private attached to the One-oh-sixth."

Renaud's slim fingers stroked his jawline. "I'm sorry, Corporal, but I'm not at liberty to discuss troop deployments with you."

Indy made his lips a thin line. "I understand, sir." He saluted and was half into an about-face when the captain spoke again.

"One last thing, Corporal: Get a haircut."

"Sir," Indy snapped.

Five minutes later Indy was still searching for Corridor B. At the intersection of two side galleries, the ambulance corps volunteer caught up with him. "*Par ici . . . tout droit*," he said, gesturing with a heavily stubbled chin. "Straight ahead." Then, in English, he added, "Just keep going. You can't miss it."

"Thanks," Indy said, smiling. "I appreciate it."

The man's eyes lit up. "Hey, you parley-voo English?"

"Among other languages."

"Well, that's great. These French guys—I mean, you're not French, right?"

Indy indicated his collar stripes. "Belgian."

"Oh, yeah, I heard you say something about Belgium back with Renaud. You're looking for a buddy of yours, huh?"

Indy stopped. "Yeah. His name is Remy Baudouin. With the One-oh-six Light Infantry."

The volunteer glanced about him and lowered his voice. "Don't figure he's on French leave, do you? You know, absent without—AWOL."

"No. I'm sure he's not."

The man nodded. "What's your name, soldier?"

"Henri Defense," Indy said, keeping up appearances.

"Tom Carren," the volunteer told him. He held out a hand. "Put her there, Henry." Adding, as they shook: "You ever been in New Jersey, Henry? You look kind of familiar."

"Is that where you're from?"

"Newark, kid." Tom grinned. "Born and bred."

Two Americans in one day, Indy thought. This one from practically next door to the last place Indy had lived before leaving the States.

Tom pinched the leather sleeve of Indy's jacket. "Nice look, Henry. You a fly-boy?"

"A courier."

"Oh, a motorcycle rider, huh? Yeah, I didn't figure you for a regular blisterfoot. But, listen, Henry, if you ever want to sell that jacket, you let me know, all right?"

"Sure."

"And about your friend—whatsizname again?"

"Remy Baudouin."

Tom repeated it to himself. "I know this guy, see, this looey with the Hundred-and-first, and he knows a guy . . . Well, anyway, to make a long story short, I can probably get the inside dope on where your buddy's hanging his tin hat, you know what I mean. I mean, I can probably find him for you."

"That'd be swell," Indy said, falling back into old habits.

Tom's thick eyebrows went up. "Henry, you sure you never been in Jersey?" Without waiting for a reply, he continued: "Got time for a cup of java or are you all in?"

Indy shook his head. "I'm all in."

"I'm hep. Between this weather and the bucketheads, it's tough for a guy to find a spot of shade."

Indy parted company with the American at the mouth of Corridor B and eventually found his way to the scullery. The cook was a well-fed Frenchman in a soiled toque who told him to take a chair at the table in the adjoining room. No sooner did he step through the doorless passageway than a pair of familiar hellos rang out.

Two Belgians he'd met on his first day in Verdun were seated at the table among a dozen or so others of mixed nationality. The pair—Claude and Alex—had been sent south from the Ypres Salient at about the same time Indy and Remy had been ordered from the Somme when the

"camaraderie program" had gone into effect. Or the coun-
terinfiltration program meant to rid the French courier corps
of German spies—like so much else with the war, it de-
pended on whom you listened to.

In Indy's case, the recommendation for the courier post-
ing had come about as a result of his bicycle escape from a
German internment camp in Bavaria—the account of which,
much to his secret satisfaction, had taken on legendary
proportions. Once in Verdun—under the watchful eye of
General Nivelle's adjutant—he'd also had a chance to demonstrate his prowess on horseback, a talent he'd perfected
when the Joneses had lived for a time in Utah. It was there,
in 1912, that he'd earned his Life Badge in the Boy Scouts,
acquired the scar that marred an otherwise noble chin, and
developed a fondness for sporting a brown fedora in his
civilian life.

"Where did they assign you, Henri?" Claude was asking
now. He was exceedingly tall and narrowly built, with a
rudder of a nose and close-set hazel eyes.

"To Souilly," Indy told him. "General Nivelle's staff."

"Of all the luck. What do they have you doing, driving
one of the general's limo-coupes?"

"They gave me a motorcycle and a leather jacket and told
me not to expect any special privileges."

"But a motorcycle," Alex said wistfully. He was
Claude's physical opposite in every way imaginable. "We
spend all our time on bicycles. Right here in Verdun."

"Then consider yourselves the lucky ones," Indy said,
making a place for himself at the table. He didn't know
either of the Belgians very well. He asked after Remy, but
neither could tell him anything. Nearly twice Indy's age and
ill-suited for either motorcycle or bicycle duty, Remy was
the one who had really drawn the short straw. Along with
two hundred other Belgians, he had been sent directly to the
frontline trenches hear Thiaumont.

"Hey, Cook," the Frenchman at Indy's left directed toward the kitchen. "What's taking you so long? You're making soup, not wine."

"Take yourself to a restaurant if you don't like waiting," the fat cook responded peevishly. "I hear there's still one open in Paris."

As if what was already on the table wasn't feast enough, Indy thought, running suddenly hungry eyes over the spread.

At the Somme everyone had subsisted on bully—tinned corned beef—and "Maconochie," which was a meat-and-vegetable stew named after the manufacturer. Then there were the Pearl biscuits, which if not tops on anyone's list were at least good for passing out to French children. Goods from Britain flowed in relative unending variety to the front—sardines, condensed café-au-lait, bars of chocolate—but in the Citadel, with Paris only 125 miles west, the traffic in perishables was extraordinary. Even without the welcome addition of Jean-Marc's soup, the dinner table boasted tinned oysters, butter, cheese, hard-boiled eggs, fresh fruit—even a bouquet of primroses and violets in an empty Beaujolais bottle.

Indy began to heap things onto his plate, salivating like a dog. And yet one bite into the repast and he was through. He couldn't eat. Had he really been in the trenches only that morning? He closed his eyes to make sure, and the visions that danced behind his lids confirmed that he most certainly had been there. Over and over again, in nickelodeon flicker, he saw the young soldier falling, struggling to get up, dying. And he saw the one he'd thrown over his shoulder and carried in, the man's tear-streaked face, blood-soaked legs . . .

He regarded the food and the men beginning to tear into it, and asked himself if anyone stationed in the Citadel, with its soft cots and officers' bars, cared if the war ended.

From the inner pocket of the leather jacket, he pulled out the box the young soldier had given him, and he turned the thing about in his hands. If nothing else, he had to find someone who could take it to Paris and deliver it to the soldier's wife. Someone on furlough.

He thought briefly about Paris. He'd been there eight years earlier with his mother and father, in the midst of a grand tour around the world. And what a time he'd had! He wondered if the city had changed much, or if any of the artists he'd met—some of them quite famous now—would remember the ten-year-old boy who'd capered with them in the Moulin Rouge.

"Claude tells us you were at the Somme," said one of the Belgians Indy didn't know.

"That's right."

"Did you see any of those land battleships?" another soldier asked. "The things are said to be able to flatten barbed wire and crush machine gun nests."

"I heard about them."

"How bad was it there?" a third wanted to know.

Indy forced an exhale. "About as bad as it is here. There were twenty thousand casualties the first day of fighting."

Collective murmurings of commiseration rose from the table.

"*C'est triste, n'est-ce pas,*" a French corporal said.

It was one of the stock responses you were likely to hear whenever anyone talked about the war. It's sad, isn't it.

"Sad isn't the word," Claude said. "I can't comprehend how it has come to this point."

"Nobody can comprehend that," the French soldier told him.

But Alex apparently could. "It's simple: The Germans invaded Belgium." He jerked a thumb at Claude and Indy. "Our homeland."

"So they could invade France," the cook said, appearing suddenly from his kitchen. "*My* homeland."

"Then how did Russia get into it?" someone asked.

"Because Russia and France are allies." The cook cleared a place on the table and threw down two baguettes. "Look: the one on the left is France, the other is Russia." He placed a length of sausage between them. "This is Germany and Austria-Hungary."

"Here's Belgium," Alex said, passing him the bouquet of flowers. A tin of kippers soon became England; a tray of salt, Serbia.

The cook regarded the results of his culinary cartography

and grunted. "Now, when the king of Austria was assassinated in—"

"The archduke," Indy interrupted. "Not the king. The heir to the throne."

Jean-Marc nodded and began again. "All right, when the archduke was assassinated in Belgrade—"

"In Sarajevo."

The cook looked at him. "Perhaps you should explain."

Indy glanced at the faces turned to him and cleared his throat professorially—the way his father might.

"Serbia wanted to break ties with Vienna. Archduke Franz Ferdinand thought there was more to gain by loaning money to Serbia than threatening it. He was also worried about getting Russia stirred up. But when he and his wife were in Sarajevo, three Bosnian Serbs were waiting for him.

Indy paused to take a sip of water. When he continued with more details of the war's beginnings, his tone of voice was flat, absent of any emotion.

A bomb had been thrown at the skiff the couple was riding in. Ferdinand was wearing a cocked hat with green feathers. The bomb was the size of a cake of soap. But instead of detonating on impact, it had hit the folded roof of the car, rolled into the street, and exploded under another car in the motorcade. Twelve people had been seriously injured.

A few blocks further along Appel Quay, a young man named Gavrilo Princip also affiliated with the Serbian Black Hand terrorist group, had drawn his Browning revolver and fired two shots. The first round hit Sophie, killing her instantly. The second hit Ferdinand, who had his arms wrapped around his wife and was imploring her to live for the sake of their three children. He was dead by the time the motorcade reached the governor's residence.

The Austrian emperor had been devastated by the news. He had already lost his brother, Maximilian, in Mexico. His wife, Elisabeth, had been killed by a knife-wielding assassin in Geneva. And his only son, Rudolf, had killed himself in a suicide pact at Mayerling. Now his nephew and heir was dead.

"War was declared on Serbia," Indy said, wrapping up his brief lecture. "Russia came to Serbia's aid, and Germany came to Austria's. With Russia involved, France and Great Britain had to honor the terms of the Triple Entente and join the fight. Kaiser Wilhelm II, the grandson of Queen Victoria, had the excuse he needed to invade France. He did it by the least fortified route: through Holland and Belgium.

"Now half the world is at war."

No one spoke for a long moment. Then Claude said: "All to protect the rights of a tiny country in the Balkans."

Again the group fell silent. But several of the French were regarding Indy with interest. "How is it you know so much, Corporal?" the cook finally asked.

"Because Henri's never without a book," Claude told him. "Reading, reading, reading . . . Each time I see him."

One of the French snorted. "It's a pity reading doesn't kill Germans."

Everyone stared at the cook's arrangement of bread and sausage, kippers and salt. "To me, that doesn't look at all like a map of Europe," someone commented.

"So what *does* it look like?" Jean-Marc said warily.

"Dinner," the soldier replied.

And once more everyone but Indy dug in.

7

Indy found an unoccupied cot in the dormitory where Claude, Alex, and a couple of the French soldiers from dinner slept. There was a gramophone going at the far end of the room; earlier on, a cylinder of Elgar, then Schubert. Indy would have favored ragtime, or Irving Berlin, or even some of that George Cohan stuff—but he wasn't complaining. The bed was soft, and it came equipped with a pillow and a scratchy wool blanket.

He had his back to the stone wall just now and a writing tablet in his lap. The cook had lent him a quill and a bottle of ink. Indy had been sitting that way for some time, trying without success to compose a letter to his father. But what was there to tell, really? The Oxford-educated Professor Henry Jones certainly wouldn't want to hear about the war, or about the events that had motivated Indy to enlist. He wasn't interested in anything that didn't have to do with the pursuit of knowledge—medieval scholasticism especially, legends pertaining to the Holy Grail even more so. The relationship between father and son had never been exactly "loving," but ever since the death of Indy's mother, Anna, four years earlier, the situation had worsened. Anna Jones had believed in magic and miracle cures; but in the end, when even faith had failed her, her husband had withdrawn into his studies. Indy had done the opposite, seeking to define himself in terms of the tangible world. And now they hardly spoke.

This was subject to change should Indy be able to report finally having mastered Mandarin or some obscure Himalayan dialect, or if he could say that he'd visited the site where the Piltdown man had been unearthed. Otherwise, Indy—

who could speak a dozen thriving languages and four dead ones—would be judged lacking and given a failing grade.

As though it were yesterday, Indy could hear his father telling him, "Count to twenty in Quechua. Now do it backward."

Always some next field of study to master, some thick new text to digest: James Frazer's *Golden Bough*, Albert Einstein's *Theory of Special Relativity*, Sigmund Freud's *The Interpretation of Dreams*. When all Indy had wanted to do was ride horses and master the art of the bullwhip. And now all he could talk about were the trenches, the war, the killing machine . . .

He set the writing pad aside and stretched out on the cot. Glued to the dormitory walls wherever his eyes roamed were photos of wives, lovers, mothers, children . . . He thought back to the dinner discussion about the war, the assassination of Franz Ferdinand; and he tried in earnest to recall details of the visit the Joneses had paid Vienna in 1908, on the same round-the-world tour that had brought them to Paris. He pictured Franz Ferdinand, whom he'd met—tall and sad-eyed and mustachioed. And he remembered—and always would—ice-skating on a lake with the archduke's daughter, Sophie, Indy's childhood sweetheart.

How indeed had the world arrived at such a point?

How had *he*?

In the seventeen years since his birth, the world had seen the assassination of a U.S. president; earthquakes that had destroyed entire cities; volcanoes that had wiped away entire mountains; the passing of Halley's Comet. There had been great engineering achievements, like the Panama Canal and the eight-hundred-foot high Woolworth building. And wondrous if not quite so grand achievements in the arts, like comic strips and the birth of movies with actual titles and words on the screen.

Fearless adventurers were exploring the heights of Tibet, venturing into the heart of the Amazon basin, journeying to the frozen poles. Ancient civilizations in Crete and in Peru were at long last revealing their secrets. The modern world was filled with wonder: rayon, neon, bakelite, submarines, racing cars, aeroplanes—all the things a young person could dream of. And all subordinated to the service of world war . . .

Indy cast his eye to the wall above the adjacent bed and there found—among illustrated postcards of the Folies Bergère, a *La Vie Parisienne* rendering of a naked woman, posters of Theda Bara as "the Vamp," Pearl White in pith helmet, Isadora Duncan in veils—a faded hand-colored photograph of the exotic dancer, Mata Hari, in her bejeweled headdress, bracelets, and breast cups. She was tall, large-boned, and dark-haired, with the profile of a cinema star.

He'd first seen a photograph of her a year earlier, on his way to Mexico and the excursion he most blamed for having landed him in the middle of the war. A carefree search for good times had led to anything but. Several eye-opening days with Pancho Villa's rebels, the solving of an archaeological puzzle, the beginning of his friendship with Remy. But he might as well blame Ned Lawrence for landing him in the war if he was going to blame Mexico—Ned and his grandiloquent letters about "the war worth fighting." Or why not simply blame his father. If his father hadn't taken him on that grand tour, introducing him to people like Lawrence and Teddy Roosevelt and Krishnamurti . . .

All that really mattered was that here he was, an American in Verdun. And everyone knew the things that could befall Americans in foreign lands. Just look what had become of Butch Cassidy and the Sundance Kid in Bolivia.

Indy wondered where he had gone wrong. In addition to the tomes his father had forced on him, he'd read all the usual boyhood classics: *The Call of the Wild, Tarzan of the Apes, The Four Feathers, Peter Pan*. But perhaps his course to misadventure had resulted from a few too many midnight hours spent with dime novels, huddled under the sheets with Nick Carter, Bowery Billy, and of course Frank Merriwell. The handsome, muscular, agile Merriwell, who could outsmart cattle rustlers, Asian thugs, bad guys, and bullies of all make and manner; who could box, pass, run, shoot, hit, bicycle, and match cue sticks with the best of them.

All for love of mother, school, and country.

8

Tom Carren, the ambulance corps volunteer, shook Indy awake. It was impossible to tell if it was day or night. But judging from the way he felt, Indy knew it had to be before dawn; and that for all intents and purposes he'd only just closed his eyes.

In the scant electric light of the subterranean dormitory, Indy saw that Tom was wearing French khakis and, of all things, a baseball cap. His breath smelled faintly of cigarettes. "The One-oh-six went into action yesterday," the American whispered. "Over the top. They captured some ground but got their butts beaten pretty bad. Your buddy, Remy, he took a round."

Indy sat bolt upright on the cot. "Is he dead?"

"That much I don't know, Henry. But if you want to come with me, we can probably find out."

Going with Tom meant sitting beside him on the hard bench of an ambulance and speeding out of Verdun in the predawn light. The truck was one of a dozen similar vehicles posted at the Saint Paul barracks. There were a dozen more at what was left of Bras, about three miles distant, a pickup station for casualties along the Fleury front. An American named Lovering Hill and a French doctor supervised the operation. The trucks would leave each point at ten-minute intervals, sometimes twenty-four hours a day, so that there would never be more than two loaded vehicles on the road at any one time. The drivers decided who would go by drawing lots.

That morning, Tom was at the wheel of a Ford, which he

53

said was a gift from Henry Ford himself, an outspoken opponent of the war. Indy was tempted to reveal his nationality, but he held his tongue. It wouldn't do to have word reach General Nivelle's staff that an *American* had now infiltrated the courier corps.

Tom drove the truck like a fireman—at full speed, blowing the whistle, every running light and headlamp lit—trusting that the big red cross painted on the roof would deter German pilots from targeting him with a bomb or a cartridge drum of machine gun rounds. Not that many pilots, German or Allied, had the nerve to fly in the dark. As for the blind unthinking artillery shell, that of course was another matter.

The ambulance bounced from one crater to the next, splashing mud and water in all directions. Indy had a hand vised on the flat windscreen's tubular support, but there was no way to anchor himself on the seat. Tom at least had the outsized steering wheel.

They crossed the Meuse just north of the fork. The shell-holed half mile between Verdun and the former village of Belleville was a mire of horse remains and jettisoned supplies. If it was true that five thousand horses were required to support one division of men in the trenches, Indy reckoned that two divisions worth of steeds must have succumbed along the stretch of road.

The trip was a rodeo ride through hell.

Indy was trying to keep himself from thinking about Remy. He'd said little from the moment he'd climbed into the cab of the truck, buttoned up in the leather jacket, his side cap pulled low on his forehead. What dreams he'd had during the short night were punctuated with scenes of the young soldier's death outside the Souville trenches. Tom, on the other hand, couldn't keep quiet. And when he wasn't talking about New York City, he was talking about his experiences in the field.

"It works out to be sixty percent casualties from artillery fire," he was saying now, "thirty percent from small arms, and the rest from grenades, gas, and disease. Seeing how your buddy ended up taking a round, he must have been right in the thick of things.''

The terrain of limbless, charcoaled trees began to rise, and Tom shifted the truck into a lower gear. Every so often the headlamps would give spectral life to scenes along the side of the road: groups of exhausted soldiers, steaming horses dragging caissons or wheeled cannons, stretcher-bearers and their horses or mules hauling carts filled with wounded men. Some of the animals wore gas masks that resembled coarsely woven feed bags.

At first light, they arrived at a place called Quatre-Chiminées, an underground shelter that had been carved into a hillside between the ravines of Les Vignes—''the vines''—and Froideterre—''cold earth.'' Quatre-Chiminées meant ''Four Chimneys,'' so named because of the quartet of air shafts that had been drilled straight through the hilltop to provide ventilation. It was through those same chimneys, Tom told Indy, that the Germans had dropped hand grenades when they had overrun the shelter several months earlier. Now the site served as a kind of triage center for casualties brought in from the frontline first-aid posts and dressing stations.

''What usually happens is that the *brancardiers*, the stretcher-bearers, bring the wounded only as far as the Pied du Gravier ravine,'' Tom said, pointing toward the northeast. ''Then whoever's strong enough has to get himself down here on foot—assuming he has any. The rest have to stay in du Gravier until the *brancardiers* get time for them.''

An icy shiver passed through Indy as he contemplated Remy lying injured, unattended. He gripped Tom tightly by the shoulders. ''We've gotta find him.''

Tom nodded gravely. ''We will. But sometime you've gotta explain to me where you learned to jaw like an American.''

A narrow flight of cement steps led down into the hillside. At the foot of the stairway was a damp chamber fifty feet wide and two hundred feet long, lined end to end with the *blessés*, the wounded. On stretchers lay men with missing limbs; men riddled with bullet holes and jagged pieces of shrapnel; men with spouting head wounds and torn-open abdomens; men with faces blackened by explosions; men with red swollen lips and singed hair; men with clucking coughs and pink foam at the edges of their mouths.

Pained cries filled the fetid, sickly sweet air.

The stretchers lay side by side, with scarcely twelve inches separating them. A central aisle had been left for a doctor and a medical corpsman. Bloody dressings were heaped in all corners. An operating table and the floor around it were sodden with blood and unidentifiable bits of flesh.

Indy walked down the line in numbed dismay, glancing at each face he passed, not certain that he would be able to identify Remy even if he saw him. Light was provided by a combination of acetylene lamps, encrusted oil stoves, flashlights, and candles. But the horror of war had subverted the normal order of things; in a sense, every man resembled the next. And for once even the slit-open uniforms didn't seem to matter. Indy saw Belgians alongside French alongside Germans alongside Moroccans . . .

Early on in the war, bullet wounds—so-called "clean" wounds—were thought best left untreated. Such was the opinion of surgeons who had served in the Boer War. But it was soon discovered that the dung-laden soil of northern France was a far cry from the sterile clay of the Natal and the Transvaal. A condition known as "gas gangrene" could occur to wounds that had been infiltrated with contaminated mud and muck. So now the practice was to extract the bullets and clean the holes as quickly as possible.

Still there was only so much that could be accomplished—especially by a single doctor with hundreds of men to treat. The one at Quatre-Chiminées applied tourniquets, pressure bandages, and dressings; he stitched together flaps of violently parted flesh and he extracted fragments of rusted iron and shell casing. There were indirect transfusions for some, spinal analgesics for a fortunate few. But what the surgeon mainly did was divide the ones who might make it from the ones who didn't stand a chance. And he was generous with the morphia to both groups.

Indy walked the length of the chamber and back and didn't find Remy. He was about to begin a second trip when Tom took him by the elbow and steered him toward the cold stairway.

Indy's gut spasmed in anguish.

He feared the worst had happened.

Morning coffee had just been served at Souilly. Robert Nivelle would have been hard-pressed to summon praise for the British, but he did enjoy their habit of breakfasting. The morning meal had recently become a staple in the better hotels in Paris. Coffee and perhaps a few pieces of yesterday's bread, toasted to conceal the staleness. Breakfast was a habit he had brought with him into the field, and—all credit to Mangin's black majordomo, Baba—he could scarcely begin the day without it.

The brocade drapes in the tall windows were parted, and sunlight poured into the room. The sunlight heightened the rich colors of the Persian carpets and exaggerated the surface textures of the large oil paintings that dressed the walls. A Tintoretto, a Titian, a pair by Delacroix—all selected by Mangin, who had a keen eye for such things.

It was Mangin, in fact, who entered a moment later, announced by Major Marat.

Nivelle remained seated at the breakfast table. "Good morning, Charles," he said with some exuberance. "What news have you brought?"

"Mixed, at best," Mangin said, sitting down and accepting the coffee Marat poured for him.

"Suppose you begin with the good."

Mangin indulged in a long swallow of the steaming brew. "All four German observation balloons around Fort Douaumont have been brought down in a dawn raid by our Storks."

Nivelle sent a fist into the palm of his hand. "Good for

the *Cigognes*! This more than makes up for the sloppy efforts of Captain Thenault's squadron.''

Thenault commanded the Lafayette Escadrille, out of the aerodrome at Bar-le-Duc. ''It wasn't sloppy flying, Robert,'' Mangin said. ''There were problems with the Vickers machine guns.''

Nivelle's face wrinkled in disapproval. ''One can't fight a proper war with volunteers, Charles, no matter how honorable their intentions. The Lafayette Escadrille is made up of Americans, after all, and America has yet to grasp the value of the aeroplane as both a reconnaissance instrument and a fighting machine.''

Mangin tugged at his mustachio and smiled. ''Were Pétain only present to hear you say that.''

''You have my permission to tell him,'' Nivelle said offhandedly. ''Now, you announced that your news was mixed . . .''

Mangin nodded. ''Fleury has been retaken.''

''But as of last night it was ours!''

''And this morning it belongs to the Germans once again. The damn place has changed hands seven times in the past two weeks.''

''To hell with it, then. This constant taking and retaking only strengthens my resolve to concentrate our efforts on storming Douaumont from the west.''

Mangin didn't respond immediately. He gathered his thoughts for what he was about to say. ''Now that we've both had time to reflect, Robert, do you find any justification in Pétain's concerns about Douaumont?''

Nivelle compressed his lips in petty annoyance. ''Naturally, there is *some* justification. However, I see little hope of improving our lot with the artillery we have. Oh, the seventy-five millimeter looks fine on postcards or when it hangs in brass miniature between the breasts of a lovely *cocotte* on the Champs-Elysées, but the cannon is ill-suited to these goddamned hills. Our volleys continually fall short of their mark.''

''We could have the guns moved forward,'' Mangin said.

"Do you realize what you are suggesting? As it stands, our artillery salient is being ceaselessly bombarded on three sides. The battery commanders don't dare go to the latrines for fear of being hit. They're defecating into their helmets. It would require a massive effort to reposition the cannons at this time." He regarded Mangin with suspicion. "Furthermore, we can't allow ourselves to be distracted from our principal objective: Douaumont. I say it again, Charles: *Douaumont*. Keep the name squarely in your thoughts at all times. The counteroffensive must begin on schedule."

"I was only thinking that if we could hold off for a day or so," Mangin said. "Perhaps give the frontline companies a chance to rest—"

"Come now, Charles, there will be ample time for all of us to rest when we're dead. For the moment—this historical moment—we must seize the initiative and go forward."

Mangin rocked his head from side to side, momentarily tight-lipped. "*D'accord*. But I do have one further recommendation to make. It requires no repositioning of guns or troops; nor does it pose any threats to our operation. In fact, it requires nothing more than the risk of a few lives."

Nivelle leaned back in his chair, steepling pudgy fingers. "Tell me."

Remy had been moved to the field hospital of Château d'Esnes, on the left bank of the Meuse. What Indy saw upon arriving there—after helping Tom load four stretcher-bound men into the back of the ambulance and hurry them back into Verdun—was no less revolting than what he had witnessed at Quatre-Chiminées. In the courtyard of the ruined castle, wounded men lay like so many discarded weapons. The dead and the dying, shoulder to shoulder at the base of a mountain of freshly painted crosses. Orderlies carted the corpses to a rat-filled barn and stacked them inside like firewood. Indy would never have believed that one place could support such a dense population of flies.

Triage and surgeries were performed in the basement, where two doctors and a chaplain were on call round the clock. Postoperatives, tended to by volunteer *infirmiers* and nuns in winged caps, were then moved to wherever they could be squeezed in: the wine cellar, the arched passageways, the horse stables.

Indy was directed to a sickroom at the rear of the enclosure. Eight beds of different sizes were positioned along one wall, ten along the other, all culled from bombed-out houses in the area. He recognized Remy by his scream.

Two hospital attendants and a nun were struggling to keep the Belgian immobilized while he tore at the wound dressing that blanketed his abdomen.

"They didn't get it out!" Remy was saying. "It's still in there!"

The nun called for additional support and a third orderly hurried over to drape his body over Remy's flailing legs. "The doctor removed the bullet," the nun tried to tell him. "You have to calm yourself, or the wound will never knit properly."

"I can feel it," Remy said. "They have to operate again."

Two of the orderlies began to lash Remy's arms to the bed, but he continued to strain at the binds, exhausting himself in the process. Indy ran to the bed and pulled one of the men away, more roughly than he meant to.

"I'm his friend," he explained as the others suddenly turned on him. "You don't need to tie him down. Just let me talk to him."

The nun, young and round-faced, looked skeptical. "He's a danger to himself. And to others here."

Indy shook his head. "I can talk to him. I can calm him."

The nun nodded to the orderlies, who one by one eased their weight off Remy. Remy was breathing rapidly.

"Hey, pal," Indy said. "The Germans finally managed to get you, huh?"

"Indy," Remy said, opening his eyes. He was a powerfully built man of thirty-one, with close-cropped, thinning hair and a medicine ball of a gut. Indy supposed that his round wire-rimmed spectacles had been put aside for safe-keeping.

"How are you?" Indy asked.

"I've been better, friend."

"I've got a surprise." Indy's hand went to the inner pocket of the jacket and emerged with a packet of cigarettes. He glanced at the nun for approval, and she nodded her head. He prized a cigarette from the pack and lit it, placing it between Remy's cracked lips. The Belgian drew deeply and managed a smile.

"Turkish?"

"I got them off an Alsatian prisoner at Quatre-Chiminées. Traded him for a tin of bully beef."

"God help him," Remy said.

"Naw, they love the stuff."

"I always said you were a lucky kid."

"Yeah, Remy, and you once told me there's only one rule: 'Stay alive.' "

Remy smiled wanly.

He had indeed looked better, but he wasn't going to die, Indy decided. He was pale, scratched up, and bruised, but his brown eyes were only slightly less lively than normal.

Indy recalled when he'd first laid eyes on him in Mexico—moments after Pancho Villa himself had commuted Indy's sentence of death by firing squad. Misinterpreting the rebel leader's remark, Remy had almost carried out the sentence nonetheless.

The Belgian had led quite an eventful life even before tying up with Villa. A former seaman who hated the sea, he'd jumped ship in Veracruz, married a mestiza named Lupe, and opened up a cantina in Mazatlán. It was the murder of Lupe by federales that had compelled him to enlist in Villa's army.

"Did the surgeon really leave something inside you?" Indy asked when Remy had finished the cigarette. Remy averted his eyes. "Remy?" Indy asked again.

"They got it out," Remy said at last. "But you have to keep them from sending me back to the trenches, Indy." His voice faltered, and he began to shake from head to foot. The look in his eyes was one of stark terror. "They'll send me back if I get well, so I'm not going to get well. I'm not going to let them put me out there again. I'm not, I swear I'm not—"

Indy had to force him back down onto the bed. He put his face close to Remy's and lowered his voice to a seething whisper. "You don't know what your saying. You *have* to let yourself heal. If they find out you're malingering, you'll wind up in front of a firing squad."

"I don't care! Anything's better than being out there. Death is better. They can brand me a coward if they want, but I know that I *fought*. I charged when the order was given. I killed, Indy. I killed—"

Indy clamped a hand over his friend's mouth. It took all the strength he could muster to keep Remy pinned. When at last he felt Remy beginning to relax beneath his hold, he threw a cautious glance around the room. Two orderlies were eyeing him with wary distrust.

Indy wrapped his arms around Remy and held him tight.

Belgium had already been invaded when Remy joined Villa, but when news of the German atrocities reached him, he began to understand there was a war closer to his heart that had to be fought. Germany, in a brutal attempt to terrify the French early on, had reduced Belgium to an enclave of some five hundred square miles. The rest of the nation was literally stripped of machinery, food, and clothing. As a result, some 200,000 Belgian refugees had found shelter in France; more in England, Switzerland, and Holland.

Remy's sudden passion for the Great Cause had proved contagious, and—much to Professor Jones's consternation—Indy had traveled with him to England, where the two had enlisted in the Belgian army. The Belgian recruiters were said to ask fewer questions than the British; but in truth no one at that point was being particular. In May 1914, an enlistee in the British Expeditionary Force had to stand five-foot-eight; two months later the height requirement was five-five; and by November—thirty thousand casualties later—it was five-three.

Indy, on a miscalculated whim, had taken the name "Defense" from the sign in the recruitment office that read, "Défense de Fumer"—No Smoking.

"Are you all right?" he asked Remy now, loosening his hold somewhat.

Remy nodded stiffly, his cheeks streaked with glistening tears.

"What happened to you out there?"

Remy's eyes glazed over. When he spoke, the words came tumbling out of his mouth.

"We made it safely from the fire trench to the approach trench. But then we found ourselves trapped between overlapping fire from our own guns and from the Germans'. We couldn't advance, and we couldn't retreat. We sat there for twelve hours while the land exploded around us. Then the *boche* got wind of us. They began to hurl gas canisters into our laps. Only a few of us had masks. We fired at the Germans until our ammunition was depleted. A lot of men died.

"The ones who didn't moved the corpses to the edge of the trench, positioning everyone in fire attitudes, with rifles protruding over the parapets. We thought we could fool the *boche*. You always think that you'll shit your pants in a situation like that, but you don't. You're so terrified that your insides lock up tight as a drum. But you get thirsty—very thirsty—when you've been shot. So thirsty that you'll lap from muddy puddles like a dog. So thirsty that you'll drink your own urine.

"I lay there and prayed I would die. Sometimes I thought the artillery shells were fireworks. I thought I heard people laughing and singing, as though they were at a country fair. I lay there and prayed I would die. But they found me. And they resurrected me. So they could send me out to fight again."

Indy tried to speak, but no words came. He swallowed dryly. "Let your wound heal, Remy. Stay here and get well. They won't send you back."

Remy gazed at him and snorted a thin laugh. "Oh, but they will, friend. You'll see that they will."

Indy gave Remy's shoulder an affectionate squeeze and stood up. "I'll try to visit you tomorrow."

Resolutely, he walked away from the bed. At the end of the room he encountered the nun, whose white habit was now stained with fresh blood.

"I'm sorry about your friend," she said.

"How long will he be allowed to stay?"

Her grim expression supplied the answer: Not long enough.

Indy climbed the stairs to the courtyard, wondering if he could snag a ride back to the Citadel. Two military police were just arriving in a motorcycle and sidecar. They drove past him and circled back for a closer look at his uniform.

"Are you Corporal Henri Defense, General Nivelle's courier?" the one in the sidecar asked.

Indy nodded. "That's me."

The two regarded one another. The one on the bike spoke. "Then you had better come with us, Corporal."

9

"It has come to our attention that you speak German, Corporal Defense," General Mangin was telling Indy half an hour later.

Indy wondered how exactly that little piece of news had come to the general's attention. But in looking around the room Indy recognized Major Gaston, and he immediately grasped what had happened. One of Gaston's grenadiers must have mentioned the brief verbal exchange they'd had with the German frontliners, and how Indy had translated.

Mangin was seated behind a rickety wooden desk in a briefing room at the heart of the Citadel. He toyed with his waxed mustachio as he continued to appraise Indy. "Would you say that you speak German well enough to get by, or are you quite fluent?"

"Quite fluent, sir. I've read Schopenhauer and Nietzsche in German."

"Bravo, Corporal," Mangin said with obvious amusement.

"And not only is the corporal fluent in German. He has the distinction of being one of the few to have escaped from the Jerries' internment camp at Dusterstadt."

The speaker was a British officer, a major, with ruddy cheeks and a thin gray mustache. He wore pristine khakis, a peaked field service cap, and a polished Sam Brown. Indy guessed that the holstered revolver was a Webley Mark IV.

"Is this true, Corporal?" Mangin asked.

"Yes, sir," Indy told him. "Although the account of my escape has been greatly exaggerated. Sir."

The general exchanged meaningful glances with the major and with Major Gaston. Also present in the room were two Negro soldiers, North African colonials by the look of them. Missing, though, were the elaborate uniforms and red fezzes typical of the Zouaves. Instead, the two wore twilled-cotton trousers, black aviators' sweaters, and blue berets.

"Corporal Defense," Gaston said, "I want you to meet Corporals Tuak and Remann of the Three hundred and twenty-first Infantry. The corporals are from the Algerian Brigade. They have been receiving special training at a camp near Bar-le-Duc."

Indy's brows went up. He'd heard rumors about the camp; that the terrain there simulated that of no-man's-land, right down to the unexploded projectiles and dead horses. The troops were said to be able to see in the dark and hump twice their own weight in supplies: sandbags, tents, canteens of water, canteens of wine, two gas masks . . . When laying spools of barbed wire, they worked with teams of donkeys that had had their vocal chords severed. That certainly explained the lack of field uniforms, Indy thought.

"Stand at ease, Corporal Defense," Mangin said; then, to Gaston: "Major, if you would."

Gaston stepped forward with a map that he unrolled and pinned to a canvas bulletin board. He directed his comments to Indy and the Algerians.

"What you hear must not go beyond this room." Gaston's right forefinger found Fort Douaumont. "A counteroffensive is planned for tomorrow morning along this entire front. We have been apprised, however, that the enemy has refortified supply lines to the fort and moved in additional batteries—perhaps by railroad. We need to ascertain if this is the case."

Indy gaped at Gaston. Was the major including him in that *we*? His heart began to race.

"General Nivelle has ordered a night reconnaissance, departing from the trench line here, at the Ravine of Death." Gaston's finger indicated a spot west of the redoubt. "The objective is the German forward observation bunker, here, at the southern edge of the Chaufour Woods. Sappers have swept the area of mines, clear to the German wire. Intelligence will be gathered from the bunker by sight and sound. The return to our trench follows the same route through no-man's-land. Our listening posts will be advised of the mission and provided with the appropriate code words. Searchlights in this sector will be switched off to facilitate the mission, but flares will continue to be launched at ten-minute intervals, so as not to arouse undue suspicion on the other side.''

Gaston glanced about the room. ''Any questions?''

Just one, Indy wanted to say. *Is it too late to rescind that remark about speaking fluent German?*

''Observation balloons?'' the Brit said. He used the German word *drachen*, which literally meant ''sausage.''

''None,'' Gaston told him. ''Our aeroplanes took four of them down early this morning. No new ones have been raised.''

''Has there been aerial reconnaissance?'' one of the Algerians asked. Tall and thinly built, he had a wide mouth and sculpted cheekbones.

''Photographs have revealed nothing unusual. A group of Alsatian deserters mentioned seeing newly poured concrete firing platforms in the woods north of the fort, but that information has yet to be corroborated.'' Gaston's finger returned to the map momentarily. ''Intelligence gained by body exhumers working between the ravine and the fort indicates that some reinforcing has been done to the machine gun nests and *stollen*, but this, too, is anecdotal.''

The major turned to the Brit. ''You had something you wanted to add, Major Twinbury?''

''Indeed I do.'' Twinbury's French was grammatically weak and thickly accented. He drew a telescoping pointer from his pocket as he approached the map.

''Jerry certainly has something up his sleeve. Aside from the rumors about fresh gun emplacements, the listening posts have reported a marked increase in tunneling operations. Now, this could be nothing more than improvements to the underground bunkers. But at the same time, we want to be on the lookout for tunnelers, what we in the Expeditionary Force have termed 'moles.' Up at Festubert, a team of Jerry moles tunneled right under our trenches and seeded an entire area with mines. The Sirhind Brigade sustained heavy casualties as a result. So you'll have to be on the listen for talk of moles as well as talk of artillery.''

He dragged a duffel bag forward and opened the drawstring top. ''I've brought along some special equipment for your use . . .''

And Twinbury began to pass the items along to Indy, Tuak, and Remann: modified gas masks, wire shears, hedging gloves, antisniper face guards, German grenades equipped with throwing handles, a folding trench knife . . .

Ultimately he displayed three shiny Webley revolvers. ''And mind you, men, these come with the new Mark VII bullets, which tumble some as they enter their targets. All the better for putting the fear into Jerry.''

Indy hefted the handgun. It was nothing at all like the guns he'd fired in Utah—the Winchesters and Colt Peacemakers. Although once he'd had an opportunity to try out a Sharps Buffalo Rifle.

As for the Mark VII bullet, Twinbury made it sound as though it could turn the war around. But then there had been so many previous developments that were supposed to accomplish that—red phosphorous smoke screens, for example, or Livens projectors, which fired time-fused barrels of oil and cotton waste. And of course the introduction of land battleships—tanks.

General Mangin by this time had come around the desk and was standing in front of Indy, regarding him somberly.

''I would like to hear your reactions to what has been said, Corporal Defense.''

''Sir?'' Indy said.

''Well, soldier, Corporals Tuak and Remann have been trained for just this sort of mission. You, on the other hand, are a courier—a Belgian courier, at that—who happens to have read Schopenhauer and Nietzsche in the original German.''

Perhaps it wasn't too late to back out, Indy thought.

"What I mean to say," Mangin continued, "is that we can't *order* you to belly your way across no-man's-land and press your ear to the wall of an enemy bunker. The choice is completely up to you. Understand, though, that should you choose to do it, the French army will be indebted to you. More, the French Republic will be indebted to you."

More flag waving, Indy thought. "I appreciate that, General," he said after a moment. "But I do have one question, sir."

Mangin stiffened. "Go ahead, soldier, ask it."

"Will the mission save lives, General?"

Mangin quirked a grin. "It could."

"Then I'll do it."

10

At twenty-two hundred hours, with a half moon lighting the sky, Indy and the two Algerian reconnaissance specialists bellied down into the Ravine of Death. Behind them, in the forward fire trench, sat snipers with scoped rifles, sappers with holstered flare guns, and listening experts with their mechanical ears to the ground. Indy's face was blackened with a paste of coal dust and gun oil. He wore black trousers, a black ribbed sweater, knee boots, and a beret. On his belt and cross strap he carried the Webley, wire cutters, a sole ammo pouch, and a grenade. The folding trench knife rode in a scabbard lashed to his right thigh.

Tuak had given him a length of bark to gnaw on. "It will keep you awake and alert," the Algerian had said. The three-inch-long strip looked like cinnamon but tasted like bitter almonds. Indy's mouth tingled, numbed by whatever alkaloids the bark contained. But he was as awake as he would have been on four cups of Turkish coffee.

The ravine retained vestiges of undergrowth, scorched, to be sure, but thick and difficult to maneuver through. At the top of the embankment the land leveled off and was relatively flat, except where torn up by shellfire. No-man's-land, indeed. The stumps of Normandy poplars looked like charred stakes that had been driven into the ground.

You couldn't allow yourself to consider what you were crawling through—any more than you could allow yourself to dwell on what could become of you out there. Heaved skyward by explosions, the soil was more suited to the environs of a long-active volcano: it was crisped and fused into a kind of soft gravel. But far worse was the mixture of decaying flesh and bone. No-man's-land was a composite of human remains, rusting iron, abandoned weapons and haversacks . . . It was one huge graveyard, exhumed time and time again by the fall of artillery shells.

At the bottom of every gully were corpses that looked to have been belched from the earth. There were so many, in fact, that you became inured to their presence, along with the flies they summoned, the maggots they birthed. Ever since the Somme, Indy found that he could sometimes gaze at a dead man as dispassionately as he could one of the Egyptian mummies he'd seen as a nine-year-old in the Valley of the Kings.

If you were so inclined you could restructure the very circumstances in which they had died: this one to machine gun fire while charging the wire; that one to an enemy bayonet. Over here, a shell—German or French, it made little difference—had flattened a circle of men; they lay sprawled in impossibly stiff postures like the numerals on the face of a clock. Over there, two men had been shot while they crouched in a foxhole. Some were fully dressed in greatcoats and harnesses; others had been laid bare by the sheer physical forces that had felled them. Still others were mere bundles of tattered clothing, smaller than they should have been, as though life itself had mass that fled with death.

Indy speculated that archaeologists in the year 2000 would be able to read the entire history of the war from a single parcel of ravaged ground.

He thought about Stephen Crane's *Red Badge of Courage*, which he had read only months earlier.

"Look at the grin on this one," Remann whispered in Indy's ear, motioning off to the left. The corpse was lying on its back, with hands crossed over its chest as though in slumber. Around its neck was tied a black-and-white training handkerchief that gave written instructions for the care of one's rifle. A young man had once inhabited the shell.

They had reached the wire now, and Tuak was already busy cutting a path. Indy always experienced a twinge of national guilt at the sight of wire. The barbed coils, as thick as a thumb, were one of two American contributions to the stalemate; the other being the machine gun, which had been invented by Hiram Maxim back in 1889.

Remann forced Indy's head to the ground as a flare blossomed overhead, drifting back to earth on its small parachute, like a falling star. The German bunker was plainly visible in the red afterglow, one hundred yards distant at the far side of a severely holed stretch of ground.

"Remember to stay low," Tuak told Indy. "The Germans don't take spies alive."

"Where are you two going to be?"

"We'll be where we need to be," Remann said cryptically. He was plucking grenades from a canvas bag and lining them up in the dirt eighteen inches from his chin.

Tuak wedged a forked stick under the top strands of barbed wire and Indy snaked through on knees and elbows, as Charles de Gaulle had taught him to do.

He had met the towering, large-beaked Frenchman at Dusterstadt, a camp the Germans reserved for determined escapees. De Gaulle, who could quote poetry as easily as he could discuss philosophy, the history of France, or battle tactics, had held that firepower and mechanization were the keys to successful modern warfare—a stand that had alienated him from Joffre and several other shortsighted generals of the French High Command. But de Gaulle had nothing but admiration for Philippe Pétain, another staunch advocate of big guns and aeroplanes.

So what would either man make of a lone soldier bellying his way through the mud on an eavesdropping mission, Indy wondered. Was there a place for both man and machine in the war? Could one man or one machine make a difference?

He was fifty yards from the bunker when he became aware of a rasping sound emerging from a shell hole directly in his path. He peeked over the rim and could just discern a French soldier flat on his back in the muck. The man's eyes seemed to find Indy in the darkness.

"Help me," he croaked. "I'm shot in the legs, and in the stomach, I think. Take me home. Please."

Indy could barely make out the words. He eased himself down into the hole and alongside the man. He reeked of vomit and diarrhea. "Don't speak," Indy whispered in his ear.

But just his voice was enough to give the soldier hope.

"Yesterday a visitor arrived, but he doesn't want to talk to me." The soldier's hand gestured weakly, and Indy saw the body of a German a few feet away, face first to the ground.

"I said that he was being impolite, I *told* him he was being impolite, but he wouldn't talk, he just made sounds. So I had to stick him with my knife." The soldier's left hand reached out to stroke the bloodied tricorner blade of a bayonet.

Indy fished a hard candy from his pants pocket and slipped it into the soldier's mouth. "Keep quiet. I'll be back for you." He had just started to move off when the man grabbed a handful of his sweater.

"You're going the wrong way, friend. It's the other way, the other way."

Indy pried the soldier's fingers free and covered the final fifty yards to the bunker. Constructed of concrete and timber, the blockish enclosure was roofed with steel plate. Littering the ground were the remains of sandbags fashioned from pillowcases, slips, and blouses looted from nearby farmhouses. Indy rolled over onto his back and wormed his way to a fire slit in the bunker wall. Carefully, he raised his head and peered into the dimly lit interior.

Below him, two Germans in field gray uniforms and snap-brim caps were bent over a table, entering notations on a map. A kerosene lantern and a field radio sat on a table by the wooden door.

One man was round and slack-jawed; the other, tall and barrel-chested. They both wore Mausers on their hips. The tall one was singing in German, while he worked.

"Dry your tears, Louise, wipe your eyes; in spite of what they say, a soldier never dies . . ."

"Don't, Gunter," the round one interrupted. "Not tonight."

"You're weary of my singing, huh?"

"I'm weary of the war."

"The war? But surely the war must have ended by now," Gunter said with theatrical concern. "Don't you recall what the kaiser promised? 'Two months and you will be singing in Paris.' *Nach Paris!* Don't you recall?"

The round man walked away from the map table and hunkered down on the earthen floor. Indy lowered his head some.

"Tonight, you can be jolly for the two of us. If the French hold off on their attack, I'll gladly join you in song tomorrow. We'll sing *Du Wunderschone Stadt*, *Deutchland uber Alles*, whatever you wish."

"But that's the last thing we want them to do," Gunter said. "We're ready for them now. Two days, three days more, our bellies even emptier than they are tonight, who knows if we'll have the strength to send them scurrying back to their holes. It's not like the old days, Werner. *Then* we had a fighting army, hardened by the Marne, Yser, Ypres, Champagne, Artois . . . Now, now we march schoolboys to the front and feed them to the French *poilu* for lunch."

Indy stifled a yawn. The effect of the mysterious bark was wearing off, and he felt hollow. The mental and physical stress of the past several days was suddenly catching up with him. He thought he could fall asleep right there, right there in the mud surrounding a German bunker . . . He could simply shut his eyes, curl up into the ground—

He gave a start and snapped back to consciousness. Christ, he actually had fallen asleep! For a moment, anyway. Once more he raised his ear to the opening.

"Don't know whether to applaud their courage or laugh at their stupidity," Gunter was saying. "But believe me, the attack will come tomorrow. And our four-twenty howitzers will make them sorry they did. The French don't even know they are there."

"You don't know that."

"I do know that. Those guns have been assembled in complete secret. Even now they're draped with so much canvas and camouflage you can't distinguish them from the rest of the Chaufour Woods. So let the French come. We'll *give* them the west casements of Fort Douaumont, while we resupply the east. The moat will make for an accommodating grave."

So the rumors were accurate, Indy thought. The Krupp siege howitzer had been named for the Czech word for catapult because of the way the huge guns lobbed their fourteen-hundred-pound shells. The shells contained two hundred pounds of Ammatol explosive—a mix of TNT and ammonium nitrate—and were fused to explode on impact. The craters they blasted were often as much as twelve feet deep and fifteen feet across. The Germans had called the guns die diche Bere— Big Bertha. Nivelle's forces were in for a pounding.

Indy was moving closer to the opening when, from somewhere, a bird sang. Indy couldn't believe his ears. A nightingale? One very confused loon? He wasn't very good with birdcalls. In any case, it was the first bird he'd heard in a week. And Gunter and Werner had heard it, too.

"I'm sure it was only a bird," Werner said.

Gunter went to the opening and peered outside, his face not a foot from where Indy lay curled on the ground. "A bird, or a Frenchman trying to sound like a bird. I'm going out to have a look."

"You're wasting your time," Werner told him.

"We'll see."

Indy waited until he heard the sound of the bunker door scraping the ground to make his move. Then he was up and running for the wire in a crouch.

"Werner! There's someone here," Gunter said behind him.

The Mauser coughed twice and rounds whizzed past Indy's right ear. He dropped to his face and slid down into a crater.

"I'm going after him," Gunter said. "Tell the trench—"

The German made a plosive sound, followed by a series of mournful grunts.

"Gunter?" Werner asked. "Gunter?"

And all at once, out of nowhere, Tuak was alongside Indy in the shell hole, his trench knife glistening darkly in the moonlight. He drew a forefinger across his throat and gestured with his chin to the bunker. He tapped Indy into motion and crawled rapidly from the hole.

Indy started to follow but suddenly remembered the wounded French soldier. He stopped to take his bearings. Two holes to the right, he decided, and headed that way.

"All right, comrade, we're going home," he said as he rolled into the hole. But the soldier only grinned at him. Indy touched him lightly on the shoulder, and he toppled over, the way only dead men could. Indy forced an exhale and made a quick search of the body for documents, turning up an identity card and a couple of crimped and blood-streaked photographs. He shoved everything into his pants pocket and was turning to go when a hand latched onto his arm.

Indy gave a terrified start, fearing that the dead soldier had somehow become reanimated. But as he turned he found himself confronting the ghostly face of the bayonetted German soldier who'd been lying facedown when Indy saw him last.

Stumbling forward like a zombie, the German had a knife in his hand and was making feeble plunging motions in Indy's direction. The man's eyes were rolled up into his head and the front of his uniform was drenched in blood. Indy crabwalked backward, a shriek lodged in his throat. The German pitched forward, falling across Indy's legs and continuing to stab at him with the knife. The blade grazed Indy's raised arm and slammed into the earth near his head. Indy dragged himself backward up the slope of the hole, his fingers raking the ground; the German was still sprawled across him, his left arm hugging Indy's legs. Indy unsheathed his knife and plunged it between the German's shoulder blades. The German arched his back like a swimmer performing a swan dive, his arms flailing at the knife buried in his back. Indy kicked at him and the man rolled to the bottom of the crater, driving the knife through his back to emerge at his chest.

Indy fought for breath, shaking where he lay.

Without warning, flares lit the sky like a fireworks display and machine gun fire splintered the silence. Indy was tunneling a hole for himself when Remann got to him.

"Come, man, let's go, let's go!"

The Algerian grabbed him around the waist, and Indy began to tussle with him as though he were the enemy. Tuak appeared over the rim of the crater as rounds stung the ground on all sides.

Someone threw grenades.

Someone responded with mortars.

The Algerians put Indy between them and ran him back to the wire.

11

Indy raced down the road to Souilly, maneuvering the motorcycle through a steady stream of supply trucks, some with mascots painted on the sides: "The Cock," "The Girl from Cannes," "The Little Colonel" . . . It was no wonder Citadel staffers referred to the Road as "the conveyor belt." Six thousand vehicles per day were said to cover the fifty-seven kilometers between the railway terminal at Bar-le-Duc and the Verdun military zone. There were right-hand drive, four-cylinder Berliet CBAs with bench seats and diamond-plate running boards; and there were Ford and Fiat ambulances with solid rubber tires. There were mail trucks and gun carriages and flatbeds topped with searchlights; and then there were the lighter trucks of the engineers corps, the artillery corps, the air force. On cold overnight runs, the drivers would glove their hands with Vaseline and keep themselves going with sweetened black coffee.

The Road had recently been widened to accept two lines of vehicles. Roadcrews comprised of civilians and displaced territorials in uniforms twenty years out of date were constantly topping off potholes and washouts with crushed stone, quarried locally and transported to the Road by horse-drawn carts. Thirty tow trucks, working round the clock, saw to the one out of every hundred vehicles that broke down. Others that succumbed to enemy bombing runs were left to burn in the rutted ground on either side of the route.

The drivers were under orders not to pass one another, but couriers were free to do as they pleased. Especially those conveying urgent messages between the Citadel and

General Staff headquarters at Souilly, less than twenty kilometers south.

It was seven A.M. on the morning following the recon mission. Much earlier on, Indy, Tuak, and Remann had been debriefed by majors Gaston and Twinbury, but at dawn Indy had received orders to report in person to General Nivelle at the commandeered town hall.

General Mangin's bright-red Opel limo-coupe was parked in front of the building when Indy arrived. A team of privates was working to rid it of mud.

Indy presented himself to Nivelle's adjutant, Major Marat, who escorted him to the briefing room on the second floor. Indy, back in khaki breeches and tunic, gaiters, and thigh-length leather jacket, clicked his heels and saluted smartly, palm outward.

"Corporal Defense reporting as ordered, sir."

It was Mangin who told him to stand at ease. General Nivelle was standing with his back to the room at one of the tall east-facing windows. Major Gaston, looking agitated and in sore need of sleep, was at the map table with Mangin. The room was unpleasantly warm and noisy with truck traffic.

Without bothering to turn around, Nivelle asked Indy to repeat, word for word, what he'd overheard the previous night behind enemy lines. Only when Indy had run through everything twice did the general finally show his face.

The look he directed at Indy was withering.

"You're Belgian, are you not, Corporal?"

"Yes, sir," Indy said.

"From what part of Belgium. Exactly."

"Why, from Evergem, sir. A small town just north of Ghent." Speaking in French, Indy used the Belgian name *Gand*. He'd made a fool of himself in the recruiting office in London when asked a similar question, but now, with Remy's help, he had a credible counterfeit history worked out.

"And the name 'Defense,' " Nivelle continued. "That's Belgian?"

"My father was French, sir."

Nivelle cocked an eyebrow. "Really, Corporal. And where is your father from?"

"He's dead, sir. But his family was from Paris."

Nivelle shot Mangin a glance. "Well, Charles, did you hear him? French. When I specifically requested a *Belgian* courier. And you know damn well why."

Mangin looked momentarily nonplussed, then compressed his lips in frustration. "Surely, you're not suggesting that the corporal has had intelligence with the enemy, General."

Indy swallowed hard. Nivelle had yet to be convinced that his courier corps was free of spies. He looked to Gaston for support, but the major only stared glumly at the map.

"I'm not suggesting anything of the sort," Nivelle said. "I'm simply trying to determine something of the lad's background. After all, Charles, this bunker conversation he alleges to have overheard could undo everything we've set in motion here."

"May I submit, General, that our objective was to investigate the possibility that something had been overlooked," Mangin replied. "Now we know that that is in fact the case. We have corroboration of Pét—er, our concerns. The enemy has indeed moved heavy artillery into the area of Douaumont, and means to ensnare our troops. It's plain that they mean to give us the western casements while they refortify from the east."

"So you say, Charles."

Mangin reddened. "So the *Germans* say, General. You heard the corporal."

Nivelle glanced at Indy. "What I hear and what I choose to believe are two entirely separate matters."

"But what could he stand to gain by lying, for God's sake?"

Nivelle glared at his second-in-command. "I repeat: I am not accusing him of lying. But given the conditions under which the mission was executed—the last-minute nature of it, the quite normal fears and misgivings that attend such operations—well, we must be prudent about what we accept as truth. We must take care not to exaggerate the importance of one late-night conversation between two apparently exhausted German soldiers."

Mangin stormed through a quick circle around the map table. "With all due respect, General, we can't afford to *understate* the importance. If nothing else, we have found justification to be circumspect in our actions. More than enough to warrant additional aerial reconnaissance of the area before we begin."

"And announce our intentions?"

"The Germans have already grasped our intentions."

"I hope, Charles, that you're not proposing we alter our plans. The cautious approach works well for Pétain, but it doesn't suit you at all."

It was obvious that Mangin didn't relish the comparison. "An attack on Douaumont at this juncture will place our troops in an untenable position—isolated, with the western counterscarps of the fort to their backs and Krupp howitzers to the north." He paused briefly to fold his arms across his chest. "That's why I've taken the liberty of consulting with General Pétain. I concurred with him that the frontline troops should stand down from the attack. I have already given the order."

Nivelle was speechless for a long moment. "You what?" he said at last. "You took it upon yourself, you say. Well, we'll see about *that*, General, when the time comes. But as to the present . . ."

He whirled on Gaston. "Major, raise Colonel Barc on the phone immediately." Then he threw Mangin a piercing look. "I'm going to countermand your stand-down order, Charles. And if you don't like it, you're welcome to file a report to Joffre and the High Command."

Indy could scarcely believe the gall of the man. To think Indy a liar was one thing, but to ignore invaluable intelligence simply to stay on schedule . . . Nivelle made him think of George Armstrong Custer, always riding to the sound of the guns, regardless of what he was riding into. Did that mean Verdun could become Nivelle's Little Big Horn?

"Sir," Gaston interjected with grim reluctance, "in accordance with command protocols, Colonel Barc will not be able to act on your order."

"Raise him on the phone, Major," Nivelle snarled. "That is a direct order."

Mangin waved Gaston away from the telephone. "What the major is trying to tell you is that Barc will require a written countermand to my order."

Nivelle held Mangin's gaze. "Then consider it done, General." Four rigid steps took him quickly to the desk, where he took up a fountain pen and began to write.

Mangin watched him for a moment before going over to the desk. "Do what you will with me, General, but I'm afraid it's too late to reverse the actions I've taken."

"Don't tell me what I can and can't do, Charles. You're beginning to sound like Pétain, and frankly I'm disappointed. I thought you understood that there are bigger issues at stake than Fort Douaumont. Verdun has emerged as a symbol of national pride, and what we are about to do is restore that pride to its full glory. Is that clear enough for you?"

Mangin was narrow-eyed. It was as though Nivelle had accused him of cowardice or worse. "By too late, I only meant that the appropriate time to launch an attack has passed. Ordering the men to leave the trenches now would be like sentencing them to death."

Nivelle glanced at his wristwatch, then hurried his hand. He pressed a blotter to the finished note and sealed the paper in a dispatch envelope.

"Corporal," he said to Indy. "Once more you have an opportunity to distinguish yourself." He flourished the dispatch. "Deliver this to Colonel Barc. As quickly as is humanly possible."

Indy took the Road back to Verdun. Just short of the turn-off toward Fleury, he saw a line of troops marching towards the front. Limping along in the line was Remy. Indy climbed off the bike and ran up to him.

"Remy!" He fell in line alongside.

"Off to the front again, *mon ami*," Remy said weakly. "About the other day in the hospital . . . Thank you."

"For what?" Indy said, feigning ignorance.

Remy managed a smile. "For the Turkish cigarettes."

Indy smiled back.

"You see," Remy told him, "they *are* sending me back to the trenches. Some big build-up—everyone got orders."

"Those bastards. You're not even healed yet!"

"I have to go," Remy said. "I'm making it easy for the Germans this time—I'm half dead already."

Indy fell out of line and watched Remy march off. "For God's sake, keep your head down, Remy!" he shouted, and turned away.

Sometimes you had to venture off the map to find your way.

He knew this terrain by heart now, these shell holes, these mutilated trees, these fields ruined by fire, this no-man's-land. He could probably have arrived at his destination without thinking, with eyes closed. As against that, he needed to see where he was going.

Just short of the *chemin-de-fer* crossing—the stretch of narrow gauge railway that led to the munitions dump at Fort Tavannes—close, in fact, to where the German Fokker had almost had its way with him and whose water-filled bomb craters still dimpled the landscape, something odd happened to the motorcycle: it began to buck and stutter. And one hundred yards further on the machine gave up the ghost entirely and slowed to a halt.

Indy dismounted, raised the bike on its rear kickstand, and went down on one knee to look for what might be wrong. It was likely a blockage of some sort, a problem with fuel flow to the carburetor. He had watched Claude and Alex fieldstrip a similar machine that had a clogged fuel line, and he reckoned he could do as good a job as they had with only the tools in the kit, which amounted to a couple of metrical wrenches and a screwdriver.

General Nivelle wouldn't look kindly on a delay, more so in light of his evident suspicions about Indy.

Indy bent to his task, the metal parts of the single-cylinder engine pinging and ticking as they cooled, and considered the irony of having been entrusted to deliver a message that clearly contradicted what he knew to be the truth. Niville had said that one had to be prudent about deciding what was true and what wasn't, implying that there was something tantamount to situational ethics at work in the war. Akin to the tacit agreement between allies and enemy not to bomb latrines or red-crossed ambulances or exhumers carting bodies from no-man's-land.

In the end it was left to each man to decide when there had been killing enough; when to give up the ghost and allow only one's body to go over the top. Indy thought about Remy on his way back to the front, and he thought about the countless deaths he'd seen so close at hand in the trenches these past few days. In a never-ending war it made little difference who or how many climbed from the trenches; the war would always have its tomorrow. But the humans tasked by who knew what order of demons to implement the war's demands should have a say in what went on.

There were breaking points.

Just as Indy's own machine had discovered.

He stood up and took a deep, cleansing breath. In the distance he could hear the ever-present sounds of guns, and he knew that men were dying there. He could feel the dispatch envelope in the jacket pocket, close to his heart. Nivelle had said to deliver it as quickly as was humanly possible.

Quickly he pulled an oil-stained rag from beneath the motorcycle's saddle, fashioned it into a kind of wick, and inserted one end of it into the gas tank. When the gas-oil mixture had saturated the rag, he struck a match and touched it to his fuse. He pushed the bike off its kickstand and let it roll down into one of the craters left by the Fokker's bombs. The thing hit bottom, skidded in the mud, and tipped over on its side, a moment later exploding in a swirling ball of flame.

Indy hadn't expected quite so much heat and fury from the surrendered machine. The force of the explosion knocked him backward, head over heels, down into another hole. When he picked himself up, he found that his knee had been torn open by a piece of shrapnel protruding from the earth.

For several moments he stood and watched the machine burn. Then he began to walk the dispatch toward the front. He would go as quickly as was humanly possible, but it was doubtful he would get the message there on time.

Some men would live to see another day.

PART II

Paris

"Then there was the bad weather . . ."
—Ernest Hemingway
A Moveable Feast

12

First out of the passenger carriage, Indy set down his duffel to marvel at his new circumstances. Above him arched light-filled glass panels and rose-medallioned support columns. Left and right the concrete platforms of the *gare* thronged with people, mingling in the chuffing steam of the locomotives. Furloughed soldiers and the civilians who had come to greet them exchanged loving embraces and kisses on both cheeks. Children in bright clothing ran about. Men and women in fancy dress, just emerged from *wagons-lits*—sleeper compartments—shouted instructions to luggage handlers who were wrestling steamer trunks onto handcars or balancing armloads of rectangular wicker baskets.

"I never thought I'd live to see this again," Remy said at Indy's back, mournfully at first but grinning like a happy child when Indy turned to him. Recovered from the wound he'd suffered at Verdun, Remy was his old self again, an indefatigable mix of bruised romantic and *bon vivant*. His brown eyes glowed behind wire-rimmed spectacles.

"Take a lungful of it, Indy," he was saying. "No stink of piss or shit or death in the air. Just the pure sweetness of the City of Light." He clapped Indy on the back. "Oh, the time we're going to have, eh?"

Indy hefted his duffel up onto a shoulder. "No stink of Captain Gautier's breath."

"That too, *mon ami*, that too."

They were both in uniform—khakis, ankle boots, and side caps—as was required of all soldiers on leave in the city. Hundreds of others crowded the beautiful station, many on crutches, some with missing limbs, some in wheeled chairs. Remy was right, the stench of the trenches was behind them—but there was no easy escape from the war itself.

They did, however, have almost fifteen hundred francs between them—about seventy-five U.S. dollars—and ten full days in which to blow it.

Reluctantly approving their leaves, Captain Gautier had said to Indy, "You must have some very influential friends, Corporal Defense." Adding, as he waved a pink telegraph slip in Indy's face, "I understand this was sent down from the office of Clemenceau himself."

For a time Indy had feared that General Mangin, or worse still Nivelle, would learn that the force behind Indy's "influential" friend was none other than his father. *Uh, not the father I said was dead*, he had pictured himself explaining to the general staff. *This, uh*, other *father* . . . Not that he had heard directly from Professor Jones. But rather from the senior Henry's intermediary in arranging for the furloughs, an old family friend named Jacques Levi, who taught at the Sorbonne and with whom Indy was expected to stay while in Paris.

Indy had been transferred out of the courier corps to Captain Gautier's grenadiers shortly after the incident involving the allegedly bombed motorcycle. There had been an investigation, but in the end even Nivelle's experts had been forced to agree that it was at least "conceivable" that the bike had been destroyed in the manner Indy had insisted upon. Of course, that didn't excuse the fact that Indy had been late in delivering Nivelle's dispatch to the front.

Much to Colonel Barc's relief, as it had turned out. Apprised that a countermand order was on its way to him, Barc had been praying for just such a delay; so when Indy finally arrived at Fort Souville, breathless from the long uphill slog and offering apologies for what had befallen the motorcycle, the colonel had said: "That Fokker pilot should be awarded a citation." Indy didn't have to be told that the men in the trenches felt likewise, though Barc's comment was to become a well-kept secret.

Nevertheless, in the six waves of attacks that followed the delay, tens of thousands of men had been killed. But Fort Douaumont was at last back in French hands.

"Indy, stop right where you are," Remy said suddenly, holding out an arm to restrain him. "Now, look to the right, there, going up the stairs . . ."

Indy did, and was rewarded with a sight for sore eyes: a trim young woman showing shapely ankles sheathed in silk. She couldn't have been more than twenty years old and was wearing a dress Indy had heard referred to as a *chemise*, hanging loosely from the shoulders and ending at mid-calf. Under a squashy Pearl White beret, she had her blond hair bobbed in the once popular Irene Castle style.

"French women have the world's most beautiful legs," Remy said, his voice wistful, without taking his eyes off the woman.

Indy hardly heard him. All at once he couldn't stop his eyes from roving. On all sides were women whose dresses seemed inspired more by archaeology than the movies: Egyptian- and Greek- and Oriental-looking tunics, complemented by moleskin turbans and drum major's hats and wide-brimmed things studded with vulture quills. Still other outfits, cut from broadcloth and serge and obviously sprung from the war, were replete with epaulettes, gauntlet cuffs, tartans, braid, and sword belts. A woman standing nearby had on a trench coat and a black felt tricorne that made her look like Napoleon . . .

"Indy," Remy shouted, shaking him. "Take it easy, Romeo, you're drooling all over your boots."

Indy closed his mouth and gave his head a quick shake. "Sorry. But, Remy: So many girls, and so little time . . ."

The Belgian tucked in his chin and grinned. "Ah, young Indiana Jones is going to set the town on fire these next ten days, is that it?"

"You bet," Indy affirmed enthusiastically.

Remy pulled him aside and lowered his duffel to the floor. "I'm glad to hear you say that, my friend, because I've been preparing for just such an occasion." He pulled a tattered writing tablet from a rear pocket and slapped it with the back of his fingers. "A list of the finest *maisons closes* in Paris. I began jotting down names the day we arrived in Verdun."

"*Maisons closes?*"

"*Bordels*, Indy—brothels."

Indy flashed a wolfish grin. "And all this time I thought you were collecting recipes."

Remy opened the tablet. "Look here: the One Two Two, Le Sphinx, La Poste . . ." He took stock of Indy's rapt expression. "You know, *jeune maestro*, perhaps it's a good thing you've waited as long as you have."

Indy frowned. "Hey, it's not like I planned it that way."

His friend wagged a cautionary finger. "The first thing you must understand is that, where sex is concerned, women do the planning."

Indy's brow furrowed. It wasn't women so much as the *search* for women, *chercher la femme*, that had gotten him into trouble in the past. Women were the reason he and his cousin had been on the Mexican border that fateful day Villa's men had ridden into town. And then there'd been London . . .

Shortly, Indy found himself outside the station, standing in brilliant sunshine on a boulevard bustling with activity. Finding a cab wasn't going to be easy.

"Where do you think we should begin?" Remy asked while Indy was busy signaling to every *fiacre* that passed. Horse-drawn, the four-wheeled open carriages were manned by top-hatted *cochers* and roomy enough to accommodate a party of four. Or two soldiers laden with overfilled duffels.

"There's the one on the rue du Perre in Pigalle," Remy continued. "That's fairly close to where we are now. But I've heard great things about the one on rue de Londres. Of course, we could start with the one on boulevard Edgar Quinet . . ."

"Do you mean now?" Indy said, turning from the street. "As in right now?"

"Well, of course I do."

Indy showed the palms of his hands. "Professor Levi and his wife are expecting me to go directly to their house. I don't have time to stop by a . . . *brothel*."

"Come on, Indy. There'll be plenty of time for your father's scholarly friend *after* you've had your ashes hauled."

"I'm already a day late, Remy—thanks to your last-minute 'note taking' in Verdun."

"Listen to me, *mon ami*, I'm not talking about spending hours. For your first woman, you'll need only minutes." Remy chortled. "You say you're already overdue, so what's a few minutes, more or less?"

Indy tapped his foot on the sidewalk in mounting annoyance. "Professor Levi helped arrange for our leave and for the train tickets. I owe him a visit, at least."

Remy rocked his head from side to side. "Good point, good point. But according to my notes, the One Two Two is only a few blocks from here in the ninth *arrondissement* and—"

"Forget it, Remy," Indy enjoined. "Besides, I have a feeling there'll be a letter from my father waiting for me." Indy hadn't heard from him since leaving the States almost six months earlier; and he hadn't written to him since London, after his enlistment—at his former tutor's insistence. "He's bound to be concerned about me if he went to all the trouble of writing to Jacques Levi. That's his way of communicating his feelings."

Remy sniffed disapprovingly. "Asking a friend of his to check up on you hardly seems like concerned communication between a father and son."

"Maybe, but I don't think he was too thrilled with my dropping out of high school to enlist in *your* army."

Remy twitched in amusement. "Oh, it's *my* army, is it?"

Indy allowed a smile. "I have to let Professor Levi know I'm all right. He can tell my father."

"I think even your father would agree that virginity is unhealthy for a boy your age. You know what they say, Indy: Old enough to fight fritz, old enough to . . ." Remy made an obscene gesture with his right forefinger and left fist. "And this is the city to learn all about . . . well, women." He appraised Indy for a moment. "Think about what's waiting for us back at the front, and then tell me that you're prepared to let this opportunity slip by."

Indy rolled his eyes. "I don't have to be reminded what's waiting for us, Remy. And I don't intend to let any 'opportunity' go by. I know I can get out of staying with the Levis, I just have to think of an excuse." He gnawed at his lower lip in thought. "I let them see that I'm all right; then I figure a way out . . ."

"That's the spirit," Remy said. "Meanwhile, I'll, um, keep the girls warmed up and waiting." He laughed unexpectedly. "Just promise me you won't fall in love like you did in London."

Indy scowled. "You're the one who got married."

"*Touché, mon ami*. And I'm missing her every minute."

"Yeah, it looks it, Remy."

Remy put his fingers in his mouth and whistled shrilly for a passing *fiacre*; the coachman heard the call and brought his rig to a halt a few yards away.

"You take it, Indy," Remy said.

"What about you?"

Remy slapped the pocket that held the writing tablet. "I'm not going far. I can walk."

Indy picked up the duffel and ran for the carriage. Remy called out to him as he was climbing aboard.

"Look for me at Restaurant Chodu in Clichy. I'll leave a note for you there."

"Restaurant Chodu in Clichy," Indy repeated.

"And don't forget about the cigarette trick."

Indy shook his head in bafflement.

Remy threw his hands in the air in transparent frustration. "Ten seconds out of my care, and he's already forgetting his lessons."

"So repeat the lesson, professor."

"If a woman accepts a cigarette from you, it's a signal. It means she's . . . of easy virtue, Indy."

Indy grinned. "I won't forget."

He gave the driver an address on the Left Bank as the coach pulled away.

Indy considered Remy's comment about love as the *cocher* was reining his horse into the traffic along the boulevard. How dare Remy think him an easy mark for love because of what had happened in London with Vicky Prentiss? It was just that there he was, a recent enlistee in the Belgian army, and suddenly surrounded by a bevy of desirable women: Suzette Chambin, Lady Lavina, and of course Vicky, the feisty polyglot and suffragette . . . "Spirited," Indy's former tutor, Helen Seymour, had called her. Indy had certainly been ready to propose marriage the night they'd dined in London—he had had the engagement ring and all, though the Thames had the thing now. But Vicky had stopped him before he had gotten the words out. She wanted a writing career, not a husband. And ever since, Indy had been asking himself whether what he felt for her was true love or a mild case of self-delusion. A kind of reaction to having made up his mind to enlist, coupled with a week of dramatic events that had encompassed everything from a zeppelin raid to a dinner with Winston Churchill. Instead, it was Remy who'd gotten himself hitched—to Suzette! Not that anyone would know he was married from the way he was carrying on now.

But if there existed a setting for love in this time of world war, it was Paris, Indy decided. Paris, which had seemed so distant from Verdun, now real, tangible all around him.

He let his eyes and ears drink in the hurried life of the streets: the darting *fiacres*, the trundling double-decker trams with their differently sized front and rear wheels, the gum-tired Brassard and Clement bicycles, the market wagons and three-wheeled delivery carts . . . The war had forced the return to the streets of horse-drawn vehicles that had been withdrawn in 1913. Nearly all of the motorized taxis and trucks had been conscripted for service on the front, and the few cars you did see about were dilapidated

ten-year-old Renaults, Citroens, Delages, even a Tin Lizzie
or two.

Indy tried to summon memories of the city from his earlier visit, in 1908. What with two million Frenchmen com-
mitted to the war and an exodus of civilians for London and
Spain and various sanitariums, Paris hardly felt like a city of
three and a half million—the city he remembered. Now the
boulevard was lined on both sides with shuttered shops,
some with signs that read: *Pour cause de mobilisation*. On
the door of a closed mattress shop, someone had scrawled:
"Sleep peacefully, your mattress maker is at the front."

Even so, much of Paris was as he remembered it. The
tree-lined boulevards and macadam streets hadn't changed,
nor had the *kiosques*, the cast-iron gas lamp posts, or the
omnipresent cone-topped Moriss columns. The sidewalk
cafés still flew striped awnings above their myriad of round
tables and caned chairs. And even the men sitting at those
tables seemed unchanged: dandies in pinched black coats,
spats, and panamas; peasants in corduroys and scarves,
smoking and playing hands of *belote*.

Paris had an architectural consistency seldom found in
cities stateside. Unlike New York, which seemed each year
to be growing more canyonlike, the nineteenth-century
buildings of Paris were sized to human scale. Five stories
tall, more or less, they had mansard roofs and tall windows
barred with twisting wrought iron. And in lieu of brick, the
structural material was an almost ivory-colored marble
called *pierre de taille*—freestone.

It was hard to accept that the place had nearly been overrun
by the Germans only two years earlier. At that time, dozens
of old trees had been felled and laid across the avenues to
slow the advance of General Alexander von Kluck's army.
But instead of entering Paris, von Kluck had turned southeast
at the last moment. French aviators detected the vulnerability
of the Germans' right flank, and von Kluck was met at
Meaux, twenty-three miles east of Paris, by the French Sixth
Army. Some five thousand French reinforcements stationed
in Paris had been rushed to the front in a fleet of little red

Renaults donated by the G7 Taxi Company, and von Kluck was not only stopped but pushed back to the continuous trench line known as the Hindenburg. But gunfire had been heard in Paris, and a church near the place de la Bastille had been damaged by German aerial bombs.

Indy fell forward in the leather seat as the *cocher* brought his carriage to a sudden halt. At an intersection of several broad streets, about a hundred chanting women were holding up traffic. A group of gendarmes in short capes and braided kepis were trying to keep things moving.

"*Qu'est-ce qui se passe?*" Indy asked the driver. What's going on?

"*Une manifestation, monsieur,*" the man said, doffing his top hat to run a gloved hand over a balding pate. A strike. "The girls are *midinettes*—seamstresses, dressmakers, some milliners. They want more pay and shorter work hours in the ateliers and shops. An 'English week,' with Saturday afternoons free to do as they wish."

Indy leaned out of the *fiacre* for a better view of the scene. Young and old, the women wore plain dresses, boots that buttoned at the ankles, and forage caps that gave everyone a somewhat militant look. They made him think of the suffragettes he had encountered in London, and an article he'd seen in a British magazine that showed photographs of French women working in the Citroen munitions factory, women driving ambulances, women driving trucks . . . The war was wreaking havoc with the old order of things. Gone were the crinolines, pagoda hips, and S-curves to which the women of Anna Jones's generation had been expected to conform. Something new was afoot, and it was going to change the way men and women dealt with each other.

Indy noticed several *gueules cassées*—disfigured soldiers—among the crowd as well, and asked about them.

"The soldiers want what we all want, *monsieur,*" the driver told him. "An end to the fighting."

They crossed the Seine at the Pont Louis Philippe, then angled across the northern tip of the Ile St. Louis and the southern tip of the Ile de la Cité before arriving on the Left

Bank. Keeping to the river, the driver steered them north along the Quai de Montebello, past fine old homes with tiny balconies that overlooked Notre-Dame.

Barges laden with lumber were plying the Seine's yellow-brown waters. Fishermen sat at the water's edge with their fish baskets beside them. In makeshift stalls along the concrete *quai*, knife grinders, umbrella vendors, and vegetable sellers hawked their wares.

Indy asked the *cocher* to stop so he could purchase a bag of roasted chestnuts; a bit further on he requested a stop for oysters; then a bouquet of wildflowers for the Levis. There was barrel-organ music in the autumn air, and the smell of pink sausage, green pistachios, and strong red wine. An old man wearing a black beret was leading a herd of milch goats to market.

Indy gazed across the river at the spires of Notre-Dame and the roofs of the Hôtel de Ville beyond that. He filled his lungs with the *plein air*, the sweetness of Paris.

He was beginning to feel alive again.

13

" 'War is a fool's game,' " Professor Jacques Levi read from Henry Jones's letter to his son. Levi was a thin man with an angular face and a shock of white hair. His reading glasses perched at the tip of a bulbous nose. " 'If Henry hasn't already figured this out, take faith that he soon will. But just in case, suggest to him for me that he reread the Russians, beginning with Tolstoy and Dostoevski. Tell him then to reread his Stephen Crane. If he still insists on poking his nose into speculative fiction, he might try George Bernard Shaw's *The Shape of Things to Come*.' "

"I have read it," Indy mumbled, mostly to himself.

They were seated in the parlor of the Levis' spacious apartment in the *beau quartier* of St-Germain, a Left Bank neighborhood of stately dwellings for the well-to-do bourgeoisie. The room had high ceilings and elaborate plasterwork detailing on the walls. The armchairs and drapes were heavily brocaded, and the rugs fairly vibrated with floral motifs. Indy's cane-backed chair was placed near the fireplace, which was cast iron with a marble mantel. The professor sat at an ornate period table with *bombé* legs. His wife, Annabel, had served English tea and was just now making crucial adjustments to an arrangement of fringed pillows that crowned the couch. A kind-faced, fastidious woman of about fifty, she'd given Indy a maternal hug when he showed up at the door, telling him how much he'd changed, how handsome he'd become. The flowers had gone over well.

" 'This war to end all wars is not some knight's crusade,' " Levi went on reading. " 'Rather than restoring vigor to the world, it is creating a wasteland which may well require generations to renew. This modern grail is a chalice filled not with the blood of Christ but the sacrificial blood of innocents—among which Henry may yet be counted. Be that as it may, old friend, any assistance you might render in helping him to see the light and to free himself from his obligations to the Belgian army would of course be most appreciated.' ''

Indy recognized his father's grail reference right off. Ever since Anna Jones's death, Professor Jones had been holed up in his office in Princeton, filling notebooks with cryptic drawings and notations related to what had become an obsession with the Holy Grail. Indy balanced the china tea cup and saucer on his left leg and raised a forefinger in protest. ''But I—''

'' 'You may inform him, too, that I am strongly in favor of his renewing his educational pursuits as quickly as possible after his retirement from the services. Since I do not, however, imagine him especially keen—in the modern parlance—on the notion of returning to Princeton, those academic pursuits may be undertaken at a university of his own choosing. He need have no concerns regarding my personal choice for what is best for him in this matter.' ''

''He's not expecting me to return home?''

Levi gestured for him to keep silent until he had finished with the handwritten missive. '' 'Thank you once again, dear friend, for all that you have already accomplished on his behalf in arranging for the—' ''

Levi scanned the remainder of the page and set it aside. ''Well, this last part isn't relevant.''

Indy broke an awkward silence by spilling tea all over the carpet.

He'd only meant to put the cup down but had ended up missing the table entirely. The edge of the saucer caught the arm of the chair and flipped out of sight. When Indy jerked forward to catch the falling cup, hot liquid sloshed over his hands and into his lap. He yelped, snatched his hands back, and in so doing sent the cup flying. The cup sailed straight up, struck the chandelier, and fell, hitting the floor with a wet crash.

Indy was bending to pick up the pieces just as Annabel Levi zoomed in with a doily clenched in her fist.

"No, don't trouble yourself, Henry," she said. "Let me."

But of course he did, and the two of them butted heads.

Annabel fell backward, a hand raised to her forehead, then decided to brave a second attempt and practically dove at the spreading spill, mopping at it with the doily.

Indy had the sense to keep out of her way.

Jacques Levi watched the scene without expression. When Indy finally turned to him, the professor merely shook his head in disappointment. He removed his glasses with exaggerated care and slipped them into a velvet-lined case.

"Well, Henry, is there anything you wish me to pass along to your father? Or are you planning to write him yourself?"

Indy pinched drenched breeches away from his thighs. "Well, sure. I mean, not immediately, but eventually, yes. It's just that I haven't . . . ." He took a moment to collect his thoughts, then grinned. "I'm amazed that he's given up on having me attend Princeton. But he's right, I'm not keen on returning to New Jersey just yet."

"And as to the other matters?"

Indy directed a quiet apology to Annabel, who was still on her hands and knees. "You mean my enlistment," he said to the professor.

"What else."

"Actually, I don't need my father or Tolstoy or Crane to tell me about the insanity of war." Indy said it with more force than he meant to. "But I have no intention of 'retiring' from service just because he's worried I'll get myself shot. It doesn't work that way. This war has to be won by people who are going to do right by the world and respect the sovereignty of international borders. The alternative is unthinkable. I'm sorry if I'm a disappointment to him. But the best-laid plans . . . ."

Levi offered a tolerant nod. "I'm certain your father will be sorry as well."

Out of the corner of his eye, Indy saw Annabel send her husband a censuring look. "Your father will be greatly relieved to learn that you are well, Henry," she said, pushing herself up from the floor.

"That goes without saying," Levi said high-handedly. But some of the hardness had already left his face. He beckoned Indy to the plush chair alongside the writing table. "How bad has it been for you thus far? Have you seen much killing?"

"More than I can recount."

"And are you glad to be away from it now?"

"In Paris?" Indy grinned again. "It's like heaven."

Levi folded his arms. "Don't be taken in by appearances, Henry. Paris is far from paradisical at the moment. It is in fact what some are calling a 'retrenched city,' brimming with discontent. The *belle époque* has ended. Unemployment is on the increase, and there have been numerous strikes. People have to endure long lines to purchase coal, sugar, even candles. Moreover, there are the blackouts, the fears of enemy raids by aeroplane or zeppelin, the searchlights probing the night skies . . ."

Annabel exhaled in weary agreement. "When I think back to the wonderful city this was." She gazed at her husband. "Remember, Jacques, when cows used to graze at the Auteuil in the Bois de Boulogne? Remember the windmills in Montmartre, the gardens in Passy? Our picnics *en famille* at Neuilly?"

Levi waved a hand. "I'm not referring to those changes, Annabel. That the city is marching in step with the times is to be expected. What I'm talking about is the political climate—this climate of repression and suspicion. Poincaré's government seems bent on extinguishing defeatism by arresting anyone who speaks out against the war."

"Jacques, please," Annabel said worriedly.

Levi only glared at her. "Who can blame people for being dismayed? The Allies have failed to push the Germans back across the Rhine; Joffre's army is utterly demoralized; the Russians are on the brink of overthrowing the czar; Italy is considering neutrality; Britain now has Ireland to add to its troubles . . . Europe as a whole is simply exhausted.

"And yet we're still asked to wave the flag and sing the *Marseillaise* every time it's asked of us. The government expects us to believe that the mutilated children they parade through the streets have been killed by the *boche* butchers, when we all know that many of those mutilations were inflicted by our own bombs and artillery shells. Poincaré tries however he can to raise the war spirit to a feverish pitch, despite the obvious need for a reevaluation of the issues. And behind it all lurks a group of small-minded militant politicians and generals who are still brooding over the indignities France suffered at Prussian hands in 1870. It simply has to end."

"Jacques," Annabel said, more firmly now. "Henry doesn't want to hear this. He's on leave."

"Henry *has* to hear this," Levi said. He swung to Indy with serious intent. "You'll see the slogans on the walls: 'Be careful, enemy ears are listening.' But the thing to bear in mind, Henry, is that it is growing difficult to know just who 'the enemy' is. To travel anywhere in the République now requires stamped permissions from the Ministry of Foreign Affairs, the Ministry of War, G.H.Q. at Chantilly, the Bureau of Movements in the Military Zone, the Aliens Control Office. The government is obsessed with ferreting out traitors and spies, and the terms that define those types are loosening. Almost every day sees accused citizens executed at the Bois de Vincennes—including women."

"Honestly, Jacques," Annabel said, "you talk as though the Germans aren't guilty of doing the same. What about that poor English woman who was put to death for trying to help a group of Belgian prisoners of war reach Holland?"

"Her name was Edith Cavell, Annabel," the professor snapped. "It behooves us to keep the names of these victims fresh in our memories."

Annabel sighed again. *"C'est triste, n'est-ce pas?"*

Levi looked at her in disbelief and snorted. "Sad for

France, yes. Remember what I'm telling you, Henry: Take care who you are seen with and with whom you converse. And watch what you say."

"I'll remember," Indy told him. In the same way he'd told Remy he would remember the cigarette trick.

Annabel approached the table. "Can't we talk of anything but the war? Can't I at least tell Henry about the marvelous week we have planned for him?"

"Go ahead," the professor said moodily. "I'm sure Henry will be overjoyed."

Annabel didn't respond to the sarcasm. Instead she grew animated.

"Well, Henry, first there's the revival of Stravinsky's *Firebird* at the Theater de Champs-Elysées—everyone who is anyone will be there. That's tomorrow. Then I thought we might take in a rehearsal of Jean Cocteau's *Parade*—my friend Mrs. Toufours can get us in. Picasso's cubist sets are said to be marvelous and the music is ragtime. Then, next week—well, there are simply so many things to choose from! Marcel Proust is giving a reading from his *Du Côte de Chez Swann*. Select pieces of René Lalique's Art Nouveau jewelry is on display. Several galleries around the city are featuring works by noted Fauvists, futurists, and vorticists.

"Of course I would have loved to show you through the Louvre, but most of the good paintings remain locked away in iron crates in case of an enemy sneak attack." She glanced meaningfully at her husband. "After all, the Germans did destroy the cathedral at Rheims. So who knows what manner of like atrocities lie in wait for us?"

Indy's thoughts reeled. First the letter from his father, then the professor's warnings about France's sudden case of spy fever, now a cultural tour that almost made the Verdun trenches seem like a holiday vacation. And Annabel was trying hard to make it sound as much fun as a chautauqua: those stateside educational entertainments that included a bit of big band marching music, an inspirational lecture or two, a couple of yodelers, Hawaiians in native costume . . .

When all Indy wanted to do was get his ashes hauled.

"Uh, it all sounds great, madame," he said at last. "But there is one small problem."

"Why, what's that, Henry?"

"Well, you see, the truth is, I'm actually in Paris on assignment."

Jacques Levi peered at him. "On assignment? For whom? And why wasn't I informed of this?"

"It came up last minute, sir. It's a . . . a secret assignment."

The professor looked skeptical.

"It has to do with a certain . . . penetration operation."

Annabel, utterly bewildered, glanced at Indy, then at her husband.

"I'm not free to discuss the details," Indy went on, "but I have to tell you that the operation will necessitate my being billeted elsewhere."

"Billeted?" Annabel said.

"Where?" the professor wanted to know.

"In, uh, in Clichy."

Annabel's manicured fingers flew to her mouth. "Good heavens. That hardly seems a suitable area for a secret military assignment."

"It doesn't?" Indy said.

Jacques Levi threw him a secretive smile and turned to his wife. "Annabel," he said consolingly, "I think I understand. The location was obviously chosen to confuse would-be spies. Isn't that right, Henry."

"Yes, sir," Indy said, instantly forgiving the professor for the paternal stance he had assumed earlier on.

"What a pity," Annabel was saying. "And we were so looking forward to your staying with us. I had a room all prepared." She forced an exhale. "But I suppose an assignment has to take precedence over home-cooked meals and a comfortable bed."

"I'm afraid so, madame."

"But, Henry," she said earnestly, "at least allow us this evening. A ball is being held at the Hôtel d'Orsay for the undersecretary to the minister of war. Several prominent people will be in attendance, including, I'm told, some celebrities.'' She looked imploringly at him. ''Please say yes. Permit us to tell your father we spent *one* evening with you.''

Indy mulled it over. Remy could manage without his company for the night, after all. And the professor had gone to the trouble of seeing to the furloughs . . . ''I think I can convince my superiors to allow me a free evening.''

Annabel applauded. ''That's wonderful.''

Jacques regarded him in obvious amusement. ''Who knows, Henry, you might even enjoy yourself.''

14

The name of the young soldier who had died in front of Indy's eyes at Verdun was Marcel de Mourney. Indy used the afternoon to deliver the soldier's inlaid box of letters and photographs to his widow.

Still a courier in the trenches.

The rue Jacob address Indy read off an unposted letter wasn't far from the Levis' apartment, but the neighborhood on the river side of the boulevard St-Germain may as well have been a different world. The de Mourneys' Paris—the Latin Quarter—was a labyrinth of unswept cobbled streets lined with ramshackle buildings. In place of *haut monde* women in mink stoles and tan leather high heels ornamented with pom-poms, Indy encountered example after example of the kiss-curled new breed, smartly simple in their wide-pocketed dresses, mannish hats, lace-up boots, and walking sticks. So many, in fact, that he began to wonder if men and women wouldn't be sharing the same clothes before too long.

The area had recently become the haunt of artists who'd turned their backs on Montmartre, and of penniless expatriates who had turned their backs on America. Indy had learned that Pablo Picasso was renting a studio a few blocks from rue Jacob, but no one answered the bell when he stopped by to say hello.

Perhaps Picasso wouldn't even remember him, Indy decided.

The de Mourneys' flat was near the church of St-Germain-des-Prés, at the top of five long flights of wooden stairs in an ancient building that had settled every which way, making for an even more difficult climb. The two small rooms, crowded with salvaged furniture, had gas but no running water. Not much older than Indy, the soldier's wife, Nicole, was a slight, dark-haired girl who had pretty features beneath evident fatigue. She had two young children, one of whom must have been born while Marcel was at the front.

She had already been notified of his death, so Indy was spared the gruesome task of telling her. When she asked him if he had known Marcel well, he told her no, that they'd only met for a moment. She didn't ask about how he had died.

Indy handed her the box, and she took it over to a table and opened it. She leafed through the letters and photographs in silent dispassion, absently, as though they belonged to a far distant past. When she came at last to the ring Marcel had bought for her in Vittel, she slipped it on her finger and regarded it with awakened interest.

"Do you think it was expensive, *monsieur*?" she asked Indy. "Do you think it will fetch much?"

Back on the street once more, Indy wandered about, stopping into one café for a cup of coffee, another for a plate of *quenelles*. He bought another bag of roasted chestnuts from a street vendor and sampled fresh goat cheese at a stall along the Quai des Grands Augustins. He eyed the velvet-clad women on their bicycles and saluted the fancy-uniformed *flics* on theirs.

At a Moriss column whose forest green top was decorated with lion's heads, he read advertisements for two American movies that were showing in the city: D. W. Griffith's *Birth of a Nation* and *A Fool There Was*, with Theda Bara starring as a dark-eyed vamp.

He also read the slogans scrawled on the walls, but he didn't find any urging him to be mindful—as Jacques Levi had—that enemy ears were listening. He did, however, come across an old enlistment poster affixed to the iron door of a building constructed in Art Nouveau style, with exaggerated bow windows and floral-shaped panels of colored glass tiles.

The poster depicted a bright-eyed and confident French soldier in a clean uniform, advancing into battle with one arm gripping a rifle and the other raised in assured victory. In script across the top ran the phrase *On les aura*—"We'll get them!"

To the same door someone had glued a political cartoon cut from a recent newspaper. It showed a skeleton sprawled at the foot of a German in a spiked helmet, who was holding a butcher knife and wearing an apron stained with bloody handprints. "*Remplace-moi, je suis fatigué*," the skeleton was saying, with one arm raised in supplication.

Replace me, I'm tired.

15

The afternoon had left Indy in no mood to attend a reception for the undersecretary to the minister of war. Nevertheless, he kept his promise to the Levis and went with them by carriage to the Hôtel d'Orsay, which fronted the river on the north side of the grand *chemin-de-fer* station of the same name. The gala was held in a ballroom of incomprehensible size and opulence, whose forty-foot-high beamed ceilings were decorated with murals and whose every inch of wall space was lustrous *boiserie*. There was enough food to feed an infantry division, and the band played fox trots and tangos.

Indy's khakis, though neatly pressed by the Levis' chambermaid, seemed ill at ease among the heavily braided dress uniforms that speckled the room, some dating back to the war of 1870. He had never seen so many *Légion d'Honneur* uniform rosettes gathered under one roof. Otherwise, the crowd was a blend of *haut monde* and Quai d'Orsay, as France's foreign office was known, with scarcely an attendee of either sex under forty years of age.

To say nothing of twenty.

Not that that in any way deterred Annabel Levi from introducing him to every *grande dame* and dowager in the place, ever on the alert for opportunities to mention Indy's age and talk of his "travails" at the front, but ever cautious to present him as Henri Defense, son of an esteemed friend, rather than Junior Jones, son of same.

The previous year, Poincaré's government had banned the wearing of costly gowns and jewelry at the Opéra, the Odeon, and the Comédie Française, but those restrictions had since been relaxed as a means of cheering "the boys commuting to the front." It was a thin line, however, between being thought fashionable or hopelessly *démodé*— ostentatious and very "prewar." Consequently, most of the women Indy was introduced to were attired in a style that had come to be called "deluxe poverty." He touched the gloved fingertips of a lot of well-fed bodies sheathed in satin georgette and organdy, balanced atop two-inch heels shaped something like toilet bowls. Several carried cigarette holders and lorgnettes, and more than a few sported bits of war jewelry and other items that had been fashioned in the trenches: cigarette lighters made of polished English pennies, rings and bracelets and arm bands cut from the copper jackets of fragmented artillery shells. All to offset the Egyptian and Greek tunics and tall cylindrical turbans.

As for the men, those not in uniform wore loose-fitting trousers and black coats pinched at the waist. Their felt gloves matched their hats, and sometimes their spats, with their worked buttonholes and shank buttons.

And nearly everyone was talking about the war.

"Well of course we should have listened to what Georges Clemenceau was saying in *L'Homme Libre*," Indy heard someone remark. "He was warning us about Germany years before the war began."

Indy smiled in recollection. Georges Clemenceau had been in politics for more than thirty-five years, but his reputation had been hurt by a public love affair with an American woman and by charges of financial impropriety. A *belle-époque* duellist of the first order—he had ranked first in twenty-two duels—he was known as "Tiger" to the frontliners at Verdun.

A former soldier off to Indy's left was speculating about "the Americans" joining the fight. "They're as pushy and barbaric a people as one could meet, but I sometimes think them destined to inherit and devour the world."

"One sees more and more of them lately," the soldier's gray-haired woman companion responded. "Crowding every other café you pass in the Latin Quarter, sitting there with their notebooks and their working-class attitudes. And hanging around that tiny bookstore on the rue de l'Odeon that Gide and Breton like to frequent. What is it called, Girard, the one owned by that chubby Monnier woman?''

''La Maison des Amis des Livres,'' Girard supplied.

''A war needs good ambulance drivers,'' a second old soldier thought to point out.

The woman sniffed at him. ''Ambulance drivers are one thing, bohemians with artistic pretensions are something else again.''

Annabel steered Indy around a gaggle of women listening attentively to a general who was expounding on the merits of the 75-mm cannon.

''Ah, there is Minister Lyautey,'' Annabel said, pointing toward the windows along the north wall. ''The small one in uniform with him is General Cartier.''

There were actually several small men in uniform, but Indy thought he knew which one Annabel was talking about. Lyautey was straight-backed and distinguished-looking, with slicked hair and a natty black mustache. Cartier had the build of a wrestler.

But it was only when the soldierly circle opened some that Indy understood what had brought so many diverse uniforms together: At the center stood a very tall, striking woman of voluptuous proportions. Perhaps in her mid-thirties, she had a prominent nose and bobbed dark brown hair. She wore a wide ankle-length skirt, high heels, and an osprey-plumed brimmed hat.

''Who is that woman?'' Indy asked Annabel just as several women he had already met were gathering round to ply him with questions about his experiences at the front.

Annabel adopted a long-suffering expression. ''That, Henry, is Madame Marguerite Zelle. You may have heard of her by her *nom de guerre*, Mata Hari—the exotic dancer.''

Indy looked again, wide-eyed. It *was* her, though he would never have recognized her with all her clothes on. In the photos he'd seen—on the way to Mexico and again in

Verdun—she was wearing little more than a peignoir through which her wonderfully rounded *derrière* could be clearly seen.

"I'd hardly call her a dancer," one of Annabel's Salonnière friends interjected. Her name was Mrs. Toufours, and she was dressed in a Turkish-style sleeveless tango frock and white satin tango pumps with clusters of diamant. "More a vaudevillian performer."

"More a courtesan, from what I understand," offered another—a Mrs. Pontamin, in a gold-embroidered Grecian tunic, an orange *crêpe de chine* wrap, and thonged footwear.

"What is a *demimondaine* doing here, anyway?"

Indy couldn't recall this latest speaker's name, but she was wearing a so-called "minaret dress" that fit her like a lamp shade and high-cut kid vamps with lizard stripes. Suddenly Annabel's outfit of *décolleté* tea gown and picture hat was beginning to look ordinary.

"You need to ask what she's doing here, Monique? The war has brought all of us together."

"Yes," Mrs. Pontamin said in grudging sympathy. "And look at the way Madame 'Mata Hari' hangs on the minister's arm."

Mrs. Toufours lowered her voice to a gossipy whisper. "She's involved with more than Lyautey, I can tell you. I understand she was van der Linden's lover before the war."

Indy knew he'd heard the name, then recalled why: van der Linden was the prime minister of Holland.

"I was told she was the mistress of Friedrich Wilhelm."

Indy started. As in Crown Prince of Germany Wilhelm? he wondered.

"She's lately been seen with someone closer to home," Annabel contributed with patent distaste.

"Who?" a trio of voices asked simultaneously.

"I don't want to spread rumors, but let's just say that he was a former minister of war."

"Not *Gallieni*?" one of the women asked, gasping.

Annabel shook her head. "Before Monsieur Gallieni."

Again there were gasps. "General Messimy?" Mrs. Pontamin said in shocked indignation.

But Mrs. Toufours waved a hand at her. "All politicians take mistresses. The Belgian, Leopold, had his Cleo de Merolde. Ludwig of Bavaria had his Lola Montes—"

"Another 'dancer,' " Annabel sneered.

"So much the better for the wives if they don't have to deal with the base needs of their husbands."

Mrs. Toufours leaned covertly into the circle. "I understand Madame Mata Hari earns one thousand francs for an evening," she said just loud enough to be heard.

Lip-rouged mouths dropped. The women watched Madame Zelle and Minister Lyautey for a long moment.

"Such a superficial, arrogant creature. An aging *cocotte*."

"Very *belle époque*, very prewar," Mrs. Pontamin said.

"I once saw her dance onstage with a live python," Annabel said. "It must have been ten or twelve years ago."

The woman in the minaret gown nodded knowingly. "An acquaintance of mine—and I won't name names—saw her dance at one of Natalie Clifford Barney's 'all-women affairs' only three years ago."

"Lesbian affairs, she means," Mrs. Toufours clarified for everyone's sake. "At the Doric Temple of Friendship, no doubt."

Indy reddened and tried to move to the edge of the circle, but Annabel blocked his escape. No one seemed at all inhibited by his presence.

"Precisely," the woman continued. "She rode in on horseback—sans costume, of course, like Lady Godiva."

"Not really."

"I remember seeing her at the Guimet," Mrs. Toufours said. "Or perhaps it was at one of Madame Kireyevsky's *salons* . . . In any case, she appeared swathed in veils I'm certain she had purchased on the rue St-Honore, and proceeded to rid herself of them, prostrating herself in front of this statue of an Indian god while she writhed those generous hips of hers. I must admit, the audience seemed quite taken with her. They showered crimson scarves upon the stage, and Madame Mata Hari—draped afterward in a gold *lamé* cape—graced them with a humble bow."

"Is that why she was known as 'the Red Dancer'?"

"Well, as for the dancing, it was merely tolerated. Everyone was primarily interested in seeing her in *déshabille*. And yet even then she kept her breasts concealed. She's absolutely flat-chested, you know, nothing at all on top. But enviable thighs and buttocks in those days, I will grant that much."

"No wonder the Germans were so fond of her."

Mrs. Toufours laughed nastily. "Well, it's not as though she were the other one—you know, Isadora Duncan."

"Absolutely," Annabel said. "It was simply Madame Zelle's Javanese lineage that people responded to."

"Javanese? I thought she was Indian—a Hindu?"

"Certainly not. She was the offspring of a Javanese nurse and a Dutch official stationed in the East Indies."

"You're mistaken, Annabel," the lamp-shaded woman countered. "She was the daughter of a Buddhist priest in Java and a temple neophyte."

"You're both wrong," said a fifth woman who'd recently entered the circle. "Her father was a British lord, and her mother was Indian. She was raised as a sacred dancer in a Hindu temple on the Ganges River."

"Oh, come now," Mrs. Toufours said. "That's the legend of Mata Hari, not the truth of Madame Zelle. In fact, she's Dutch, but she was born in Java. Her *grandmother* was the daughter of a Javanese priest, and her father was a Dutch aristocrat and scholar who read the Vedas and had been naturalized as an Indian."

"Whatever the case," Annabel said, "she apparently shot the servant who poisoned her son."

"Her son? A woman like that actually bore a child?"

Indy glanced over Mrs. Pontamin's shoulder and saw that Jacques Levi was leading Minister Lyautey and Madame Zelle over to the group. He tried to warn Mrs. Pontamin, who was going on about what she called Madame Zelle's "service record," but the woman only shushed him, and so wound up face-to-face with the former dancer just as she was saying, ". . . wherever one finds soldiers, one will find the Mata Haris of the world—"

"Ah, Monsieur Lyautey," Annabel said, fairly choking on the words and breaking a protracted silence. "May I say how wonderful it is to know that you now have the helm of the ministry."

"You are too kind, Madame Levi," Lyautey said gallantly, bending to kiss her fingertips. "And may I present Madame Marguerite Zelle."

Hardly missing a beat, the women said how charmed they were to make her acquaintance.

Annabel tugged Indy forward. "Minister Lyautey, please meet Corporal Henry . . . Defense, who has only today arrived from the Verdun front."

Lyautey bowed slightly from the waist and extended a hand to Indy. "A Belgian fighting at Verdun . . . I am greatly honored, Corporal Defense. Your involvement in France's struggle is a credit to Belgians everywhere."

"France's struggle is Belgium's survival," Indy said, taking even himself by surprise.

"Well spoken," Mata Hari told him.

Lyautey introduced her as Madame Marguerite Zelle and made no mention of her stage name. Up close she was even taller than Indy had guessed from across the room—five-eleven at least in her buckled and beribboned Louis heels. Indy also noticed that her round face was heavily made up. But her skin was a dusky amber, her mouth wide and tantalizing, and there was just . . . *so much* of her.

"My pleasure, madame," he managed. *You great big beautiful doll . . .*

"And mine, Corporal."

He couldn't take his eyes from her. And oddly enough, she seemed to be inviting him to meet her luminous gaze.

He was still watching her as she and Lyautey moved off.

"So what are your impressions, Henry?" Jacques Levi asked, regarding Indy with amused interest. "Of this room, I mean."

"Grand," Indy said, plainly distracted.

"And have you taken note of the sculptures?"

"Every last one of them."

"Wonderful statue of Aphrodite in the foyer, don't you think?"

Indy heaved a lovesick sigh, his eyes fixed on M'Greet Zelle's backside. "Just remarkable," he told Jacques.

From the center of her huddle of uniformed gentlemen, M'Greet watched the young Belgian corporal fairly tiptoe from the ballroom, free at last of the sexagenarian rumor-mongers who had gotten their claws into him. She gave him a few moments, then excused herself from Layautey's company and followed. After a short search, she found him in a small drawing room decorated with statues and assorted *fin de siècle* bric-a-brac. Henri Defense had a book in hand.

"Affairs like this demand a certain tolerance for *des mondanités*, Corporal. But I can well understand your having had your fill of Mrs. Toufours and her friends."

Defense turned to her in innocent surprise, as though he'd been caught sneaking a sweet before dinner. "I'm sorry, madame, I didn't hear you—"

"I was only saying that it seemed to me that you had reached your limit with Mrs. Toufours's sophisticated chit-chat."

"Well, yes. That is—"

"And you've found something more interesting in that book?"

Defense regarded it as though he hadn't realized it was there. "Not exactly. But when I realized it was written in Classical Greek—"

M'Greet narrowed her eyes. "You can read Classical Greek? Read to me, then."

Defense spoke a sentence of what certainly *sounded* like Greek, then offered a translation in French: " 'The goddess Artemis stood under the archways, the moonlight shining above her . . .' It scans better in the original."

M'Greet looked over his shoulder. "I suppose I'll just

have to trust that you're telling the truth," she said, close to his ear.

The corporal made an unsteady turn to face her, swallowing hard before he spoke. "Of course I'm telling the truth. As a matter of fact, I'm fluent in several languages."

M'Greet toyed with her garland of pearls. "Which languages would those be?" she asked in Dutch, her native tongue.

"Dutch is one of them," he answered in kind.

She switched to German. "And what others?"

"German, of course. Along with English, French, Spanish, Italian, Latin, and some Japanese."

M'Greet was pleased to see his confidence building. "Then you're either very well schooled or very widely traveled for someone your age."

The corporal was only momentarily chagrined. "The answer is both. I even know a few words in the Javanese language," he retorted. "Your stage name, Mata Hari, it means 'Eye of the Morning'—dawn."

M'Greet couldn't suppress a faint smile, though smiling was not something that came naturally to her. "You could have read that in any newspaper or magazine."

"I would say so if I did."

She gave him a coy look. "Yes, but perhaps you're simply trying to impress me."

The corporal returned a roguish grin that favored the right side of his upper lip. "How am I doing so far?"

She circled him, appraising him with theatrical scrutiny. "You cut a fine figure. But those khakis of yours could use a touch of braid and brass."

Defense wedged a finger into the collar of his shirt. "I know I'm out of place here. But no more than you are: the goddess Diana, walking among mortals . . ."

M'Greet touched spread fingers to her bosom in feigned abashment. "I beg your pardon."

Defense blushed. "I was only—"

"No, do go on, Corporal," she told him. "Please go on

with what you were going to say.'' She loved the fact that he had blushed.

"It's just that when I was young I had the privilege of seeing the palace dancers of Raj at Punjab, and they didn't compare to your extraordinary gift.''

"My gift? You don't mean to say that you've seen me perform?''

"Naturally. It was several years ago at the, um, Guimet. I was captivated.''

M'Greet pretended to reflect. "The Guimet, you say. And you were 'captivated.' '' She looked him up and down. "You must have been, what, twelve, thirteen at the time?'' She drew another blush from him. "Which dance did I perform, do you recall?''

Now it was Defense who pretended to reflect. "Uh, it may have been the one with the snake.''

"The snake? Oh, I hardly think so—not at the Guimet.''

"Then it might have been at one of Madame Kiyevsky's *salons* that I saw you.''

"Madame *Kire*yevsky's, you mean.''

Defense averted lovely eyes. "Of course. Anyway, I remember you in veils, and the scarves the audience threw—er, showered on you.''

M'Greet held her tongue, afraid her continued flirtation might be misconstrued as sarcasm. The last thing she wanted, after all, was to frighten him off. "I'm very flattered by your recognition of my meager efforts,'' she told him.

"Madame,'' the corporal said, smartly clicking his heels. As though it just then occurred to him, he withdrew a packet of cigarettes from his pants pocket and offered her one.

She smiled inwardly, accepted the cigarette, and squeezed it into an ivory holder. "Why, thank you, Corporal.'' It was an American cigarette—a Camel—when all she preferred to smoke were Turkish cigarettes. But she didn't suppose it would matter, this once.

What struck her most about Henri Defense was his youthful exuberance and naiveté—his *élan vital*. The uniform notwithstanding, he was hardly her usual type; he was not as tall as she would have liked, and he certainly wouldn't be one to fold his dress tunic neatly before sliding between the sheets with her. But perhaps that was at the center of the sudden attraction she felt for him.

With increasing frequency of late, she found herself attracted to younger and younger men. Or was that simply a measure of how deeply she missed her dear Russian officer, her dear sweet Vladimir, who had been wounded at the front and lay convalescing in a hospital in Vittel, in the heart of the war zone? Indeed there was something about Henri Defense especially that made her think all the more of Vladimir, whom she had taken into her arms only a few short weeks earlier, and whom she yearned to see.

As she drew on the American cigarette, she began to study the young corporal in a new light. Despite his rank, he was obviously well connected or he wouldn't have been among those invited to the affair for Minister Lyautey's undersecretary. Of course it could be nothing more than his being in the care of the Sorbonne professor, Levi, and the man's awful wife. But perhaps there was more to it. Perhaps Henri Defense held some secret rank among the Belgians. Or better yet, perhaps he was the scion of some influential Belgian family living as refugees in France.

The name 'Defense' afforded no hint at an aristocratic upbringing, M'Greet reminded herself. But what was a mere name, in any case? And if Henri Defense *did* have pull in high circles, then he might be able to help her secure the *carnet d'étranger* she needed to enter the war zone and visit her wounded young lover.

She at least had to find out. And given the broadness of the corporal's shoulders, his boyish good looks, and obviously strong arms, the task she set herself was not without its appeal.

"Tell me, Henri, do you have plans for later this evening?" she asked when she had crushed out the cigarette.

"Uh, no, I don't."

"Then would you care to join me for an *assiette anglaise* at my hotel?"

Defense's mouth dropped, perceptibly. "But what about—I mean, aren't you with . . ."

"You mean Lyautey? Oh, don't worry about him. We'll be through with our, um, business by no later than eight-thirty."

"Swell," Defense said in English.

You had to love the boy's enthusiasm.

"Now, listen carefully," she told him. "Go to the Grand Hôtel on rue Scribe and tell the front desk that you are my nephew, and that I want you to have the room next to my apartment."

Defense took his lower lip between his teeth. "Uh, I only have a couple of hundred francs . . ."

M'Greet wondered whether he was worried about the cost of the room or the cost of what he expected the evening to bring. "Don't worry about the room," she said leadingly.

He simply nodded.

She dug a room key from her purse. "Order an *assiette à deux* for eight-thirty and have it sent to my apartment." She pressed the key into his hand. "Take this, and let yourself in. Be discreet, Henri, but make yourself comfortable while you wait for me."

"Yes, Madame Zelle."

"And please, call me M'Greet."

"Yes . . . M'Greet."

She summoned another faint smile. "Perhaps I'll have something Greek for you to read."

16

Two hours later, outside the main entrance to the Hôtel d'Orsay, Indy said good-bye and thank-you to the Levis. Annabel tried to prevail upon him to join her for high tea the following day at a *salon* on the Champs-Elysées, but he said he was certain "his superiors" wouldn't be as forgiving of his absence a second time. He waited until their carriage was out of sight, then turned and walked in the opposite direction along the *quai*, west toward the Pont de la Concorde. He didn't hurry his steps, but neither did he linger at the stalls where the Moroccan vendors had their silver and brass merchandise spread out on hand-dyed bolts of fabric. He crossed the bridge without looking at—or spitting into—the Seine, and he shuffled through the place de la Concorde without taking note of the Egyptian obelisk from Luxor, the bronze-tailed mermaids and bare-breasted sea nymphs adorning the twin fountains, or the black draped statue of Strausbourg at the octagon's northeast corner. Nor, for that matter, did he note that the electric lights he had marveled at as a ten-year-old were switched off.

I'm having dinner with Mata Hari, he told himself, still waiting for the reality of it to sink in.

He continued in the sickly blue glow of the gas globes to the far side of the place, between the one-hundred-and-fifty-year-old palaces built by Gabriél, and on up the rue Royale, past the restaurant Larue and the Rosy Cross tea *salon* to the Eglise de la Madeleine. But he barely glanced at that masterpiece of Athenian architecture as he moved through the square and angled into the boulevard Madeleine in the direction of the Opéra. Horse-drawn carriages and trams rumbled by him, the music of violins wafted from the fronts of cafés, people approached him with black-market goods concealed under their coats, but he was oblivious to all of it. Until, that was, he had entered the vaulted and garishly gilded lobby of the Grand Hôtel and was standing mutely before the front desk.

"May I help you?" a tall man with finely drawn eyebrows was suddenly asking him.

"Help me?" Indy said, his voice cracking some.

"Yes, *monsieur*. Are you looking for someone?"

Indy swung from the lacquered mahogany counter as though he had forgotten something. Two uniformed bellhops were watching him, as were a few prosperously attired civilians and military officers and a hotel Pinkerton or two. "I, uh, would like a room," he said on completion of his spin on the marble floor.

The clerk read Indy's rank from his collar. "Do you have a reservation—Corporal?"

"No. But Mata—that is, Madame Zelle . . ." He cleared his throat and squared his shoulders. "Madame Zelle wishes me to instruct you that I'm to occupy the vacant room adjoining her suite."

The man lifted one of those narrow brows. "And you are?"

"Corporal Henri Defense. Madame Zelle's . . . nephew."

The clerk swapped looks with a replica of himself positioned further along the counter at a boxy telephone with a brass crank. "Of course, *monsieur*." He slid forward a registration card. "If you would fill this out. And of course I will need to see your passport and *carnet d'étranger*."

Indy handed over the requested documents and put his name and ID number on the card. Under "Arriving from" he wrote "Verdun." The clerk checked the information on the card against the passport and travel permit and handed back the documents. He then took a key from a rack and signaled for a bellhop. The kid who showed up an instant

later was approximately Indy's age and height, with a de-
fiant sparkle in his blue eyes.

"Miguel, show Madame Zelle's nephew to room twenty-
two," the clerk instructed. Indy could practically hear the
quotes he put around the word *nephew*.

The bellhop turned to him, a knowing smirk already
forming. "Your bags, sir?"

"My what?" Indy said, prepared for trouble.

"Your luggage."

Indy glanced away for a moment, then flashed his grin.
"You mean my duffel isn't here yet? The *wagon-lit* porter
at the station promised he would have it sent along." In
fact, the damn thing was back at the Levis' apartment.

The bellhop looked uncertain all at once. "I'll make the
necessary inquiries, Monsieur Defense," he said deferen-
tially. "And please allow me to show you to your room,
nonetheless."

Indy followed him through the lobby, past a sumptuous
dining room with tall, round-topped windows and rock-
crystal chandeliers, then through a spacious central courtyard—the "winter garden," it was called—ceilinged in
turn-of-the-century iron and stained glass and furnished with
Art Nouveau tables and chairs. It was in the Grand's *salle
de lecture*, Indy recalled, that his father had given a talk in
1908 on Arthurian legend. Taking up the whole of a near-
triangular block across from the Opéra, the hotel was world-
renowned, and often the choice of celebrated travelers from
around the globe. Henry Stanley, among numerous others,
had stayed there before steaming off to East Africa to search
for Dr. David Livingstone.

They rode an elevator to the third floor and walked for
some time down a carpeted corridor. The bellhop opened the
paneled door to room 22 and asked if Indy lacked for anything. Indy told him no and tipped him a sou. Then he closed
the door, put his back to it, and allowed himself to slide gently down to the floor, where he shook his head and laughed
at the utter strangeness, the *unreality* of his situation.

But only for a moment. Then he was up on his feet and

fishing from his pocket the key Mata Hari had given him. Opening the door a crack, he peeked out into the corridor; when he was certain it was deserted, he edged out of the room and hurried like a burglar to Madame Zelle's apartment.

The foyer opened on a small drawing room containing a *chaise-longue*, several Louis XIV chairs, a Coromandel screen, and a polar bear rug. A stunning view of the Opéra could be had from the balcony. Rich tapestries and gilt-frame mirrors graced the walls of a somewhat larger bedroom, but Indy thought the furniture a bit frowzy for his taste—too much velvet and brocaded silk *chinoiserie*, very "prewar," as Mrs. Toufours might have said. Off the bedroom was a combination boudoir and lavatory.

The main rooms were equipped with fireplaces as well as radiators. There was a telephone in the foyer and electricity throughout. It wasn't exactly his idea of homey after so many months in the trenches, but it would certainly do until the real thing happened along.

Indy counted twenty pieces of luggage, running the gamut from individual hat boxes to enormous wardrobes over-stuffed with shoes, undergarments, and voluminous dresses and skirts. Elsewhere were scattered what M'Greet Zelle must have considered her travel essentials: a portable writing desk; a hodgepodge of pens, spare nibs, writing tablets, and bottles of ink; a library of leather-bound books; a gallery of photos encased in silver frames; several throw rugs; a pendulum clock under a bell-shaped glass cover . . .

He ambled through the dressing room and into the lavatory beyond, surprised to find a full-size bathtub on taloned feet. He thought briefly about Nicole de Mourney's fifth-floor flat with its washbasin and pitcher of cold water. But he couldn't keep his mind off that bathtub. It had been *months* since he'd indulged in an honest-to-goodness bath.

The pendulum clock in the bedroom read eight o'clock, which meant he had more than enough time to bathe and still have dinner—for two—sent up to the suite. So he opened the taps all the way, dumped a handful of bath salts into the water, and began to peel off his uniform. He stepped into the tub before it was half full, lowering himself with a pleasurable sigh into the fragrant steam and soap bubbles. Then, starting with his toes—which would never be the same after the mud of Verdun—he went to work on himself with a bar of castile soap, scrubbing, lathering, sponging, deodorizing . . . Trying all the while not to dwell on what the coming evening might or might not have in store for him. When his thoughts did turn to the wished-for possibilities—might as well call them *impossibilities*, Indy told himself—he began to quail. He was seventeen, and it was about time, but this was *Mata Hari* he was talking about! Not some haggard Pigalle streetwalker, but a woman who danced naked and fornicated with prime ministers!

Of equal concern was the fact that he and M'Greet seemed destined to have met. She was far from the first person of celebrity he had encountered, but unlike the others—Princess Sophie or Annie Besant, Freud, or Picasso, for that matter—Mata Hari held a special place in his fantasies. Growing up he had often heard her name whispered by adults, and then there had been the photographs, passed with near reverence from adolescent hand to hand, in a way even a counterfeit Honus Wagner baseball card wasn't . . .

Indy had felt he was on intimate terms with Mata Hari long before coming upon the newspaper photo he had found in Mexico or the one he had seen glued to the wall in the Verdun Citadel.

Fate was not something easily grappled with.

His comrades had told him how war and sex could sometimes be a bad mix, that warfare could so confuse the emotions that sex couldn't happen no matter who one was with: a wife, a lover, a bordello prostitute. And what if that should happen to him? What if he couldn't get aroused? What if he got aroused and didn't know what to do? Daniel Beard's *American Boys Handy Book* hadn't delved into that.

He climbed from the tub spanking clean but hopelessly befogged. Among the manifold accoutrements of Madame M'Greet's *salle de bain* was a men's shaving cabinet, complete with straight-edge razor, leather strop, badger hair brush, and a shaving mug similar to one his father had used. Indy found it disconcerting that M'Greet would include a men's kit among her travel essentials, but he wasn't naive about her past, and he decided to put the items to good use. He even slicked back his hair with pomade when he was done shaving. Now, he thought, if he only had one of those small brushes for the teeth . . .

He had just time enough to order the *assiettes*. He hastened to the suite door, made a quick survey of the corridor, and returned to his own room. An *assiette* was little more than a dish of cold *charcuterie*—pork, usually—for travelers who preferred dining later than six o'clock, the standard dinner hour. It was known as the *assiette anglaise* after the British, who were by and large responsible for having instituted the distinctly non-Parisian practice.

Not five minutes after he buzzed for room service, the same blue-eyed bellhop appeared at his door.

"Will that be one *assiette*, Monsieur Defense?" Miguel asked.

"No, *à deux*," Indy told him. "And please have them sent to Ma—Madame Zelle's apartment."

"Two meals for your aunt," the bellhop said.

"She has a large appetite."

The bellhop glanced at Indy's pomaded hair and sniffed the scented air. "So I've been given to understand, *monsieur*."

Indy came close to biffing him on the spot but managed to gain control of himself. He waited fifteen minutes for the room service trolley to go by his room, then crept back over to M'Greet's when the waiter had left.

It was eight-thirty-five on the nose. Any minute, Indy thought, she would be coming through the door.

An hour later, however, he was still thinking it.

And an hour after that, with little remaining of his portion of the *assiette*.

By then he was wandering about the suite, trying to make up his mind whether to catch up on some much-needed sleep or hit the streets in search of Remy and whomever he was keeping warm with.

He had already sorted through everything of M'Greet's worth looking at, short of invading her privacy entirely: her collections of museum brochures and theatre programs, fountain pens and cigarette lighters, the fashion-plate catalogues—*Fèmina, Le Style Parisien*—and the magazines—*Frou-Frou, l'Assiette au Beurre, La Gazette du Bon Ton.* And he'd examined the photographs in their silver frames, showing M'Greet with one famous man or another. A few bore dates ten years old or more, written in what was perhaps her own distinctive hand, with its rounded, widely spaced letters. He noticed that the name "Mata Hari" was never without upturned crescents—the accent marks called breves—above the penultimate and last *a*'s.

At long last, just short of midnight, Indy picked up a novel and began to read. The novel was entitled *The Thirty-nine Steps*, by an English author named John Buchan.

In minutes he was sound asleep in the chair.

The boom of a 75-mm cannon brought him to with a pulse-quickening start. That, at least, was what the door sounded like when M'Greet slammed it. But by then Indy had instinctively heaved himself to the floor, cracking the back of his head against the chair as he dropped. The next thing he knew, M'Greet had his head in her lap and was caressing his brow.

"Are you all right?" she was asking. "Did you hurt yourself badly?"

Indy gave her a protracted "Huh?" and decided that he was dreaming.

"But you fell so *hard*. As though you were being shot at."

"Wasn't I?"

"Why, no, of course not, you poor thing. And I'll wager you were up half the night worrying about me, weren't you?"

"Half the night?" Indy swung to the tall windows; soft light was spilling through a crack between the blackout curtains. He lifted his head from M'Greet's lap. "What time is it?"

"It's just dawn, Henri. I'm so sorry you had to wait. I lost all track of time. Then I tried and tried to call the hotel, but you know how difficult it can be to get through."

Indy frowned in anger. "Where were you?"

M'Greet's brown eyes widened. "Easy, *cheri*. It was simply that things took longer than I thought they would."

"Lyautey took longer, you mean."

Her face clouded over. "Don't be difficult, Henri. I said I was sorry."

Indy pulled himself up into the chair and gestured to the food trolley. "There's what's left of the dinner we were supposed to share. I'm *sorry*—I got hungry."

M'Greet didn't say anything for a few minutes. She stood up, removed her hat and fur-trimmed coat, and put them away. Then she lit a stick of incense and arranged herself alluringly on the sofa. "Come sit by me," she told the sulking Indy. "If you're truly upset about our not having dinner, there's always breakfast. I'll even have some Heidsieck champagne sent up. I've a friend who obtains it for me far below cost."

"I'm sure," Indy said.

But he went over to her anyway, laying his head against the back of the sofa. Once more she began to caress his brow, gradually working her fingers into his hair. He heard his heart pounding in his ears.

"About Lyautey, Henri," she said, breaking a long silence. "You have to understand, he was expecting me to stay with him. When I told him I had to leave, he grew angry— just the way you did a moment ago. That's when I left. Before he sought to take unfair advantage of our friendship."

"Unfair how?" Indy wanted to know.

"By treating me as his property and thinking he could do with me whatever he wished. Why is that, Henri? Why are men constantly trying to control women?"

"I don't know, M'Greet." He looked at her. "Maybe because we want to possess the things we find beautiful. We're afraid to share them."

"And do you find me beautiful, Henri?"

"Very." He was certain she heard him gulp.

"And would you too try to control me?"

He shook his head.

"Even though I'm weak and can be easily controlled?"

"I wouldn't. I'd—"

She had taken hold of his hand and was tugging him toward him, tugging him *onto* her. Indy spread his hands, placing them on either side of M'Greet's face, so as to hold himself away.

"Don't worry about crushing me, darling," she said softly, closing her eyes. "I want to feel you fully against me."

"But I, I . . ." Indy stammered. "I don't know if I can do—"

She pressed a finger to his lips, silencing him. "Don't tease me, Henri. A soldier like you, returned from the front—I know what goes on there. Only promise you won't take advantage of me."

Indy's face was inches from hers. He could feel her loins making circular motions against his. He felt her arms encircling him. "I won't take advantage. But I can't—"

"You can," she said breathily, touching him.

"Whoa!" Indy said.

"You see? You can."

Indy leaned into her deep kiss. She took his tongue into her mouth, then took his face between her hands and kissed his cheek, his neck.

"Take me to bed, Henri," she whispered.

Indy lay spooned against her back in the suite's huge bed, with its half canopy and velvet curtains. The pendulum clock read seven-thirty and the light coming through the part in the blackout drapes was golden and aswirl with motes of dust. M'Greet was asleep, snoring faintly. Her amber skin was smooth and smelled of musk and perfume.

"In the east, I would bathe daily in milk," she had told him. Stirred by the nearness of her now, he began to kiss the back of her neck. He nuzzled her wavy hair.

The first time they had made love it was over almost as soon as it began. Remy had been right about that. But the second time, all credit to M'Greet's instructions, Indy had held out. *The secret is to take the slowest, sweetest route*, M'Greet had said. *Let me show you what a woman likes . . .*

Strangely, though, she hadn't allowed him to touch her breasts or to remove the satiny *cache-seins* she wore. Not that he minded all that much; it was arousing, in fact, to see her partly clothed. And M'Greet's lingerie was nothing at all like the corsets women had once worn, those wool things with bones and watch-spring steels. Now women weren't so much buttoned into their undergarments as they were gently hugged and lusciously contained by them.

It had occurred to him that M'Greet was almost as old as his mother would have been had she lived. But far from instilling in him any sense of misgiving, the difference in their ages only stimulated him all the more. Older women were experienced, and they knew how to be seductive. And as for Indy's older woman, Madame Marguerite Zelle, the exotic and celebrated Mata Hari . . .

He could hardly wait to tell Remy who *he* had warmed.

M'Greet moaned and rolled over to face him. Her eyes and hands roamed over him. "You're so lovely," she said.

"Are you hungry?" he asked, for want of a response. "I could go out and get us something."

The smile she returned was ambiguous. "You're so sweet. But there will be plenty of time to eat . . . afterward."

Indy gravitated to her once again.

The war had disappeared. For a time, at least.

17

Save for the satin bust bodice, M'Greet walked naked from the bed to the bathroom, where she performed her *toilette*. While the tub was filling, she douched with a spermicide solution prepared from a powder supplied to her by an English druggist on rue de la Paix. She luxuriated in the warm bathwater, wishing it really were milk; then, wrapped in a large towel she had purchased in Cairo and always brought along on her travels, she returned to the boudoir to dress.

First, however, she took a moment to study her reflection in the anteroom's full-length mirror. She turned one way, then the other, holding up a hand mirror to gaze at her callipygian backside. She had grown accustomed these past few years to her full face and rounded limbs, her Rubenesque stature—and the graying hair she kept dyed to its normal dark brown. She felt *entitled* to the added weight after her long career. Wasn't the same happening to Isadora Duncan, with her pert nose and double chins? It was only that the current styles for women stressed slimness over the full figure, and she was beginning to feel slightly out of step. One had only to think of the greyhound-sleek Coco Chanel, who dressed like a hospital nurse in her *chemise* dresses and little black frocks made of wool jersey. It was very boyish, this *sportif* style, but many men seemed to favor it. The talk on everyone's lips was about dieting and exercise, a pared-down shape for an age of fast-motoring flying machines, and world war.

M'Greet faced front and ran her hands over her body. Her shoulders were broad, her complexion dusky; then there was her towering height of one meter seventy-five. But the main problem, a perpetual source of embarrassment, were her breasts—mere raised nipples on her flat chest.

Of the many memories anchored to her shame, one stood out in particular. The year was 1907, and she was a newcomer to Paris. It wasn't the Grand Hôtel in those days, but a tiny *pension de famille* with a washbasin for a sink. On the advice of a friend she went to see the artist Jean Guillaumet in the hope of posing for him. But after she had summoned the courage to disrobe, he took one look at her and said that he couldn't use her. She had seen in his eyes how displeased he was with her breasts. And later she heard that he had described them to café friends as "*blettes*"—fruits gone bad and squashy. Others had even referred to them as tobacco pouches.

She had never uncovered them again—neither onstage nor in bed. In the absence of any cleavage, however, she couldn't wear a *soutien-gorge*, or "brassiere," as the new American version was being called; so she had had to improvise. For her performances, she wore specially designed metallic and bejeweled breast cups; and for bed, whether in sleep or love-making, the *cache-seins* stuffed with cotton—or with the belly down of geese now that the war had made cotton a source of explosive power and driven it from the markets.

But for all the adolescent embarrassment over her size and her chest, it was precisely those distinguishing features that had allowed her to see the world differently from her peers, and to develop her gifts as an interpretive dancer. While the girls in secondary school had been of a kind in their black uniforms, she had been wearing red dresses with bold yellow stripes or handmade robes of crimson velvet.

And it was plain that men continued to find her desirable, even as she approached forty. Including her latest conquest, her dashing young virgin Henri Defense. Former virgin, now. And how different *he* was from the run-of-the-mill elder statesmen and officers with whom she most often cavorted. No, Henri did not fold his clothes neatly before retiring to her arms, but Henri had the stamina of youth, rising to the occasion, as it were, time and time again.

Unlike the Italian captain from Genoa she had spent the night with after she had left Lyautey. The man was an inadequate lover and an insufferable bore; but he had promised to send her some money as soon as he returned to Italy—enough to cover her mounting costs in the Grand, including the room for her "nephew." Older friends, former lovers, were also promising funds, but none had arrived as yet, and the situation was becoming desperate.

It was unlikely that Henri Defense could assist her on that front.

It pleased her to see that he was already quite smitten with her—though she might end up picking up after him like a mother with her child. Henri was certainly young enough to *be* her child, in any case—just about the age her own son would have been, had he lived. But she was beginning to understand that true happiness was more in loving than being placed atop a pedestal and worshiped.

And how different Henri was, too, from her dear Russian officer, de Masloff, with his halting French and horribly wounded body. Gassed by the Germans, Vadim's scorched throat had scarcely allowed him to speak when last they'd seen one another; and one of his eyes, ruined, had been covered by a patch.

They had been introduced in the Grand Hôtel *salon* by another officer, and the three of them had gone to a get-together at Madame Dangeville's, where M'Greet and the twenty-one-year-old Vadim had fallen in love. He was a thin man, and he was soft and slight compared to Henri, who had a strong back and hard muscles. But Vadim suited her more than Henri did. Henri was innocent and unblemished by war; Vladimir was flawed, as M'Greet felt herself to be.

His eye patch, her concealing *cache-seins*; they were a perfect fit. And she wanted to do things for him: buy him fancy clothes and exquisite meals, pay off his gambling debts, rent an apartment where she could care for him . . .

The need to see him again preyed on her. The only thing standing in her way was the *carnet* that would permit her to travel through the war zone to Vittel. No one thus far, however, had seemed the least inclined to help her obtain one. Not the head of the Russian liaison post in Paris, not the local police commissariat. On the advice of a friend, she had even gone to see the head of the Section de Centralisation des Renseignements—France's counterintelligence bureau. But she wasn't sure she could agree to the exchange of services Captain George Ladoux was demanding.

The risks that strategy presented were too great. More than she felt she could undertake.

A few potential paths remained open in any event. She could appeal to her old friend Jules Cambon, who was now secretary-general of the Quai d'Orsay; or to Henry de Marguérie, whom she could still call Robert.

And there was the well-meaning, well-built, and—with luck—well-connected Belgian corporal, Henri Defense.

M'Greet knew it would require a certain delicacy.

She put on a robe, a feather boa, and blue leather slippers. Then she dabbed Poiret perfume on her pulse points and went to her new lover.

At nine-thirty, a hotel employee had walked the corridors ringing the warning bell that announced breakfast. As an alternative to donning proper attire and heading for the dining room, guests could request that coffee and toasted bread—a *petit déjuner*—be sent to the room.

M'Greet had insisted on the latter, as a means of avoiding the hordes of British and French officers who had turned the Grand into a kind of military hostel. Just now she and Indy were sitting at a fold-away table a waiter had positioned in front of the open doors to the balcony. The view took in the place de l'Opéra and a portion of the busy boulevard des Capucines.

Indy, back in his khakis, had asked how M'Greet Zelle had become "Mata Hari," and—between sips of coffee and nibbles of dry bread—she was enlightening him.

"My father was a wealthy Dutch banker. But as influential as he was in Holland, he could do nothing to prevent my mother from making me a servant of the temple. After all, she was Javanese, and the two of them were living in Java at the time. So as a result, normal home life ended for me at fourteen. I was turned over to the custody of the priests and trained in the ways of a dancing priestess, dedicated to a life of chastity. It was the temple priests who named me 'Mata Hari'—Eye of the Morning.''

"Then it's not just a *nom de guerre*," Indy said. "Like Mary Pickford or someone.''

M'Greet adopted a haughty expression and shook her head. "When I was sixteen, a Scottish military officer named Sir Campbell MacLeod visited the temple and saw me dance. He became completely infatuated and arranged for me to be taken from the temple by force. He took me to India and made me his wife. We lived lavishly for a time, and I bore him two children, a son and a daughter. But MacLeod was a brutal, abusive man with a horrible temper. When he drank, he would beat me for no reason. He used to make me perform for his friends—my temple dances and more. Do you understand, Henri?''

Indy made his lips a thin line and nodded.

"Then my son was poisoned by a female servant whose lover MacLeod had thrown from our household. I located MacLeod's revolver and killed her. Nevertheless, MacLeod blamed me for our son's death. He said that I'd been negligent.''

"That's horrible.''

"But of course we had to leave India.''

"I imagine so.''

"We returned to Europe, and I asked him for a divorce. He wouldn't grant me one, so I took my daughter, Non, and went to live with my father in Amsterdam. Then . . .'' M'Greet paused for a moment. "Then one night MacLeod came to the house in a drunken rage. He attacked me where I slept, raped me, and . . . bit the nipples from my breasts.''

Indy winced and averted his eyes, realizing then why she hadn't let him touch her there, or remove the bust bodice.

"That same night, MacLeod made off with Non and left

the country. Years later he divorced me. I've seen Non only once these past ten years.''

Indy took a breath. You didn't need to have spent time in the trenches to have war stories. ''When did you begin to perform in Europe?''

''Shortly after Non was taken,'' M'Greet said. ''I had decided to interpret the soul of the Orient, by means of dance, to the rest of the world.'' She glanced over her shoulder at something. ''Would you care to see an album of some of my photographs and newspaper clippings?''

The album was bound in red leather and a good four inches thick. M'Greet showed him a photo taken in 1903, in Paris, when she'd first danced at Madame Kireyevsky's *salon*; then another from that same year that showed her swathed in veils, dancing before a statue of the four-armed Indian god, Siva.

''This was taken at the Musée Guimet on the place d'Iena,'' she explained. ''The audience wore evening jackets and ballroom gowns, and I wore practically nothing at all— scarves, breast cups, a headdress, bands on my arms and legs. The stage was lit by oil lamps and festooned with jungle vines. Four dancers vied with me for Siva's eye, only to slink away in humiliation. I writhed my hips in sexual ecstasy, as I had been taught to do in Java, and one by one I rid myself of the scarves. When finally I threw myself at Siva's feet, the applause went on for five minutes. Later, I entertained everyone with a puppet I had brought from my native land.''

M'Greet showed Indy the glowing page-one review that had appeared in *Le Matin*. She showed him photographs of Mata Hari's appearance at the Cercle Royal, an aristocratic all-men's club; Mata Hari at the Olympia; Mata Hari in Monte Carlo, in Vienna, Cairo, Berlin, and Madrid, where she'd worn a kind of skin-tight body suit—a *collant*—to appease her Catholic audience.

The album contained excerpts from a Mata Hari biography, as well as an aged, flattened packet of Mata Hari Cigarettes, which Indy saw featured ''a blend of Turkish and Javanese tobaccos.''

Indy recognized the photos he'd seen in Mexico and in Verdun.

And how here she was in person.

But the photos he kept finding his attention drawn to were those of M'Greet in the company of famous men: with Baron de Rothschild; with Jules Cambon; with Fred Karno, the mime who had discovered Charlie Chaplin; with generals and politicians and businessmen from a dozen different nations . . . It seemed to go on and on. And he began to wonder which and how many of the men had been her lovers. Ten? Twenty? *Fifty?*

And what the hell was she doing with a counterfeit Belgian corporal? He gazed at her in wonderment, unbelieving—but wanting at the same time to hear her say that he could make her forget all the others; that he was the one she wanted. As much as he wanted her . . .

"Henri," M'Greet said suddenly. "You're not even listening to me."

"I'm listening," he told her.

"Don't you want to see any more photographs?"

"They don't do you justice."

She tilted her head to one side and grinned. "Are you so taken with me already?"

"Yes."

"And I'll remain in your thoughts when you return to the front?" She saw Indy's smile collapse, and quickly added, "I didn't mean to bring up the war."

"No, it's good you did. I have to remember what's real and what's a dream."

"Is it true about Verdun—that there are food shortages and desertions?"

"Some truth," he said, being purposely vague, as everyone on leave had been instructed.

"It's so terrible. I wish it would end. I wish that someone would sink all the German submarines and drop bombs on all the German trenches."

"You're not the only one."

"Do you think you'll be returning to Verdun soon?"

"In nine days, unless something happens to change that."

M'Greet rose from her chair and paced into the sitting room. He watched her for a moment. "But we can make the most of these days, M'Greet."

She continued to pace, then swung to him in anxious concern. "Do you think you could arrange for me to come with you?"

"To Verdun?"

"Lots of women have visited the front, Henri. Besides, I wouldn't necessarily have to stay in Verdun. I could wait for you in . . . in Vittel, for example. Vittel is close by, only one hundred twenty kilometers or so."

"It's a spa, isn't it?"

"Yes. And I understand it's very much unchanged, despite the war. I could take the waters while I wait for you."

Indy rubbed his chin. "Why do you need me to take you? Couldn't you just go there on your own?"

M'Greet hurried over to him. "I would need a *carnet d'étranger*, Henri. Do you think you could arrange for one?"

Indy thought about it. Professor Levi was the only person he knew in Paris who could probably arrange for a travel permit. And wouldn't *that* be a shock to Professor Jones: that Junior had requested a *carnet* for Mata Hari!

"Why don't you ask Minister Lyautey?" he said.

M'Greet walked away from him again. "Because . . . Things are difficult enough between us without my asking him for favors."

"I forgot about that."

"So it's up to you to help me, Henri." She looked at the floor. "If you wish to, I mean."

"Of course I do, but—"

She silenced him. "Promise only that you will think about it. But I don't wish to talk any more about the war, the thought of you returning to the trenches . . . You should ask your Belgian commanders to transfer you to Africa, Henri. I've heard the war is much safer there."

"The war is safer here, in your bed." He reached for her, and she allowed herself to be pulled into his embrace.

M'Greet locked eyes with him and grinned coquettishly. "Only for you, I think . . ."

18

M'Greet had mentioned a "sensational exhibition" she wished to attend, and Indy—being the sport he was, and deciding there was apparently no escape after all from the kind of cultural tour Annabel Levi had planned—had said, sure, he'd love to tag along.

So, by noon, after another long session in each other's arms, they were riding the elevator down to the Grand's showcase lobby, M'Greet wearing a turban, wide skirt, and short jacket trimmed with feathers, Indy feeling as though he were sporting a chestful of braid and brass.

The hotel staff—bellhops, concierge, and maître d'—positively fell over themselves in their attempts to please her, presenting her with newspapers and messages, offering to fetch carriages, motor taxis, whatever she needed. And on each occasion, regardless of whether services were actually rendered, M'Greet would turn to Indy and say, "Be a darling and give him a sou." So often, in fact, that Indy calculated he was down several francs long before they reached the front doors.

"How can you afford to stay here?" Indy hazarded to ask.

"All first-class establishments charge a reduced tariff for stars," she told him. "Strictly as a means of advertising their cachet among the *haut monde*."

Indy could see how it paid off: scarcely a man they passed failed to doff his hat to her, some bowed, and a few took her fingertips. "Madame Zelle, how charming to see you," they would say. Or, "Madame Mata Hari, what an honor it is to see you again.'' Most were handsome young men in checked trousers and waistcoats, spotless ties and gleaming boots; but many were officers in one army or another, French, Italian, Belgian, British Expeditionary Force, even an American or two, all billeted at the Grand.

And Indy wished they would all disappear.

The women stared openly or exchanged whispered remarks behind the privacy of open fans.

"And how are you and your nephew this morning?" a clerk at the front desk asked.

"Wonderful," M'Greet told him. "Simply marvelous."

No mention of Indy being other than a relative.

They exited through the arcaded winter garden, which left them on boulevard des Capucines. M'Greet said that the exhibition was only a few blocks away and suggested they walk rather than hire a taxi. Indy agreed, seeing it as money in his pocket.

They began to follow much the same course he had taken the previous night—down the boulevard toward the Madeleine—but short of the church M'Greet led them east toward the place Vendome. The rue de la Paix was one of the city's most chic streets, and Indy thought it an odd place for someone to open a gallery. But less than a block along he realized that M'Greet's "sensational exhibition" had nothing at all to do with painting, and everything to do with *haute couture*.

"I can't go in *there*," he protested at the glass door to a couturier's shop.

"Well, of course you can," she told him.

"But it's all . . . *women's* things."

"Don't you like women, Henri?"

"Sure I do, only, only . . ."

"Only nothing," M'Greet said, and dragged him inside.

As he had feared, he was the sole man in the room, and his arrival on the arm of Madame Zelle caused quite a sensation among the hundred or so women already present. But M'Greet was nothing if not the consummate cynosure;

she linked arms with Indy and found them a table at the center of the hubbub.

For decades the arbiter of high fashion, the *haute couture* of Paris was rebounding from two years of enforced hibernation. At the start of the war—as M'Greet explained it to Indy—many of the city's celebrated designers had closed their ateliers and gone off to fight at the front. Paul Poiret had enlisted in the army; the House of Worth had ceased operation; Jenny had substantially reduced her output. Clothes had gone overnight from gay to drab. But now even *couture* had been deemed vital to the war effort.

Which Indy thought went a long way toward explaining why the exhibit, the fashion show—the *café-concert*—had been imbued with such martial purpose. To the strains of patriotic music, a murder of mannequins paraded about the room, sometimes among the tables, other times onstage, against a painted backdrop of a military map of France studded with little tricolored flags that identified battle sites along the trench line. Elsewhere were posters depicting coquettish young women hanging on the arms of brave young soldiers—sans the whiskers and brown teeth that characterized the *poilus*. There were dresses named "La Marseillaise," skirts—similar to the one M'Greet was wearing—called "the war crinoline," turtleneck sweaters identical to those worn by English sailors, even silk blouses allegedly sewn from the parachutes of downed German aviators!

"Show your frontline hero how much you care," a female voice was saying over a loudspeaker. "Show him that your shortened skirts and V-neck gowns are for his eyes only. Deprive him of nothing; deprive yourself of nothing. Put a good face on the war, and be sure to wear your clothes with a youthful, carefree approach—*avec désinvolture*. 'Jaunty,' one might say . . ."

The mannequins continued to circulate, showing shapely ankles and calves, slouching as they walked. Indy saw more pieces of jewelry fashioned from artillery shells, and miniature 75-mm cannons dangling from silver or gold chains.

M'Greet heard him grumbling and leaned toward him. "This is all very *outré*. Very 'war.' "

Indy shook his head. "This has nothing to do with the war. They don't understand that the war has already created a style all its own."

"Really. And what style is that, darling?"

"Mourning wear," Indy told her.

M'Greet insisted on lunching at her favorite restaurant, the Pavillion d'Armenonville in the Bois de Boulogne. They hired a carriage to take them part way down the Champs-Elysées—the name meant Elysian Fields, home of the virtuous dead—and from there they walked, or more accurately strolled—*flaner* was the word M'Greet used—in the direction of the place Etoile.

The chestnut-lined boulevard was the ideal place to see and be seen, even on a weekday afternoon. Once more M'Greet was greeted by seemingly every other man they passed: all *boulevardiers* in Prince of Wales tweeds, wide-brimmed trilbys, and pointed nubuck shoes of the sort gangsters would affect. And once more Indy felt grabbed and shaken by jealousy. He didn't want her to have a past; he didn't want either of them to have pasts. He wanted things to be all future.

At the Arc de Triomphe, where a photographer with a box camera and tripod wanted to shoot them, they hailed another *fiacre* and this time rode it all the way to the park. Built at the edge of a small man-made lake, the Pavillion d'Armenonville was a three-story wooden structure with Victorian detailing, reminding Indy of some of the smaller resort hotels he knew from the New Jersey shore. M'Greet was well known there, and a *garçon* in a white bosom shirt immediately showed them to a table. The dining room had plush carpets, gilded brass chandeliers, and Doric-style columns; one wall was given over entirely to floor-to-ceiling windows.

M'Greet ordered oyster *apéritifs*.

During the French Revolution, the Bois de Boulogne had served as a hideout for aristocrats and others fleeing the guillotine. Baron Haussman—chief architect to Napoleon III, and the man most responsible for the layout and look of modern Paris—had used Hyde Park as his model for redesigning the bois. Now it was prized not only for its winding paths, ornamental ponds, and *kiosques*, but for the Longchamp Racecourse and the Auteuil, known for its jumps.

"Horses are my second great love," M'Greet was telling Indy when lunch arrived. "Early on, even before I achieved fame as a dancer, I worked as a riding instructor. Then on a dressage team in the circus. Of course, there wasn't much work for dressage teams once lion tamers appeared on the scene."

"I'm pretty good with a whip myself," Indy said.

"Do say."

"And I consider myself a pretty good rider as well."

She smiled in a patronizing way. "Well, we must ride together sometime soon. As for your using a whip—"

"No, seriously," Indy pressed, eager to demonstrate that there was a lot more to him than a facility for languages—that he could stand in the shoes of any of the officers or dandies they'd encountered on the boulevard. "Pancho Villa's lieutenant said I was one of the finest horsemen he'd ever seen."

M'Greet blinked. "Are you telling me that you rode with Pancho Villa?"

"I did. I was with him when he raided the Hearst hacienda."

"Well, that's something, isn't it." M'Greet took a sip of wine. "After dancing and riding, I think I would pick big-game hunting as my third great love. In India, before my marriage to MacLeod became unbearable, we would often hunt tigers in the—"

"I hunted rhinos in East Africa with Teddy Roosevelt!" Indy gushed.

M'Greet stared at him. "*President* Teddy Roosevelt?"

Indy nodded. "He used to get carried away with the killing. I finally had to tell him to stop, before he hunted the fringe-eared oryx to extinction."

"You told Theodore Roosevelt to stop hunting."

"Absolutely."

"On safari in East Africa."

"In Kenya, to be exact."

"And when was this?"

"1909."

"And you were how old at the time?"

"Te—Uh, old enough to shoot a rifle."

M'Greet watched him a moment longer, then laughed. "You're making fun of me, aren't you. Just because of the photograph album."

Indy grew worried. "No, I'm not, really," he started to say. But M'Greet wasn't listening; she was looking out the window at something. "What is it?" he asked at last.

"Those two men," M'Greet said, gesturing with her chin.

Indy pivoted in his chair. The pair to whom she had to be referring were in a rowboat in the middle of the lake. They were wearing raincoats and derbies.

"They've been following me ever since I arrived in Paris. It has been weeks now."

"Following you why?"

"Who can say? But I think it must have something to do with what happened on the boat from England. Then there was all that business on the Spanish frontier . . ."

Indy set back his chair. "Maybe you should start from the beginning."

M'Greet took another sip of wine. "Well, first England refused to issue me a passport to travel by ferry to France. I was coming from Holland, you see. In any case, without the passport to travel by ferry across the Channel I had no choice but to go the long way around—by steamer to Spain. And on the boat was this horrible British man named Hoedemaker, who described himself as a businessman but who was really on board to spy on the passengers—especially those Dutch, Danes, and Norwegians who were suspected of being en route to South America to manage German firms."

Already, Indy didn't like the sound of it, but he told her to go on.

"I had noticed this man Hoedemaker whispering to the

officials who stamped my transit papers in Falmouth—where, incidentally, I was subjected to a body search by some of those miserable suffragette women."

Indy thought about Vicky Prentiss, his almost-fiancée. If Vicky had been one of them, that meant that—

"Then, back at sea," M'Greet continued, "I learned that Hoedemaker was spreading rumors that he'd searched *my* cabin. Well, naturally, I confronted him, and I demanded an apology. When he denied it—" she clapped her hands together "—I slapped him, just like that. Right across his face. I not only drew blood for my efforts but applause from the other passengers. They had as little use for the man as I did."

Indy ran a hand over his mouth. M'Greet's story was sounding worse and worse. "So what happened at the Spanish border?"

"He made more trouble for me with the guards. Beforehand he was following me all over Madrid; then, at the French frontier, he arranged for me to be sent back to San Sebastian and detained for three days before I was permitted entry into France. I thought it would all be behind me once I reached Paris. But not two weeks later, these two *flics* show up—"

"*Flics?*" Indy interrupted. "You mean they're policemen?"

"Who else would they be? They hang around the hotel, they watch me from doorways, they follow me into cafés . . . I finally had to tell the hotel staff about them."

"And what did they tell you?"

M'Greet shrugged. "That they could do nothing. I tell you, Henri, the war has made everyone so suspicious. All these tribulations we're forced to endure."

She used the term *tracasseries*, but Indy saw them as a good deal more than petty annoyances. Or hadn't M'Greet heard about France's current dose of spy fever?

"Well, of *course* it's due to espionitis," she said after he had aired his concerns. "That's precisely what I'm saying."

"But you have to be careful, M'Greet."

She waved a hand dismissively. "It's nothing at all. They're simply keeping themselves entertained at my expense."

Indy glanced at the two men in the rowboat and wasn't so sure.

M'Greet took hold of his hand. "You mustn't let it upset you, darling. It's just the war, and you must push all that from your mind."

"That's not exactly easy when all you see around here are wounded soldiers and earrings made out of shell casings."

"Stop being morbid. For all you and I know the war could be ending right now, but the news has yet to reach us."

"What good does it do to pretend?"

M'Greet reached over and turned his face to her. "What's true is what's happening to us here, right now. All else is illusion, Henri. As a Hindu, I understand this better than most. That's the message I tried to convey with my dance: that life is for the living." Her face clouded over in anger. "I was dancing the cycle of life, sex, and death. My dances were meant to be a revelation, an unlocking of hidden doors. But people failed to understand. My message was degraded by lesser talents who believed that nudity was the single important ingredient."

Indy was attentive to her every word. He was well aware of exactly what she had unlocked in *him*. He brought her hand to his lips. "You do make it easy for me to forget the war."

She regarded him in silence for a long moment. "Tell me what you are thinking, Henri."

"It's difficult to put into words."

"You love me, isn't that it? Go ahead, tell me you love me."

"I do."

"And I do you, darling. That's why it's so important that we be together. You must try to secure the travel permit for me."

"I'll do what I can," Indy said, not knowing whether he

meant it or not, uncertain that he could be of any help. But he wanted to be with her; that much was clear.

M'Greet had signaled the waiter to prepare the bill. "When this nasty war business is over, we'll go to Biarritz, Henri. We'll swim in the ocean and drive through the Pyrénées in an Hispano-Suiza and dance until dawn at the Hôtel du Palais."

"I'm more interested in tonight," Indy said.

She averted his gaze. "Tonight is a problem, darling. I do want to stay with you, but I'm expected to attend a dinner party. The plans were made weeks ago. I'm sure you can understand."

"With whom? Whose arm are you going to be on tonight?"

"Please, darling." She patted his hand. "Let's not create a scene."

"After dinner, then."

"Absolutely. And now I must go," M'Greet said, rising. She kissed him quickly on the cheek. "Don't look so sad. It's only a matter of hours."

"I'll miss you," he said to her back as she hurried off.

The waiter delivered the bill; the sum was almost enough to break him.

He glanced out the window while he dug deep in his pocket for the money. The two men in the rowboat were no longer there.

19

Indy rode the métro to the place Clichy and asked around for Restaurant Chodu. As it happened, the restaurant was closer to Pigalle; but rather than take the subway again, Indy opted to cover the few blocks on foot. The route took him past accordion players, streetwalkers, and reeking *pissoirs*. On the left side of the street was the Red Windmill, the Moulin Rouge, whose entrance was jammed with soldiers eager for a look at lifted skirts, frilly underwear, *can-can* abandon. Indy would have been there himself, were it not for M'Greet.

He recalled walking that same stretch of boulevard almost eight years earlier, but either the street had changed or his memory of it had altered with the passage of time. In 1908 the area around Montmartre, the slopes of *le butte sacré*, had been an intoxicating mix of the rowdy and the bohemian; now the street felt forlorn somehow, in search of an identity to replace that which the artists, in their emigration to Montparnasse and the Latin Quarter, seemed to have taken with them. The rowdiness remained, but it had turned pedestrian and vaguely dangerous—especially in the diminished light of world war. So too had the *clochards*, the young women forced by circumstance to sell themselves on the street, and their pimps.

The note Indy found waiting at the Chodu contained directions to a dilapidated building on a steep, cobblestone street just west of the Basilique du Sacré Coeur, at the top of the mount. Indy surmised the place was a brothel from the fact that Remy had enclosed a code word to be used at the door.

"Coco," Indy said to a man who asked who had sent him.

The door opened, admitting him into a foyer where the same beefy man wanted to know if he was carrying a gun. Indy told him no and asked after Remy. The doorman suggested Indy look for him in the *salon de choix*—the choosing room.

Indy didn't have to be told when he'd arrived. The giveaway—aside from the plush carpets and crimson walls and velvet draperies, aside from the smell of wine and beer and brandy and the layers of cigarette, cigar, and hashish smoke—aside, in fact, from the soldiers dancing the Maxi and the Grizzly Bear with each other—were the dozen or so pedestals central to the room, atop which were perched, as if some erotic menu, a diverse assortment of partially clad women. Some round, some thin; some tall, some petite; some with black hair, some with blond; some old, and some incredibly young. Attired in short aprons and high heels, in sheer peignoirs and camisoles, in opéra vests and pure silk undies, in vivacious peach panties and slip bodices, in lacy brassieres and slim-fitting knickers . . .

"Welcome to the Baboon's Place, soldier," a woman appeared at Indy's right hand to say, loud enough to be heard over the music and song and scores of voices. "I'm Mimette."

She was forty, Indy guessed, buxom and handsome, her dark hair elaborately coiffured. He supposed she was the *maîtresse*—the madame.

"Do you see something you favor up there?" Mimette asked. "They all have their yellow health cards. Government-inspected, *comprenez-vous, monsieur*?"

Indy glanced at the pedestals. *Everything*, he wanted to tell her. But what he said was: "I'm looking for a Belgian corporal named Remy Baudouin."

Mimette planted her hands on her hips, threw her head back, and laughed. "Him!" She looked Indy over. "I never would have figured you for that one's friend, but yes, he's here all right." She took him by the elbow and gestured through the crowd to a table across the room. "Sitting there with Genevieve and Colette."

Indy thanked her and was just setting off when she yanked him back. "And no trouble, soldier, understand?"

"Yes, madame, no trouble," Indy promised. Whatever that meant. He hadn't made it halfway to Remy's table when the Belgian glimpsed him and screamed his name.

"Where the hell have you been?" Remy kissed Indy on both cheeks and bear-hugged him through a complete circle.

Indy sat down opposite one of the women, the older of the pair, a bright-eyed *brune* with lacquered fingernails. "I, uh, got here as quickly as I could."

"You mean you've been with the professor all this time?" Remy was incredulous.

"Jeez, Remy, it's only been a day and a half."

"Do you know what I've been able to do with a day and a half?" Remy put an arm around each woman and grinned.

"I don't want to know."

"Oh, yes, you do, *mon ami*."

"Oh, no, I don't."

"Oh, yes, you do," the women said together.

Indy looked from face to face in wonder.

"Girls," Remy said, "meet my best friend, Indiana Jones. Indy, meet—"

"Genevieve and Colette, I know." He kissed their hands.

"Oh-la-la, a *gentleman*," the one with the nails, Colette, said. She threw Indy a lecherous wink.

Genevieve, raven-haired and toothy, gave him the same up and down look Mimette had. "Indiana sounds like a name for a dog."

"You and my father would get along really well," Indy said.

"So, just what *have* you been doing?" Remy wanted to know.

"Uh, going to lectures, exhibitions, that sort of thing."

Indy wanted to tell Remy about M'Greet, but at the same time he worried that Remy's feelings would be hurt when he learned he would be on his own for the entire furlough.

Better to make it sound like an obligation, Indy had decided. And in fact there was a good chance Indy would be spending additional time with the Levis after all. Earlier, on the phone to Jacques Levi to say that he would be by to collect his duffel, Indy had broached the subject of procuring a travel permit for "a friend." The professor had said that something could probably be arranged, but he wanted to talk to Indy first. About the letter to his father, among other things.

"You have to learn to sidestep these obligations," Remy was saying. "Life is short, my young friend. You can't allow it to pass you by."

Indy peered at Remy, noticing for the first time that the Belgian had a shiner. "Life obviously isn't passing you by. It looks like it hit you square in the face."

Remy gently fingered the purple bruise. "I was only dancing on the piano."

Colette and Genevieve traded looks and giggled. "More like dancing *in* the piano," Colette remarked.

"The guy was playing 'Heaven Will Protect the Working Girl,' " Remy explained. "And Genevieve, here—"

"Oh, no, Remy," she cut him off. "I didn't start it."

"I distinctly recall you saying you hated Marie Dressler."

"That didn't mean you had to ruin the piano."

"He took away all the music," Colette told Indy, pouting.

Indy watched the three of them laugh. "Sounds like a wild party."

"Yes," Remy said. "And we want you there for the next one." He looked at Colette. "Isn't that right, *ma chèrie*, don't we want Indy along?"

Colette winked again.

"Uh, I'm trying, Remy," Indy began. "It's just not going to be as easy as I thought it would be. Besides, I'm having an all-right time."

"Going to lectures? Going to exhibitions? How can that be any fun?"

Indy shrugged. "I guess after the trenches and all. You know, it's . . . calming. Sitting by the river watching the boats, feeding the birds, wandering around, being reminded that life goes on, even now."

Genevieve eyed him in a knowing way. "Ha! Your friend, he's fallen in love, Remy. Probably found himself a godmother—some pretty young thing from the Faubourg St-Germain who is going to adopt him."

"No!" Remy said.

Genevieve nodded. "Look in his eyes. Look at the way he glows."

Remy adjusted the position of his round spectacles and leaned across the table in Indy's direction. "*Mon dieu*, it's true! You've fallen in love—*again*!"

Indy held up his hands. "No. I mean, this is different from last time. It's not like it was with Vicky."

"Meaning, you're having sex this time, *n'est-çe pas*?"

Indy went red with embarrassment.

Colette smirked. "He's not in love—he's in *heat*. I've seen the look many times."

"What is she like?" Remy asked.

"Incredible."

Remy hugged the women to him. "Ah, but aren't they all. But at least tell me who she is."

Indy shook his head. "That's all you get for the moment."

"And trust me, Indiana," Genevieve said with assurance, "that is all you will get—a moment. So be certain to make the most of it."

Indy recalled the two policemen in the rowboat and was instantly sobered.

20

Lying came easy to M'Greet Zelle. It was a talent she had developed early on in life, before dance, as she grew taller and taller, outsizing all her friends, larger everywhere but in her bust, which she padded to conceal the truth. Many of the Javanese women in Malang and Bandung, where she had lived with MacLeod, left their breasts exposed—something she never dared to do. But she could mimic them in other ways, especially the intricate movements of their dance: the exaggerated hand gestures, the unblinking rolling eyes, the yogic posturing. She studied them whenever she could—on moonlight nights at Candi Singosari or at ritual feasts in the pavilions, the *pendopos*, to the dreamy, melancholic songs of iron gongs, *kecapi* strings, *suling* flutes, the haunting hollowness of the bamboo *angklung* rattles. And she imitated the dancers' movements for the wives of other Dutch officers stationed in the Indies, bored to tears, half crazed from the tropical rains or the heat.

How much simpler it was for the earthy Javanese, who delighted in sensuality and promiscuous sexuality: bathing in the muddy rivers that flowed from those volcanic heights, beating their clothes clean in the shade of banyan trees. M'Greet had felt herself to be one of them from the start, and it hadn't taken long before she was sheathing herself in batik *sarongs* and *kebaya* blouses and smoking clove cigarettes.

Riding the elevator up to her suite in the Grand just now, she thought about Henri Defense and how he had been taken in by the counterfeit account of her history. But what good would have been served by telling him the truth? That she

152

had been born in Holland, not Java; that she had met Mac-Leod through a personal ad he had run in the newspaper; that it was he who had taken her to the Indies? There had been no priestess training, certainly no vows of celibacy. "Mata Hari" was a name she had created, and had used as a closing in many a letter home to her friends and her father.

But she hadn't lied about the poisoning of her son—though she hadn't shot the servant, as she told Henri. Nor had she lied about MacLeod's brutality and abuse. Only the part about his having bitten off her nipples.

But MacLeod had scarred her in other ways, chiefly by teaching her that men would always disappoint. Her dashing Scottish captain had proved to be a brute, and nearly every man she had met since had shown himself to be faithless and unprincipled. The man with whom she had spent the previous evening—a French lieutenant-general—had been no exception. He was soon going to Vittel, he had told her, and would "consider" taking her along.

Sex was the power she held over all of them, though it was important to make the man believe that he was the seducer.

She wondered how and when young Henri Defense would disappoint her. Was he telling the truth about his illustrious past, or had the stories about Pancho Villa and Roosevelt been nothing more than attempts to belittle her? Was it her karma to have finally met her match?

She let herself into the suite and found Henri waiting. She could see that he had been up half the night. At some point he had hurled a glass against the fireplace; jagged pieces lay scattered on the floor.

Careful not to betray the slightest concern, M'Greet went about removing her hat and coat while Henri glowered at her from the bedroom doorway.

"Where in blazes were you?" he asked at last. "It's six in the morning!"

She took a breath and swung to him in feigned agitation. "I'm so sorry, *cheri*, but it was simply dreadful—the entire evening. I wanted to get away, but I couldn't. I know I should have phoned, but I lost all track of—"

"Don't tell me that again!"

"Henri, please don't be angry with me." She put the back of her hand to her forehead. "I'm so tired." She went to him, but he held her away.

"Who were you with this time, M'Greet? A president? A general? One of those *boulevardiers* we met on the street?"

"That is none of your business," she said forcefully, deciding on a different tack. "We've scarcely known each other forty-eight hours, and I hardly think that entitles you to know my every move or to attempt to assume control of my life."

"But you've assumed control of mine! Don't you see that? You told me we could be together after the dinner party. I wouldn't have come otherwise. I've been waiting for *ten hours*."

"Darling, I'm sorry—truthfully." This time when she touched him he didn't flinch. She caressed his face. "Let's not waste another moment arguing."

"Just tell me how you can ask me to spend the night, then go off and spend it with someone else."

"It was a party, Henri. And it went on longer than I expected it would. You can't expect me to drop everything for you. Don't you see how unreasonable you're being?"

"I'm being unreasonable?"

"You know you are. Why do you think I've been entreating you to obtain the travel permit? Because I want to be away from here, away from all my social obligations. Then there will be nothing to stand in our way."

Indy's anger was beginning to yield to confusion.

"You know I wanted to be here with you," M'Greet continued, her momentum building now. "Knowing that you would be here was what kept me going through this horrid night. Knowing that I would be able to see you and hold you . . ."

"I've made some inquiries about the *carnet*," he said softly.

M'Greet smiled inwardly. For the moment she needed no more than to hear that he had tried. She put a finger to his lips. "Tell me later. The nearness of our bed is too great a distraction."

She gave herself over to him, making it seem like surrender.

Later M'Greet asked if he would escort her on her "rounds"—a woman on her own was easy prey for gossipers and maître d's, who would sometimes bar admission to a restaurant. And Indy, being the love-struck puppy he was, said yes, sure, he'd be glad to tag along.

M'Greet wore a shepherdess hat with a turned-up brim, tilted to one side; Indy was in clean khakis liberated from the duffel he had stowed in room 22. Once more the hotel staff fawned; the junior and senior officers bowed; the women whispered. But something novel occurred as they were about to exit the Grand's lobby: a thin man in a stylish waistcoat stepped directly into their path.

"Madame Zelle," he began. "Perhaps you remember me. My name is Johannes-Frederich Schwenker. I am the manager of the Hôtel Meurice."

Indy thought the accent he detected was Swiss.

"No, I don't seem to recall you, *monsieur*," M'Greet was saying. "Is there something I can do for you?"

Schwenker eyed Indy before going on. "I don't wish to be indelicate, Madame Zelle, but this involves the matter of a long overdue hotel bill in the amount of thirteen hundred francs."

M'Greet stiffened somewhat. "Why, whatever do you mean, *monsieur*? I have been a guest at the Grand the entire while I've been in Paris. Inquire at the desk if you doubt me."

"I don't doubt you, madame. But as I say, this bill is long overdue. In fact, it goes back more than one year."

"You must be confusing me with someone else."

"I hardly think that possible, Madame Zelle."

Schwenker was plainly angered now, and Indy stepped

in. "You heard the lady—you're confusing her with someone else."

But instead of thanking him for his efforts, M'Greet turned on him. "Please, Henri, I'm perfectly capable of handling this affair without your riding to the rescue." She looked down her nose at the hotel manager. "If you have some claim against me, than I suggest you contact my lawyer."

Schwenker pulled an official-looking envelope from his jacket pocket. "Madame Zelle," he said, flourishing the thing, "I have here a court order authorizing me to seize your luggage if this matter isn't resolved."

"And I repeat, sir: Contact my lawyer."

"I will contact the police, madame." Schwenker stormed off.

"As you will," M'Greet said to his back. "Honestly, these people . . ."

"Did you ever stay at the Meurice?" Indy asked when they were out on the street.

M'Greet threw a hand in the air. "Who can remember such things?"

They walked to the post office on rue de Burgogne, where M'Greet sent two telegrams and a *pneumatique*. At the Comptoir National d'Escompte de Paris on the place de l'Opéra, she deposited a necklace in a private box and asked the bank manager if anything had arrived for her via diplomatic pouch from Holland.

They stopped at a jewelry store, Au Colier d'Ambre, on boulevard des Capucines; then at an English pharmacy on rue de la Paix; then at a dressmaker on the same street. They had ice cream at Rumpelmeyers—Indy paid—and M'Greet had a manicure at the Hôtel Ritz, which she said was favored by the British and French officers because of its heated *salon*. Her nails newly lacquered, M'Greet argued with a French colonel about the failure of the air force to eliminate the threat of German submarines off the French and Spanish coasts.

"How is anyone supposed to travel?" she asked in a voice that could be heard throughout the *salon*.

"Remarks like that could get you in trouble with the government," Indy thought to point out later on.

But M'Greet only scoffed at his concern. "I am not one to mince words," she told him. "With politicians or generals, and certainly not with *colonels*."

Midafternoon, they called on a Madame Dangeville at her lavishly decorated apartment on rue Tronchet, a short block north of the Madeleine. The handsome Madame Dangeville, Indy was given to understand, was a former actress. M'Greet played the piano while tea was being prepared. Indy sensed that M'Greet had been expected, but didn't understand why until an hour later, when a gray-haired woman in peasant attire appeared at the door.

M'Greet introduced her to Indy as Eugenie Bazin Sorevil, and explained that Madame Sorevil was a *cartomancienne*—a reader of cards. A fortune-teller.

Indy and the three woman gathered round a table in the *salon*. M'Greet urged him to have a consultation done. "It's only five francs," she stressed, possibly in response to the faces he had made each time she'd asked him to tip someone a sou. Indy wasn't much of a believer in cards or crystal balls, but he reckoned he could use a glimpse at the future just about then—particularly since it would only be costing him the equivalent of a quarter. As instructed, he shuffled the deck of cards, but what came to mind in place of the question he meant to pose was a fragment of a dream from the postcoital nap he and M'Greet had taken. In the dream he was reaching for something on a high shelf. Each time he was sure he had hold of the object, however, it would slip from his grasp, and he would be left reaching again. He wondered how Sigmund Freud or Carl Jung or some other alienist might interpret its meaning. He wondered if he could somehow work it into the conversation that he had met both Freud and Jung in 1908.

Madame Sorevil's seventy-eight "Grand Etteilla" cards were made of stiff cardboard and were longer and narrower than the usual playing cards. When Indy had finished shuffling them, the old woman proceeded to lay them out in a circle on the tabletop.

"Here is the fair-haired young man at the beginning of his journey," Sorevil said, pointing to two cards, one depicting a man with a bundle of belongings over his shoulder and a walking stick. "It begins as a fool's errand." The card showed two crossed staffs forming an "X" on a mountainside. "Vexations, sorrows. But then—" and Indy noted the sudden light in her eyes "—but then, what marvels, what voyages!"

Indeed, one of the cards read just that—*Voyage*, an angel, an eagle, a bull, and a lion decorating its corners. The others showed twin towers of stone, a radiant five-pointed star above a stone platform, birds in flight above an eerie seashore, and flames of war or hell surmounting a tiny figure of Mercury, the messenger of the Greek pantheon.

"What a life you will have," Madame Sorevil concluded. "Filled with travel, danger, and derring-do, grand adventures."

"Now that wasn't so bad, was it, Henri?" M'Greet said.

But the cards that made up her own spread were a different matter. Madame Sorevil spent a long while ruminating over them. "I see the dark-haired *querant* facing terrible obstacles," she began. "I see crossed swords—falsehoods on all sides—love inverted, incidents, dissensions, irresistible forces at work . . ."

Indy regarded the last card she touched. Labeled *Force Majeure* at both ends, it showed a winged, torch-wielding devil atop a pedestal, to which a bare-breasted woman and a black man were chained.

"Will I undertake the journey I desire?" asked M'Greet.

Madame Sorevil thrust a finger at a card labeled *Misère* and *Prison*, a lightning-struck tower. "No, you will not."

"Then will I at least collect the money I have been promised?"

"No, you will not." *Le Justice* depicted an enthroned queen holding an upraised sword.

M'Greet's face had lost much of its amber color. "Will I be with the one I love?"

"No," the card reader said, shaking her head in a mournful way. The last card showed a monk with eyes closed, holding aloft a lighted lantern; but its title was *Traître*. "You have a better chance of being *shot* first."

Indy broke the foreboding silence. "I had a feeling we shouldn't do this," he told M'Greet.

21

Indy walked M'Greet back to the Grand Hôtel but didn't stay. The session with the card reader had left her upset, and he was feeling out of sorts as well. He wanted to prove the prognostications false. He knew he couldn't do anything about the sum of money she had asked about, but he might be able to do something about the "journey"—the trip to Vittel—which he hoped at the same time would see to M'Greet's concern about being with the man she loved. He was determined, in fact, to right that inverted love card; and if accomplishing that meant spending added time with the Levis—even attending a Fauvist exhibition or a reading by Proust—then so be it.

He was prepared to do whatever was necessary.

While he was en route to the métro station in the place de l'Opéra, however, a black Renault pulled curbside and two men stepped out to intercept him. Indy took one look at the raincoats and the derbies and knew he was in for a long evening.

The two *flics* were discreet about flashing their ID cards, and polite about asking him to accompany them crosstown in the Renault. Indy rode in the backseat with the older of the two. They asked Indy how he was enjoying Paris, talked about the new movies in town, and honked at some of the pretty women they passed. But neither offered an explanation of why they had picked him up.

The *préfecture de police* was on the Ile de la Cité, across from Notre-Dame Cathedral on the place du Parvis, the square from which all distances in France were measured. It was a huge old building with a scalloped archway entrance that opened on a cobblestone courtyard. The *flic* at the wheel parked the Renault next to a shiny Salmson coupé of the sort sometimes favored by the French military; then the two cops led Indy up several flights of marble stairs and along about half a mile of corridors to a small room that overlooked the Seine and the Quai St-Michel.

Waiting for Indy were two men, one of whom he didn't recognize. The other was Major Twinbury of the British Expeditionary Force—the officer who had briefed him for the recon mission across no-man's-land.

"Jolly good to see you again, Corporal Defense." Twinbury pumped Indy's hand. "I hope you won't mind if I speak English—my French is not what it should be. Damned nuisance getting anyone in Paris to understand even a simple sentence. Especially in the restaurants."

"English will be fine, sir," Indy said warily.

"And with you, Major?" Twinbury asked the as yet unidentified man.

The man nodded. "Go right ahead."

"So how are you enjoying Paris, Corporal? Seeing the sights, eating plenty of good food, I trust."

"It's been fun so far."

"We'll try not to take up too much of your time. Certainly don't want to impinge on a hard-earned and much-deserved furlough." He motioned Indy to a chair. "Would you care for anything—coffee, a spot of tea?"

"No, sir."

"Well, then,"—Twinbury rubbed his hands together—"down to business. I assume you've already met Detectives Tapier and Charpentier, so allow me to introduce Major Spesfant of the Belgian Intelligence Service."

Indy groaned inwardly. He must've been found out. They must know he wasn't Henri Defense but Henry Jones, Junior, and they were going to take him to task for it . . . But hold on, he thought: Twinbury had addressed him as Corporal Defense, so that meant they had something else in mind. Had they found out what had really happened on the way to the front with the attack orders? Or—

"This concerns Madame Marguerite Zelle, Corporal," the Brit said now. "The woman more popularly known as 'Mata Hari.' "

Indy waited to see where Twinbury was going.

"We are, of course, aware that you've been spending . . . *time* with the woman—not that that strikes anyone in this room as unusual."

Twinbury slid a card across the table; Indy recognized it as the one he'd filled out at the Grand Hôtel's front desk.

"All the hotel registration cards signed by foreigners are sent here, to the Service de Garnis," Detective Tapier explained. "That is how we knew who you were."

"A happy coincidence, what," Twinbury said. "You and I having worked together before."

Indy didn't return the smile. "Is there a law against my spending time with Madame Zelle?"

"Not at all, Corporal," Tapier said.

"Then what do you want from me?"

Charpentier answered. "We wonder, *monsieur*, if you realize that Madame Zelle is in a great deal of trouble."

"If this is about the unpaid hotel bill," Indy said, "I mean if that's why you two have been following her around—" He glanced first at Tapier, then Charpentier. "She's seen you, you know. She's on to you."

"We know that she has seen us, *monsieur*. And she knows likewise that she is under suspicion."

"Under suspicion for what?"

Tapier sniffed. "Of having intelligence with the enemy. She is suspected of being a German agent—a spy."

Indy gaped at him. "You're wrong, sir. You couldn't be more wrong."

"I don't think so, Corporal," Twinbury said.

The Belgian major, Spesfant, spoke. "Madame Mata Hari, code designate AF four-four, is suspected of being under the control of Germany's III-C Bureau in Antwerp. The operation is run by a German woman we call 'Fraulein doktor,' who runs all French-speaking spies."

Indy shook his head in disbelief. "But she's a . . . dancer."

"Your dancer is Dutch. And as we all know, Holland has been a nest of spies since the war began."

"She was probably recruited in Berlin," Twinbury said. "Before she was transferred to Paris, she was working there—calling herself the Countess von Linden—at a spy house on Dorotheen Strasse. The week the war broke out, she was seen lunching with Major Friedrich Gempp, head of German intelligence. Apparently they made quite a spectacle of themselves, parading around the streets in an open carriage."

"I wouldn't know anything about that," Indy said.

Twinbury threw him an earnest look. "You know, lad, she compromised one of our surprise operations up north in '14. A lot of brave men died."

Indy shook his head back and forth. "I don't believe she 'compromised' anything."

"What does she talk to you about, Corporal?" the Belgian asked. "That is, when the two of you find time to talk."

Indy blushed. "We talk about . . . life. Nothing specific."

"Has she ever mentioned Major Gempp?"

"No."

"And I suppose she told you all about how she was born in Java and kidnapped from a temple, didn't she?" Twinbury asked.

"So?"

"Well, it might interest you to know, lad, that she was born in Holland, not the Indies. She only saw Java because her husband, a Captain Campbell MacLeod, was posted there. I could cite dates and cities if it would help convince you."

Indy tried to conceal his surprise. "Convince me of what? So she exaggerated her past. She's a performer; they all do that. That doesn't make her an enemy agent."

Twinbury paced in front of him. "Has she asked you any questions about the war? About Verdun or the Somme, or anything about the air force?"

"Not specifically. Just about the rumors of food short-ages and poor morale—which I denied," Indy was quick to add.

Major Spesfant's eyes bored into him. "Before you she was seeing another Belgian—a major by the name of de Beaufort of the First Division Fourth Lancers serving at Yser. Has she asked anything about the Yser deployment?"

"No," Indy reaffirmed. "Besides, I know I'm under orders not to discuss the war."

"And we're satisfied that you haven't broken those or-ders—yet," Twinbury said. "But we also know that Mata Hari has ways of extracting the information that she needs. The Javanese taught her to do more than simply shed her clothing. Mata Hari is a trained seductress—an adven-turess."

" 'Mata Hari' is a *nom de guerre*," Indy emended.

"Quite so, but let's not mince words, Corporal: has she or has she not talked to you about taking her into the war zone?" Seeing Indy's reluctance, Twinbury pressed the point. "Come now, Corporal, must we resort to secreting a listening device in her suite? As it is we have the staff of the Grand Hôtel reporting on all her telephone calls, identifying her many visitors, and screening her mail."

Indy wondered how much they knew—whether in fact they had already planted a listening device in the suite. How embarrassing. "She did mention wanting to go to Vittel. But that's because . . . she wants to take the waters."

Twinbury and the major traded looks. "I see," Spesfant said. "And we all know how Vittel's waters are good for liver ailments."

Indy shrugged.

"Does she look ill to you, Corporal?" Twinbury asked leadingly.

"Well, no . . ."

"So there might be some other reason, then."

Indy had no intention of telling them the truth—that M'Greet wanted to be close to him. "For instance?"

"For instance, Corporal, the Contrexéville aerodrome is

close to Vittel, and it's from there that French aeroplanes depart on missions to insert allied agents behind the German lines.''

Indy was at a sudden loss for words.

"Monsieur Defense," Tapier broke in. "Would you not agree that the possibility exists for, let us say, an alternative 'interpretation' of Madame Zelle's motivation?"

"I suppose," Indy told him.

The detectives eyed one another. "Then perhaps you could be of some small service to us in getting to the truth."

"How?"

"You could begin by having a thorough look at her belongings," Tapier said.

"See if you can obtain some of her letters," Boucher added, "so we can test them for the presence of invisible ink."

Twinbury showed Indy a pocket-size Autographic Kodak camera. "If you're worried she might miss the letters, you could use this to photograph them on the spot."

"Take a close look at her fingernails," Major Spesfant suggested.

Indy regarded him in puzzlement. "Her nails?"

"German operatives are known to carry crystals under their fingernails which they can dissolve in solution to make *encre sympathique*—a first-class invisible ink."

Indy laughed shortly in disbelief. "She just had her nails manicured this afternoon! Don't you think the manicurist would have noticed?"

Spesfant whipped out a notepad. "Where did she have them manicured? The manicurist could be a German contact agent stationed here in Paris."

"The Hôtel Ritz," Indy said unwillingly.

"And find out the identity of the black man who rode with her on the train from Madrid to the French frontier."

The four went on and on with their requests, but Indy had stopped listening. All he could think of was the book he'd started to read in M'Greet's suite, that espionage novel called *The Thirty-nine Steps*.

22

Indy had a lot on his mind when he left the *préfecture*. Twinbury and the rest had to be wrong, way off base, he told himself. M'Greet was no *spy*. She was outspoken, that was all, and people tended to misinterpret her remarks. It was because of spy fever that she was suspected of having had intelligence with the enemy. Or did he need to ask Jacques Levi to deliver a lecture on the subject at the *préfecture*? The French detectives and whoever else was involved in the case simply didn't know M'Greet as well as he did—at least Indy hoped not.

The accusations aside, what bothered him most about the questioning were the constant references to M'Greet's liaisons. *Before you she was with a Belgian named de Beaufort . . . Did she ever mention Major Gempp, the German spymaster? . . . The black man who rode with her on the train from Madrid . . .* Suspects to add to the long list of dignitaries and generals to whom M'Greet had already been linked by Mrs. Toufours and her clique. Jealousy was eating away at him, fueling an anger he didn't know just what to do with.

Leaving the police building, Indy had walked north out of the place du Parvis, crossing the Seine at the Pont Notre-Dame. It was late afternoon, and a chill wind was stripping the trees along the quai of their browning leaves. He had stopped at a stall on the rue de Rivoli to ask directions to the nearest métro stop when from behind him came a jangling noise he hadn't heard for a long while, not since Mexico, at any rate: the sound of spurs.

He turned and saw a cowboy approaching from the direction of the Tour St-Jacques. Indy couldn't say for sure that the man was an American; but he did have the rangy look of a Texas cowpoke, right down to the requisite boots, hat, and spurs. And as if the day hadn't brought surprises enough, the curly-haired guy at the cowboy's side was none other than Tom Carren, the ambulance driver Indy had met at the Citadel.

Recognizing Indy at the same moment, Carren smiled and saluted; then walked up, shook Indy's hand, and clapped him on the back. "Henry Defense," he said. "Of all people to run into on the rue de Rivoli. *Damn* small world."

"And getting smaller all the time," Indy replied.

"So you got yourself furloughed, huh? Feels good to be rid of the seam squirrels, doesn't it?"

Indy raised his arms the way he'd been taught to at the trench delousing stations. "Cootie-free."

"How's that friend of yours—what was the moniker again?"

"Remy, Remy Baudouin."

"That's the one."

"He's here, too. Staying in Pigalle."

"Sampling the peaches, huh? Well, who can blame him for wanting some nookie, after taking a round and all. Just tell him for me he better report for short-arm inspection when he's through." Tom grabbed his crotch. "You know what I mean, Henry? Lot of evil surprises for the unsuspecting soldier up there in Pigalle."

"I'll be sure to remind him."

"So, where are you stowing your fleabag—your duffel?"

"Uh, downtown," Indy said, not wanting to mention the Grand Hôtel.

"Well, if you need a bed, we're only a few blocks from here."

"Swell."

Tom motioned to the cowboy. "Henry, meet a good buddy of mine, Pat Redfield. Pat flies with the Escadrille Américaine. Pat, meet Henry Defense, who claims to be

Belgian but who can chew the fat as good as any Yank I ever met.''

Redfield extended a muscular hand. "Say," Indy asked, regarding Pat's ten-gallon, "you wouldn't happen to fly a Nieuport Bébé, would you?"

"Bébé, Spad, whatever's on the ground waiting for me to climb in.''

"And you didn't by any chance down a Fokker over Troyon a couple of weeks back, did you?"

"Matter of fact, I did.''

"You pulled an Immelmann on him, then went into an inverted loop and got him from his overhead.''

Pat beamed. "You saw that, huh? I was right proud of it myself.''

"I was the guy on the motorcycle," Indy said.

Pat thought for a moment, then laughed heartily. "Well, I'll be—"

"You saved my hide, Pat." They shook hands again.

"All in a day's work, comrade.''

Indy was more tempted than ever to reveal his true identity, but he kept quiet about it.

"Henry, do you have anything on for tonight? Dames or anything?"

Indy thought about M'Greet. Again she had plans for dinner, but she'd promised the hours afterward to him. Of course, she had made the same promise that first night they met, and then again the following night . . . Even so, he needed to warn her about the hole she was digging for herself. Warn her without telling her he had been questioned by the police—the detectives had been careful to warn *him* about that. But there was one thing he wouldn't do, and that was spend the night pacing the floor of her hotel suite again. He would telephone first to make certain she was in before heading over to the Grand.

"No plans until around ten o'clock," he finally said, figuring M'Greet wasn't likely to return from dinner earlier than that.

"Then what would you say to joining us for some hi-jinks?"

"Sure thing. Where're you going?"

"To a wake," Tom told him.

The ambulance driver left it at that, and the three of them began to talk about Verdun as they walked down Rivoli toward La Bastille. They passed by the Hôtel de Ville and a couple of old churches, then turned left where Rivoli became the rue St-Antoine. The next thing Indy knew, they were in the place des Voges, which had to be one of the most beautiful squares in the city. Surrounded on all sides by pink-brick houses crowned with white fleurs-de-lis, Voges was where people had come during the ancien ré-gime to picnic, promenade, or duel—with rapier or pistol.

Now, among others, the Escadrille Américaine was bil-leted there—in luxurious fashion in apartments near the Roman baths. There must have been thirty aviators milling around in the spacious rooms when Indy, Tom, and Pat entered. Someone pressed a half-full bottle of red wine into Indy's hands.

"What's an ambulance driver doing hanging around with fliers?" Indy asked Tom when they had a moment.

"Norman—as in Prince, the guy who got this show on the road—he was always coming around to the ambulance corps to see if anyone was interested in joining the aviator unit he was trying to put together. Prince and Doc Gros, that is. Gros was the one behind the ambulance field service. We were staying at the Hôtel François. The Red Cross drivers were in the palace at Fountainbleau. And talk about sweet, Henry—it was easy street. All we could eat and drink, all the women we wanted, the works. Then we all got a look at what the war was like, and nothing's been the same since.

"Anyway, every once in a while Norman would find himself a new recruit." Tom gestured with his chin to two aviators standing nearby. "Jim and Eliot used to be ambu-lance drivers." He indicated some of the others in the room. "William, there, owned a hydroplane when he was at Yale.

Vic's a Harvard man, had his eye set on the Foreign Legion till Norman got to him. Bert was a stunt flier back in the States and did a stint with the French Air Force before signing on. Kiff was going to be a doctor or something.''

Indy recalled what he had heard about the Escadrille Américaine: that it had previously been known as the Escadrille des Volontaires, then the Escadrille Lafayette—that name still applied to the ground crews. Early on in the war, the German embassy in Washington, D.C., had raised a stink about "neutrals" fighting for France, and even the French had been resistant to the idea. However, Poincaré's government had gradually begun to see some propaganda benefit to the group, and now articles on the American Squadron were forever cropping up in magazines like *The Saturday Evening Post*.

"So why aren't you a flier instead of a driver?" Indy asked.

Tom brought his fingers to his chest. "Me—fly? Not on your life, Henry—I'm afraid of heights. It's just that I get along with these guys better than the drivers. I mean, there's as many Ivy Leaguers in the squadron as there are in the ambulance corps, but at least Pat and the rest of them don't sit around ordering brandies on the Faubourg St-Martin or spend their time writing poetry and novels and stuff. And they still smoke Camels and Piedmonts instead of those French Gauloises. 'Course, all of us do the same amount of drinking and whoring, drivers and fliers alike.''

Tom began to run down the names of some of the ambulance corps volunteers. Indy stopped him at the mention of Gertrude Stein.

"The same Gertrude Stein the writer and art collector?"

"Same-same,'' Tom said. "Except I figure she'll end up driving with the American Fund for the French Wounded.''

Indy recalled his brief encounter with Stein, her brother, Leo, and her companion, Alice B. Toklas, years before, at Picasso's studio in Montmartre. He remembered her commenting that twentieth-century art was about "the painting of one's thoughts."

Given the day he'd had, Indy wondered with misgivings what a canvas of his own thoughts might look like.

One hour and many bottles of wine later, everyone stumbled from the apartments and piled into three motorized military transports requisitioned from Indy couldn't imagine where. They drove in boisterous disregard to a *boîte* on the rue du Faubourg St-Antoine, on the far side of the place de la Bastille. The club was already crowded with drunken men and *demimondaines* singing barbership at the tops of their lungs, arguing about politics, swapping war stories, and helling around. Many were French or British aviators; others were with the ambulance corps. There were even a few Legionnaires of the new breed—volunteers in service to the République, rather than criminals of different nationalities seeking nothing more than French citizenship in exchange for a couple of years of duty in the tropics. Some of the revelers were in uniform; others were dandied up in gangster fashion, with pointed, brown calf shoes, wide trousers with turned-up cuffs, and brightly patterned socks. And Indy spotted a few more examples of shirts made from parachute silk.

Tom introduced him around to the drivers, and Indy could see how Tom didn't exactly fit in. The volunteers made Indy think of the left-wing intellectuals he had occasionally encountered on the Princeton campus, where his father taught—the ones who came from wealthy families in Saint Louis or New Orleans, but could quote George Bernard Shaw or Henri Barbusse. Romantic idealists not all that different from Indy's dad, save that Professor Henry Jones didn't drive around town in a Pierce-Arrow or a Franklin.

On the floor in the center of the club was an eight-foot replica of a DeHaviland 2 "pusher-type" biplane. The DH 2 was built more like a box kite than a true aeroplane, but its rear-mounted engine allowed for a broad field of Lewis-gunfire unobstructed by propeller blades. Stuffed into the scaled-down cockpit was a dummy clothed in aviator attire: sweater, fur-lined waterproof coverall, helmet, goggles, fur gloves over paper ones, and fleece-lined boots over paper socks.

Eventually one of the American Squadron members climbed atop a stool placed alongside the model aeroplane and called for quiet in the room.

"Now, we all know why we're gathered here tonight," he began in a mix of French and English. "And that's to honor a comrade in arms—" he motioned to the dummy "—Major Lanoe Hawker, British ace extraordinaire, who recently fell to Manfred von Richthofen in a dogfight that will surely go down in the annals of aviation history."

"Hear, hear," said a member of the British Royal Flying Corps.

"Likewise, we're all familiar with the Hawker legend: how he used to shoot Krauts out of the sky using a Westley Richards single-shot deer-stalking rifle, and how he and his pusher rid the Somme skies of many a Fokker."

The room applauded wildly.

"And my personal feeling is that he would have been with us today, that it would have been *Richthofen*'s serial number decorating the wall of *Hawker*'s quarters and not the other way around, if Hawker had been piloting a Sopwith triplane or a Pup against the Baron's Albatros."

Angry grumbles spread through the room. The twin machine-gunned, Mercedes-powered Albatros was the star of the Germans' hunting squadrons—the *jastas*. And it was an Albatros that Hawker had tangled with the day he fell.

"But I'm here to tell you," the American continued, "that it was a duel any one of us would have been proud to fight. Twenty minutes, it went on. Twenty minutes of stunning dives, vertical banks, and sideslips. Hawker's skill was remarkable in keeping his crate out of Richthofen's sights. Time after time, he would throttle back at just the right moment and duck into a turn, but Richthofen kept forcing him lower and lower to the ground.

"At the end, the two of them were practically close enough to reach up and grab, weaving around trees and silos. And that's where the Albatros gained the upper hand. Hawker was ruddering full left, preparing to meet his opponent head-on, when Richthofen throttled himself over the top. Hawker was at maximum exposure in his bank, almost motionless, and he had to know he was done for. But he came soaring into the Baron's guns all the same.'' The flyer paused for a moment. ''Hawker fell like a stone to the Albatros's Spandaus. But like a stone that makes history as it falls.''

Everyone was hoisting glasses when another aviator, a Brit, called for silence. ''Here's a bit a news that might take some of the sting out, lads: Oswald Boelcke is dead.''

Indy was as surprised as anyone in the *boîte*. Boelcke was the German ace with forty confirmed kills, the one some frontliners at Verdun had identified as ''Fantomas,'' whose skill and cunning were both widely feared and applauded.

A Legionnaire in the crowd asked how Boelcke had fallen.

''In a collision with one of his own squadron members,'' the Brit said.

The room grew silent for a moment; then someone said, ''Why not raise a glass to the *boche* as well.''

''Sure, why not,'' said a French flier. He toasted with the wine bottle he was holding. ''To Boelcke.''

''Then I say we drink to the RAF bloke who downed the Schutte-Lanz airship before it reached London,'' a Brit said. ''Used a Buckingham incendiary machine gun on the thing.''

''Here, here!''

''*Alors*, to Franz and Quenault also,'' said another Frenchman. ''Their Hotchkiss downed the first Aviatik.''

And the toasts continued, as other celebrated fliers were named: Louis Blériot, Albert Ball, Leon Morane, Mick Mannock, Roland Garros . . .

''Too bad about Hawker's going west,'' Tom Carren told Indy, appearing out of the crowd with a bottle of wine in each hand. ''But no one's going to let it put the kibosh on the jag.'' He pointed to a food-laden table. ''Feed your face, Henry; it's a lot better than the grub at the front.''

Indy helped himself to the food and downed another glass of wine—*vin blanc* this time, or, as Tom called it, ''vinegar blank.'' At ten o'clock he left the club to search for a telephone, finally locating one at a hotel not far from the place de la Bastille. But when he phoned the Grand he was told that M'Greet had not returned to her room.

Nor was she there an hour later when he placed a second call.

Nor an hour after that when the front desk clerk finally told him not to call again.

By then Indy was furious—with M'Greet for once more leaving him on the hook, and with himself for feeling so torn up about it. But he'd made up his mind to give her a dose of her own medicine: this time *he* would be the one to stay out all night.

23

Using the key M'Greet had given him the night they met, Indy let himself into the third-floor Grand suite. Hung over from the copious amounts of wine and food he'd consumed at the wake, he banged his shoulder against the doorjamb and tripped on the foyer carpet, but nevertheless he managed to ease himself into the *apartment* without waking her. He knew she was in because the clerk at the front desk had said as much. *Why, yes, Corporal Defense, your "aunt" arrived only a short time ago.* Indy could still see the man's smirk. Perhaps he was one of the staffers tasked by the police with reading M'Greet's mail and eavesdropping on her telephone calls. When all was said and done, who was really the spy?

Indy watched M'Greet sleep. Her face, turned to him where he stood in the doorway to the bedroom, looked troubled, as though by dreams of pursuit. He thought about how angry he had been that evening. He had tried to drink her from his mind and had very nearly succeeded. For at least a few hours he hadn't wondered about who she was with. At issue, though, was whether it really was a case of dinner engagements she couldn't back out of, *soirées* that went on longer than planned. Some time during the long night it had occurred to Indy that he could always go to Twinbury or the detectives if he wanted the truth.

But perhaps he didn't want to know.

He returned to the *salon* and parted the blackout curtains to peer at the street. The dawn light was soft and tinged with rose. He sat on the sofa and stared at the floor, his thoughts in a jumble. Across the room, M'Greet's purse was lying open on a Louis XIV *liseuse*—a reading table with a collapsible book rest in the top. The purse was silk brocade and had large wooden handles shaped like horseshoes. Indy regarded it for a long moment, feeling something begin to uncoil inside him. He went to the table and took the purse over to the wedge of light at the gap in the curtains. He gave the bedroom a quick over-the-shoulder glance; then, satisfied that M'Greet was soundly asleep, he began to rummage through her bag.

M'Greet's leather wallet contained several hundred francs, along with a few Dutch florins and Russian notes. Tucked into a pocket were two passports. The first had been issued in Holland years before and was a large single page folded into six. The photograph of M'Greet was one Indy remembered seeing in the album—a head-and-shoulders shot that had appeared on the back page of a Dutch magazine. The second passport was a booklet much like the one Indy carried, save that it expressly forbade travel in the *zone des armées*—the war zone. Issued in France, it bore border stamps from Holland and Spain. In the photograph, M'Greet was hatless, and her hair was combed behind her ears.

Indy dug deeper into the purse and located her toiletry bag. He went down on his haunches and emptied the contents onto the parquet floor: five face powders, three pomades, a small bar of soap, a stick of lip rouge, mascara, two cosmetic brushes, an assortment of perfumes and toilet waters, one bottle of therapeutic powder, and a small bottle of benzine that was probably for fueling her cigarette lighter.

Recalling what the police had said about invisible ink, Indy examined the therapeutic powder. It had been purchased at an English pharmacy in rue de la Paix; the label gave the contents as a mercury-potassium compound.

As he squinted at the label, guilt eased up alongside him, demonstrating the same silent care he had used to let himself into the suite. He set the bottle down. Here he was, going through her things like a thief. Now the police had succeeded in turning *him* into a spy.

He had begun to replace everything when a note he hadn't noticed earlier slipped from the wallet. He held the paper in his hand as though weighing it against his conscience, then opened it.

I'm sorry about the scene at the restaurant, it read in fine French script. *My wife behaved disgracefully. But I hope to see you and to hold you on Tuesday night. Until then,* à bientot *and much love.* Ton *Louis.*

Indy fumed as he stood there. It was only the sound of M'Greet's voice that brought him around.

"Is someone there?" she asked worriedly.

"It's just me—Henri." Quickly, but as quietly as possible, he returned the purse to its place on the antique table. M'Greet appeared in the doorway to the bedroom, clutching a velvet, fur-trimmed robe to her throat.

"What are you doing?"

"Uh, I came in and saw that you were sleeping, so I was just going to wait out here for you to wake up."

Her eyes seemed to veer to the purse for an instant before meeting his. "You weren't waiting for me last night." She sounded genuinely disappointed.

"No," Indy told her, "I couldn't get away. The party went on much longer than I expected it to." His anger was getting away from him like a wild horse. "It was dreadful, really. I wanted to be here, but I couldn't. And of course I tried to telephone, but you know how that can be . . ."

"I see," M'Greet said, narrowing her eyes somewhat. Then her expression mellowed. "Well, you're here now, Henri, and that's all that matters. Come to me, my darling."

He did. But instead of slipping between her outstretched arms as M'Greet had obviously meant him to, he took her hands in his and began to kiss the backs of her fingers, surreptitiously examining her nails at the same time.

M'Greet allowed a moment of this before snatching her hands back and pulling away from him. "What's wrong with you? You're behaving very strangely."

"Nothing's wrong."

Her brow furrowed in suspicion. "Just who were you with last night?"

"Friends. Comrades in arms."

She started to say something but changed her mind. "I'm sorry I asked. I don't own you, and I certainly don't expect you to report to me." She opened her arms once more and beckoned him in, then began to kiss his mouth and face and neck.

Despite himself, Indy grew aroused by the feel and taste and smell of her.

"I need your help today, darling," she whispered in his ear.

"Um," he said dreamily. "How's that?"

"I'm moving some of my belongings to an apartment I've rented near the Bois de Boulogne. And it's such a depressing ordeal to contemplate." She reversed out of his hold and adopted a look of theatrical helplessness. "Oh, my dashing young corporal, won't you help a damsel in distress?"

"How could anyone deny you?" Indy asked, hungry for her.

"Some manage, *mon chéri*, some manage." She led him to her bed.

M'Greet had hired an old wagon—a horse-drawn thing with slat sides and huge wooden wheels—and the services of a spindly, white-haired man who could scarcely carry himself, let alone any of the overladen trunks M'Greet wanted to move. Nevertheless, with an assist from two of the Grand's tip-hungry bellhops, the old man and Indy managed to move everything down to the lobby, and after an hour the six trunks were strapped to the bed of the wagon.

All the while, M'Greet was short-tempered with everyone involved. When she wasn't pacing angrily in the lobby, she was out on the boulevard des Capucines, gazing up and down the street in obvious concern, as though anticipating an enemy sneak attack. Or, more likely, Indy thought, the manager from the Hôtel Meurice, flourishing that seizure order of his.

The apartment M'Greet had rented was clear across town on Avenue Henri-Martin, in the western suburbs of the city. The wagon ride was a long, slow trip, made longer still by M'Greet's need to drive past the Musée Guimet, the rotunda where "Mata Hari" had made her first public appearance. From there they took Avenue Kléber south, past the Trocadero. To the left soared the Tour Eiffel, as impressive now as when Indy had first seen it in 1908—"a metaphor in steel for the spectacular ascent of man," as it had been called. M'Greet talked about herself and asked whether Indy had made any progress on procuring the travel permit for Vittel. He told her not yet, and tried to probe her urgency for ulterior motives. But all she would tell him was that the trip was *for them*.

The driver made a right turn onto Henri-Martin and followed it to the edge of the Bois de Bologne. A burgeoning street of new apartment buildings, Henri-Martin made Indy think of Manhattan's Central Park West. The building that housed M'Greet's apartment had an awning of wrought iron and frosted glass reminiscent of the Art Nouveau canopies Grimaud had designed for the métro stops.

Without the bellhops, it took as long to move one trunk upstairs as it had taken to move the lot from the suite to the Grand lobby. No sooner would Indy and the old man arrive with a trunk than M'Greet would begin to unpack it, placing items about in a futile effort to warm the two unfurnished rooms. The reason she'd given for renting the place was that she had reached her wit's end with the hotel staff snooping in her business and knowing her every move. If she only knew how deeply, Indy wanted to tell her. It was tempting, too, to confess that he'd been questioned by the police, even though the detectives had been firm in warning him not to discuss the matter with her. Which made little sense in light of their claim that M'Greet knew full well she was under suspicion. That claim in itself was enough to convince Indy of her innocence. For wouldn't a spy, apprised that she had been "surfaced" or "burned"—whatever terms were used in the espionage trade—be fleeing for the safety of Germany rather than taking a lease on an apartment in the suburbs?

The driver insisted on taking a lunch break in the middle of the unloading procedure, so Indy had no choice but to help M'Greet sort through her small mountain of yet-to-be-placed possessions. The pile he went to work on contained her collection of books, magazines, brochures, and theatre programs, along with some of the silver-framed photographs he'd seen in the hotel suite. He stopped to study one that showed a large-boned girl of five or six standing on the bank of a canal in Holland. The inscription on the back read: *Margaretha Geertruida, Amsterdam, 1882.*

M'Greet approached Indy from behind as he was holding it. She was wearing silk brocade slippers instead of the usual two-inch heels, and as a result she and Indy were about the same height.

"This is you," he said.

"Yes."

"But I thought you said you were born in Java?"

"You must have misunderstood. I said I moved to Java."

"No, I'm sure you said that your father was a Dutch officer and that your mother was Javanese."

"Yes. And we traveled from Holland to Java when I was seven."

Indy scratched his head. "No, that wasn't it—"

"Henri, I'm in no mood to argue about this," M'Greet said, taking the photo. "It's my life, after all. I should know where I was born."

Indy decided to let it go. He turned to his task in sullen silence, now discovering a ribboned packet of letters written in German.

She was in Berlin when the war broke out, the Belgian, Spesfant, had said. *She was consorting with the chief of German intelligence—*

"Give me those," M'Greet said unexpectedly. Without waiting, she reached over his shoulder and yanked the letters from his hands. "You can be a very nosy young man, do you know that?"

"From a friend or a lover?"

"A friend—from my past. You are my friend in the present."

"Your only friend?"

"My special friend. At the moment, you are the most important person in my life."

Indy recalled what Remy's prostitute friend had said about making the most of moments. "How long is this moment going to last?"

M'Greet made a motion of dismissal. "I'm a dancer, not a fortune-teller." Her face tensed for a moment, perhaps in recollection of what the card reader had told her. "Look, here is one of my old costumes." She held up a pair of gauzy pants and a kind of jewel-studded brassiere.

"Doesn't look like it covered much," Indy said.

M'Greet regarded him with a mix of anger and bemusement. "There is nothing wrong with nudity when it serves the furtherance of artistic expression." She paused momentarily. "Be truthful, Henri. You never saw me dance, did you."

Indy gestured to himself in transparent disbelief. "Of course I . . . well, actually, no. But I did see photos of you in newspapers and magazines."

"Photographs don't do me justice, isn't that what you said?" She told him to stay put, then gathered up pieces of the costume and took them into the next room. "Search the trunk by the window for the gramophone cylinder labeled 'Mystique,' " she called out.

Indy went to the trunk and rummaged around inside one of the drawers, picking up and discarding cylinders until he found the one she requested. "I have it," he said.

M'Greet poked her head around the edge of the doorway. "Turn on the machine and start the music."

Indy set up the gramophone and set the cylinder in place. The music was slow, haunting, exotic. Indy doubted that it was indigenous to Java—or anywhere in the Dutch East Indies, for that matter, but the melody had enough mean-

dering pentatonic dissonance to conjure images appropriate
to that part of the world: moonlit temples, demon-faced
icons, volcanic peaks, verdant paddies . . .

As if summoned by the sounds, Mata Hari appeared in
the doorway and danced into the room. The costume was no
longer a perfect fit, but the woman who wore it had lost
none of her sensual allure. "I'm going to dance the *ketjoe-
boeng* for you," M'Greet said in a sultry voice Indy hadn't
heard before. "The dance tells the story of a Javanese flower
that blooms and dies in a single night."

Mata Hari took striding steps around the room, waving
her scarves and spinning herself through precise circles. She
bulged her eyes and moved her head in quirky sideways
motions. She held her hands in such a way that her extended
fingers seemed to curve back on themselves. She folded
herself into yogic postures and writhed her loins the way she
did in bed. She danced with genuine passion and abandon,
making him believe that she had learned her art in a temple
in a rain forest.

He watched, mesmerized by her gyrations; and he felt
drawn to her as he had the first night they'd met. She began
to prostrate herself at Indy's feet, then rose from the floor,
ridding herself of the veils that clothed her hips. Then she
danced into his arms, wilting against him, pulling him
down, down to the floor, into her illusion.

The wagon driver returned from lunch to help Indy un-
load the three remaining trunks. They were hauling the
fourth trunk into the apartment when M'Greet emerged from
the innermost of the two rooms, outfitted in tea gown, coat,
and wide-brimmed hat.

"Henri, when you've finished bringing everything upstairs, would you see to it that the two large trunks are
moved into the back room? You needn't bother unpacking
them, but make sure they're arranged so that I have access
to the drawers."

Indy gave her a confused look. "Why? Where are you
going to be?"

"I have an appointment." She tugged on a pair of gray gloves.

"You asked for my help. You didn't say anything about having an appointment."

"Darling," she said, stroking his cheek, "must you make an issue of everything? I won't be long."

"Where is this appointment? Why is it so important?"

"There you go being nosy again. I'm sorry if I can't simply turn my life around to meet your needs."

"My needs? These trunks aren't exactly *my* needs, M'Greet."

She was already out the door. "Meet me back at the hotel this evening. If all goes well this afternoon, I promise we'll dine together."

A flustered Indy followed her down to the street, in the end only to help her hail a *fiacre*. He tried to listen for the address she gave the *cocher*, but her words were lost in the sound of the carriage wheels against the paving stones.

"I trust you have the money to pay me, *monsieur*," the old man said as Indy was returning to the wagon. "Madame still owes me five francs."

Indy got the last of the trunks upstairs and after some effort succeeded in moving the two largest into the back room. He opened them at once and began to search through the drawers. It wasn't really spying or prying this time, he decided, because he was only carrying out her orders to make everything accessible.

One drawer contained framed photographs; another, additional books, brochures, and fashion-plate magazines. In a second drawer Indy found over fifty calling cards from a wide assortment of men: from an Antoine Bernard, Fils, distiller of fine wines; from a British officer named James Plankett; from a Genovese captain of the military police; from a Lieutenant-General Maurice François Baumgarten; from a Scottish officer named James Stewart Fernie . . .

Indy threw the cards down in disgust. But the choicest items had yet to be discovered, and those he found in a bottom drawer, buried under M'Greet's lingerie. The item that initially caught his eye was a photograph of a young Russian officer, wearing the uniform and brimmed cap of a member of the Czar's Special Imperial Regiment—an elite unit stationed at the French front. The officer was slightly built but darkly handsome, with thick brows and a long nose. The photograph read: *To my Marina, with love, Vadim.*

At first Indy thought the photo belonged to someone other than M'Greet—until he came across the letter it had evidently arrived in. The envelope was addressed to Madame M. Marina Zelle. By itself, the photo would have been simply one more gift from a love-struck admirer. But Vadim de Masloff's letter to "his" Marina had been sent from Vittel.

Indy held the missive for a long while before opening it. In ungrammatical French, it began: *Dearest, I eagerly await your arrival in Vittel. I have already begun to make arrangements for the marriage ceremony* . . .

Indy didn't need to read on. He understood then why she was so desperate to obtain a travel permit.

24

"Thank you for meeting me, Robert," M'Greet said as her friend joined her at the table. He kissed her hand before he sat down.

"You sounded so desperate when you telephoned." He leaned back in his chair so as to see clear across the hotel lobby to the front entrance. "What time is the general meeting you?"

"Soon, very soon," M'Greet said. She glanced at the lobby's antique clock, an Andre-Charles Boulle *regulateur*, which showed almost six-thirty. "But I had to talk to you."

They were not in the Grand but in the Hôtel D'Antin, a few blocks away on boulevard Haussman, behind the Opéra. M'Greet was wearing an outfit Robert had bought for her two years earlier: a spirally draped skirt of taffeta, girdled in amber velvet; over that, a scarlet velvet coat trimmed in skunk and a *crêpe de chine* cape. Robert, a small natty man, an aging dandy, wore a single-breasted lounge suit with small-checked trousers, gloves the color of fresh butter, spats, and a silk top hat.

His real name was Baron Henry de Marguérie. They had first met in 1903, in the Hague. De Marguérie had been the second secretary at the French legation then, and now worked at the Quai d'Orsay, in the foreign service. They had been inconstant lovers for almost as long as they had known each other, since M'Greet's first trip to Paris when Robert had paid for her room at a *pension* on the Champs-Elysées and had romanced her with the best foods and wines and designer clothes. It was Robert, in fact, who had taken

185

such sinister delight in helping her fashion the myth of Mata Hari, introducing her at *salons* and spreading her name among the *haut monde*. And it was Robert, too, who had renamed her M'Greet, in the same way that Vadim would only call her "Marina."

"Tell me what's so important that it couldn't wait for tomorrow," de Marguérie was saying. "I'm eager to know everything you've been doing."

"I went to see Captain Ladoux again today," she said in a covert voice.

De Marguérie tapped a forefinger against his lips and trim mustache. He had had a few dealings with the notorious chief of the Centralized Intelligence Section—the "second bureau," as some called it. Captain Ladoux had always impressed him as a petty bureaucrat, but as one of General Joffre's protégés, the man was not without his influence— not all of it on the side of constitutional right.

"The captain has promised to issue me the necessary *carnet d'étranger* to visit Vittel," M'Greet said, "in exchange for my promise to see Vladimir only and to keep my distance from the aviators stationed there. As though I were going to bed the entire *escadrille*!"

De Marguérie quirked a short-lived smile. "Then you are still under suspicion?"

She sighed dramatically. "You know how these people are, Robert. They get all their facts wrong. Yes, of course, I once described myself as a 'Berliner,' but that was before the war. And, yes, I did have highly placed friends and lovers there. But look what became of me in spite of that: the swines expelled me from Berlin for being a foreigner. And what's worse, they confiscated my furs and never compensated me a single franc. I hate them, Robert. Why would I spy for them?"

De Marguérie nodded politely; the incident of the confiscated furs and alleged tiger skins was one of M'Greet's oft-repeated tales. "I know you wouldn't spy, *chère*. But just the same, you must understand that these . . . suspicions center not on what you did but what they *believe* you were doing. Truth is not the issue here. You must come to grips with this—for your own sake.''

''Oh, Robert, don't tell me this espionitis has gotten to you as well.''

The phrase that came to his mind was *au-dessus de la mêlée*—it was M'Greet's folly to believe she was out of war's reach. He took hold of her hand and forced her to meet his gaze. ''Listen to me, M'Greet. Even those of us in positions of power are not above suspicion just now. You must take care.''

She made a fanning motion with her free hand. ''You make too much of things. All you men in high office.''

De Marguérie fell silent for a moment. ''And your companions—the two *flics*—they are still following you?''

''Like my own shadow,'' M'Greet said. She looked around the lobby. ''I'm sure they're here somewhere, lurking about. But I've stopped complaining about them. To me, they have become part of the Parisian background, no different from a chestnut tree or a Moriss column.''

''Won't Ladoux call off this *filature*—this ceaseless documenting of your social movements?''

M'Greet's eyes narrowed knowingly. ''I think Captain Ladoux enjoys reading reports of my activities—outside and inside the hotel.''

''M'Greet,'' de Marguérie said in avuncular chastisement. ''Has he propositioned you?''

''Sadly, no. Or I could probably have my travel permit and be done with this business. But I think the man lacks a sexual drive. He's so buttoned-up, Robert, so . . . *slick*. So full of wax and brilliantine.''

''Don't underestimate him.''

''I know, I know.''

''And what exactly is he asking of you?''

M'Greet smiled sardonically. ''To make use of those same past associations that have made me suspect in their eyes. But now with an eye toward learning whatever I can about the *boches'* submarines and aeroplanes.''

''And you've agreed to this?''

"I'm close to agreeing to it, yes. Captain Ladoux would like to 'deploy' me—that's the word he uses, 'deploy'—in Brussels. It was partially at my instigation: I said that I could talk my old friend Wurbein into arranging an introduction to General von Bissing." Wurbein, a businessman, had been assisting the Germans in the procurement of food for its occupying forces. Von Bissing was the commander of those forces. "Or I could make use of Kroemer," M'Greet continued, "the honorary German consul in Amsterdam.

"Either way, I assured Ladoux that I could succeed in renewing my affair with the Crown Prince. Once I've accomplished that, there will be no end to what I can deliver to the Section de Centralization des Renseignements."

De Marguérie looked skeptical. "That sounds like a tall order, M'Greet—even for you. But what are you to receive in return, should you succeed?"

"One million gold francs," she told him. "But, believe me, Robert, I'd do it just to get back at the Germans for keeping my furs."

De Marguérie was nodding his head. "One million should set you up in high fashion."

"I need every sou of it, Robert," M'Greet said soberly. *"Il faut de l'argent.* I'm so tired of having to rely on *men* for my material needs—tired old men with tired old wives especially. I'm tired of the smell and the feel of them, Robert. I want to be self-reliant and rich enough not to have to deceive Vadim about how and where I get my money. I'm going to settle all my accounts and pay off his gambling debts so that both of us can be free of obligations to anyone."

De Marguérie rubbed his chin. "Are you absolutely certain about this young Russian? He could be a gigolo, you know."

"He's not. He's noble and heroic, and he loves me." M'Greet lowered her eyes to the table. "Besides, I've arrived at a point where I must face the truth of my life. I'm forty years old, Robert. I'll probably never dance again, and I don't see much hope in talking some swag-bellied old fogey into leaving his wife to marry me. I'm through deceiving myself." She looked up at her friend. "But at least I'll know real love in my remaining years."

Once more de Marguérite reached for her hand. "I remember how upset you were when you didn't get to play Salome in Strauss's play. I hear that same tone in your voice."

"That was almost ten years ago," M'Greet said in melancholy recollection. "What an ignoble end our 'Mata Hari' had—dancing for charity and for retired actors. Featured on the same bill as a dog troupe—"

"But now, now you will get to play Salome, M'Greet. Save that it will be the head of a *boche* general you'll be delivering to Ladoux."

"I suppose," she said quietly.

"You don't sound as confident as you did a moment ago."

M'Greet sighed and averted her eyes. "Madame Sorevil read my cards yesterday."

De Marguérie's face wrinkled in disapproval. "Ah, that old gypsy."

"No, Robert, she has a gift. She told me I wouldn't be making the journey to Vittel, and that I wouldn't receive the money I was looking for. When I asked about seeing Vadim, she said that I stood a better chance of being . . . shot."

De Marguérie held his concern in abeyance. "Superstitious nonsense. You are Madame Mata Hari, M'Greet, the seducer of presidents and international industrialists!"

They laughed for a moment.

"And what about your other young man—this Belgian corporal you've taken a fancy to?"

M'Greet forced an exhale, then smiled thinly. "I don't think he has any idea just how much he has done for me. He has made me feel youthful and provocative. But I'm afraid I've not been very truthful with him."

De Marguérie snorted. "For people like you and me, M'Greet, truth is a negotiable commodity. We're like Captain Ladoux in that regard."

"Well, this one I haven't enjoyed lying to," M'Greet said. Her grin broadened, blossoming into a genuine smile.

"He's so *handsome*, Robert. So preciously idealistic and vital."

"I envy you," de Marguérie said.

But his smile faded when he glanced across the lobby. "I think I see your general, M'Greet, so I will take my leave." He looked at M'Greet as he was rising. "But why this one—now of all times?"

M'Greet fluffed the back of her bob. "If he can issue the travel permit, I may decide against doing what Ladoux asks."

De Marguérie gave her a quick kiss. "Good luck, my love." Then he was gone.

25

This is war, Indy decided as he watched M'Greet and her companion from his stakeout in the overwrought lobby of the Hôtel D'Antin. Not a war of trenches and embattled middle grounds but a more subtle conflict waged in the emotions, where lies and betrayals accounted for the damage.

Once again M'Greet had set him up, just so she could knock him over. But why? he asked himself. Or was this the way it was meant to be between men and women—rolling barrages, races for the parapet, battles for control? Indy wondered if he hadn't spent too much time these past six months with machines—rapid-fire rifles, cunning aeroplanes, artillery that could zero in on a square foot of ground. He had forgotten what people could be like. Sure, machines could jam, break down, fail at a moment of need—but at least they never *deluded* you.

He thought about the women he'd encountered since leaving the States: the suffragettes and the protesters, the war widows and the *grande dames*, the Latin Quarter artistes and the Faubourg St-Honore seductresses. The tasseled forage caps and designer braid notwithstanding, women sometimes seemed to be readying their own battle plans.

And just now he felt that he had little use for the lot of them, sitting there in their Hudson seal coats and plumed hats, their generously *décolleté* restaurant frocks and chinchilla wraps, dining on *poularde Poincaré* and *bécasses flambées*, sipping their 1895 Musignys and 1904 Montrachets . . . Women were more potentially fatal than anything he'd faced in the field. It really was like a war, a battle of the sexes.

He had returned to the Grand Hôtel late that afternoon, furious at having found the letters from M'Greet's Russian lover; furious, and exhausted from the hours of physical labor. He was so sweaty and disheveled that the concierge had made him use the Grand's service entrance. Once inside, however, he'd summoned from somewhere the energy to take the stairs to the third floor at a charge.

Two steps into the suite he had known that M'Greet wasn't there, though her Poiret scent lingered in the centrally heated air. Pieces of clothing lay scattered about the boudoir as though she had been in a rush to get somewhere. A note was left on the bed:

> I apologize, darling, but we won't be able to dine together. An important matter has arisen as a result of this afternoon's appointment, and I must attend to it with all haste. Forgive me. But I do hope to see you later tonight, when I can make it up to you.

He had crumbled the note in his hand and commenced a search for clues to her possible whereabouts, a professional at it by then. The suite had yielded little, but a franc to the Grand's doorman had prompted the instant recall of M'Greet's directions to a carriage driver. "To the Hôtel D'Antin," she had told him.

And now M'Greet and her elderly companion—Minister Lyautey, from the Hôtel D'Orsay gala—had a discreet table to themselves in the hotel restaurant, separate from the long tables where most of the D'Antin's guests were indulging in a lavish dinner that included soup, hors d'oeuvres, fish, poultry, vegetables, meat, cheese, dessert, fruits, wine, and coffee. Indy, just another soldier in the lobby, watched them from behind a gilded, scroll-topped column, his stomach too knotted to acknowledge hunger.

He wandered about, feigning interest in the Ertè sculptures and waiting for the interminable meal to end. But it was only when M'Greet and Lyautey were about to leave that Indy realized he wasn't alone in observing them: a mustachioed man wearing a long coat and a derby was likewise preparing to trail the couple out the door. A *flic* or another deluded lover? Indy wondered. But, no matter, he had already made up his mind to delay any confrontations until he learned where M'Greet was headed. She had been unfaithful to her Russian officer with Indy, so it stood to reason that she was being unfaithful to him as well. It was simply a matter of *proving* that; then he'd have all the ammunition he needed to win the battle.

Indy was fifteen yards behind M'Greet when she exited the hotel, arm-in-arm with her distinguished suitor. The stranger in the derby was perhaps twenty feet behind Indy. The couple walked east on Haussman, obviously searching for a taxi. They were only a block along when a motor taxi emerged from rue Laffitte and stopped for them. Indy pursued them on foot, keeping his eye out for another motor taxi—a carriage wouldn't be able to keep up. The stranger was doing the same.

But luck was with Indy: down Haussman came a little red Renault cabriolet, which by all rights should have been at the front. Indy dove into the backseat and instructed the driver to follow M'Greet's taxi. Out the rear window, he saw the stranger flagging a *fiacre*. "Loser," he chortled.

Then he flew forward in the seat as the driver braked hard to avoid an omnibus that had trundled into their path. M'Greet's taxi was gaining distance all the time.

"*Plus vite*," Indy urged the driver after he'd reseated himself. *Faster*. The taxi picked up speed, backfiring whenever the driver shifted gears.

"They are turning, *monsieur*," the driver advised a moment later.

Up ahead, Indy saw M'Greet's taxi making a very sharp right onto boulevard des Italiens. "Take the next right," Indy said.

Rue Laffitte, the base of an isosceles triangle that included Haussman and des Italiens, was a neat shortcut. So neat in fact that Indy's taxi wound up in front of M'Greet's.

"Slow down and let them get ahead of us," Indy instructed the driver.

"*Oui, monsieur.*"

Indy slouched in the seat as M'Greet's taxi, a 1913 black Opel Puppchen, whizzed past. Out the rear window, Indy saw that the *fiacre* the stranger had hailed was trying hard to keep up.

They followed the Opel all the way down boulevard des Capucines, past the Grand Hôtel to the Madeleine, then along Royale and around the place de la Concorde to the Champs-Elysées. Just short of the Arc de Triomphe, the taxi turned left on the rue Galilée.

"Ah, perhaps an assignation, *monsieur*," the driver told Indy after they had gone two blocks. "A tryst, *n'est-ce pas?*"

"How do you mean?"

The driver gestured out the windscreen to the low buildings lining both sides of the narrow street. "This area has many *maisons closes*, you understand—"

"*Bordels*," Indy completed.

"Many, many."

When Indy had asked M'Greet why it was necessary for him to have a separate room in the Grand, she'd told him that the better hotels frowned on admitting gentleman callers to the rooms of lone women. For that reason, lovers often conducted their *affaires d'amour* in private rooms in brothels.

M'Greet's taxi came to a halt at the end of Galilée, close to where it merged with Avenue Kléber—a ten-minute walk from where Indy had spent the afternoon unloading M'Greet's trunks. Indy peered through the windscreen at the building M'Greet and her companion entered.

"Is that a—"

"Yes, *monsieur*," the driver said. "Very *exclusif*."

Indy paid him and hurried furtively down the street. The brothel building was three stories tall, with an arched doorway and balconied windows. A ledge below the third level was adorned with stone representations of the city's coat of arms—the 1210 Seal of the Waterman's Guild, whose members had administered the original township of Paris. Each medallion depicted a crescent-shaped ship with a single mast, from which ran three pairs of riggings. Concentric to the symbol ran the Latin slogan: *Fluctuat nec mergitur*— "She is buffeted by the waves but does not sink."

Marguerite Zelle or Mata Hari? Indy had time to ask himself.

From across the street, he watched for some sign of her in the tall windows; then, when an electric light came on behind the louvered shutters of one of the side rooms on the third floor, he recrossed Galilée and ducked into an alley overlooked by the room. At the same time, he heard a *fiacre* coming down the narrow street and knew without looking that it had to belong to the pot-hatted stranger. How had he caught up, Indy wondered.

He looked up at the backlit shutters and decided that the window could be reached without too much effort. There were enough crates lying about to assemble a starting platform, and the deep joints of the building's *pierre de taille* construction would make for serviceable hand- and toe-holds. Besides, all he really needed to do was get as far as the masonry ledge; from there he could ease himself along to the window itself.

The crate piling went well; and so too did the initial leg of his ascent. He soon realized, however, that he wasn't going to be able to reach the ledge—not, that was, without launching himself off his toes and making a grab for it. Briefly he considered the prospect, then took a breath and jumped, just managing to hook his fingers around the edge of the smooth stone projection. He dangled there for a moment, breaking a sweat as his fingertips began to give out; then he fell, hitting the platform with a resounding crash and rolling straight into a garbage bin.

Fortunately, no one came to the windows to investigate.

"Probably too busy with *other* things," Indy mumbled as he was picking foul-smelling vegetable matter from his khaki jacket and reevaluating the situation.

Nearby he spied a couple of flat crates that had been lashed together with a length of inch-and-a-half-thick rope. He untied the rope, coiled it the way he did his bullwhips, and fastened it to his jacket at the left epaulet. Then he recommenced his climb.

When he reached the site of his abortive launching, he used the rope as a whip to catch the wrought-iron railing of an upper story window. The rope's snake hold on the railing was tenuous at best, but Indy calculated it would hold his weight long enough for him to scramble up onto the ledge.

It did—but just. As he straightened up on the ledge, the rope unwound from the railing and plummeted into the alley. But Indy didn't bother to stop and figure out how he was going to get back down; he was on the ledge now, mission accomplished, and the shuttered window was only a few feet away.

He crept along the narrow perch and peeked through the slats just in time to see M'Greet and General Lyautey in a passionate embrace.

Shaking with anger, Indy made the mistake of trying for a more all-encompassing view by kneeling on the ledge. First one knee slipped, then the other. As he began to fall, his chin struck the window sill and a yelp of pain escaped him. But he managed in the nick of time to wedge his fingers between the downward-pointing slats of the lower portion of the tall shutter.

"What was that?" he heard the general ask.

"It sounded like a little dog," M'Greet said.

"I had better go have a look."

Indy—barely recovered from the sight of the kiss, to say nothing of the "little dog" comment—saw what was coming, but was helpless to prevent it: the building's tall windows opened into the rooms, but the shutters . . .

Lyautey gave a healthy shove to the pair, and Indy found

himself hanging out over the alley, three feet from the wall of the building.

"I don't see anything," the general said from the other side of the opened shutter. He remained at the window a moment, then returned to the room—and M'Greet's arms.

"No, don't touch me there," Indy heard her say.

Not a moment later the slats broke and he fell into the garbage again, frightening two cats who leaped yowling from the bins. Indy kept still in the event Lyautey appeared, but he didn't.

By then Indy had seen enough, or certainly as much as he wanted to. He gave the window one final glance and stamped seething from the alley, trailing organic debris. He made straight for the stranger, who was now standing across the street. Indy passed him by at first, then turned suddenly and forced him up against the wall.

"Who the hell are you?" he said into the man's face.

The man's response was to jab a revolver into Indy's ribs.

Indy took a cautious backward step and had his mouth open to say something when a car pulled up to the curb behind him. The stranger brandished the revolver. "Inside, soldier," he said, gesturing to the rear door of the car.

Here we go again, Indy thought.

26

The identity cards and badges Indy's captors showed were of a different order than the ones the *flics* had carried. Which was perhaps the reason this latest pair of government operatives conveyed him not to the *préfecture de police* on the Ile de la Cité, but to the monumental Ministry of Defense on boulevard St-Germain. And on this occasion, he was escorted to an empty room on the third floor and left there to stew for two hours.

These guys were definitely not the Keystone Kops, Indy told himself while he waited for something to happen. The only pratfalls of the past few hours had been his own.

The man who finally appeared at midnight to question him was small and mean-looking. Close-set eyes in a blockish head, a trim black beard, heavily waxed mustachio, pomaded hair . . . He introduced himself as Captain George Ladoux, but left undisclosed the agency he represented—though everything about the uniform and polished leather belt said regular French Army.

"Corporal Henri Defense," Indy said, rising and saluting. "Attached to the One hundred seventy-third Belgian Infantry, currently posted at Verdun."

"Defense," Ladoux said. "That's an odd name, isn't it?"

"You'll have to take that up with my father's father, sir. But actually my father's—"

"And your enlistment papers show you to be twenty-two years old. Is that correct?"

Indy swallowed. "Not quite twenty-two, sir, no."

The captain appraised him for a moment. "You look a

very young twenty-*one*, in any case. The rigors of war must agree with you, Corporal."

Indy kept his mouth shut.

"Speak up, Corporal. I said the war has apparently been soft on you."

"No, sir, not really, sir."

"You wouldn't lie to me, would you?"

"No, sir."

Ladoux's nostrils flared perceptibly. "Well, then, let me read you something of interest." He opened the folder he had carried in. "Your name is not 'Henri Defense,' and you are certainly not Belgian. You are Henry Jones, seventeen years of age, and you are an American."

Indy stared forward.

"A routine check of your military status showed that your furlough was issued at the behest of a Professor Jacques Levi, who teaches ancient history at the Sorbonne. Monsieur Levi was . . . kind enough to cooperate with our investigation by revealing your true identity."

Ladoux stepped into Indy's line of sight to meet his gaze. "Understand something, Corporal Jones: *Nothing*—no fact, no tidbit of information, no private thought—escapes the notice of this department. So I suggest you dispense with the games and answer my questions in an honest and forthright manner, or risk imprisonment for knowingly fraternizing with an enemy operative."

Indy wet his lips. In spite of all the anger he felt toward M'Greet, he bristled at Ladoux's accusation and felt compelled to defend her. "Sir, I was only warned not to talk about being questioned at the *préfecture*. No one said I was to stay away from her. In fact, Major Twinbury and Major Spesfant requested my assistance in procuring evidence for the case being mounted against Madame Zelle. And I can tell you—in all honesty, sir—that I found nothing in her belongings to—"

"Corporal Jones," Ladoux cut him off. "I'm not the least interested in what you found or what you failed to find among Madame Zelle's belongings. You haven't the slightest notion what's going on here. And now *I* am warning you to keep away from her, is that clear? I am not exaggerating when I say that you risk imprisonment. Moreover, your actions have already made you suspect.''

''What actions, sir? Going to restaurants and fashion shows?''

Ladoux waved the file in Indy's face. ''Perhaps you weren't listening to me earlier: I told you that *nothing* escapes our notice. We know, for example, that you were in the company of the Lafayette Escadrille last night; and that tonight you were observed attempting to spy on the activities of a high-ranking government official. As to the former case, we—meaning you and I, Corporal—we *both* know that aviators and their aeroplanes are of special interest to Madame Zelle. Do you grasp the connection now?''

Indy did, only too clearly. ''But, sir, may I say that you're mistaken if you think Madame Zelle's desire to obtain a travel permit to Vittel has anything to do with the fliers stationed at Contrexéville.''

Ladoux tilted his head to one side and snorted a laugh. ''You've learned about her young Russian lover, is that it?''

''Yes, sir,'' Indy said quietly.

Ladoux grinned. ''Yes, he's just about your age.'' He struck a match to an English pipe and blew smoke in Indy's direction. ''So you have concluded that Madame Zelle's primary motivation for reaching Vittel is this Vladimir de Masloff.''

''I have, sir.''

''Are you familiar with the term 'intoxication,' Corporal? It means to feed an enemy false or stale information. And that, I think, is what Madame Zelle has been doing to you when not feeding you bits of herself.'' Ladoux glared at him. ''She is a highly trained *agent provocateur*, Jones, and you have been her foil—her dupe.''

''Sir, if she *is* a German agent and she knows that she's under surveillance, then why hasn't she attempted to leave France before it's too late?''

Ladoux adopted a world-weary look. ''For two simple

reasons. First, because such an act would confirm our suspicions and poison her future in the espionage community. And, second, because she has herself convinced that her friends and lovers in the Quai D'Orsay can protect her from charges of hostility against the Triple Entente. But in that she is sadly mistaken, Corporal, I can assure you. Her flagrant indiscretions have only made matters worse. She is nothing but an overage, overcompensated courtesan—and a Dutch one at that.'' The captain puffed on his pipe. ''A 'neutral' country,'' he said venomously. ''As if any nation can voluntarily exempt itself from world war. You of all people should know this, Jones—your own nation equivocates. And yet Holland *profits* from the war by dealing with the very people who swept across her border to get to France.''

''But Madame Zelle doesn't think of herself as Dutch,'' Indy said. ''I mean, I know she lies about being Javanese, but she considers herself *parisienne*.''

Ladoux folded his arms across his chest. ''The trollop insults the honor of the République. A real woman does not make a spectacle of herself; she understands that her role is to care for her husband and her children. *La vraie femme* is vulnerable, irrational, and dependent. It is weakness that makes her desirable. Madame Zelle and others of her kind are what left France open to invasion to begin with. There is little hope for our winning the war abroad if we cannot win the battle of the sexes at home. These new women, these emancipated 'feminists,' are responsible for the moral decay that eats away at our society. Divorcing their husbands, going about the city unescorted, fornicating with whomever they please, shouting for shorter work hours, the right to vote, displaying their bodies . . .''

As Indy heard some of his own thoughts from earlier that evening coming back at him, he realized how wrong-headed he'd been. That M'Greet had lied to him was one thing; that women everywhere should be forced to abide by *man*-made rules of conduct was something else again.

He met Ladoux's minatory gaze. ''It's permissible for

men to go about the city unescorted, sir? To, as you say, fornicate with whomever they please? To strike for shorter hours—''

"You sound like a simpering suffragette, Jones. All you Americans do. And yes, it *is* permissible for a man to do these things, because men have always done these things. There are natural and hierarchical differences between men and women, Jones. Someday you'll understand that."

Indy squared his shoulders and composed his reply. "So is Madame Zelle under suspicion because of espionage, sir, or because she is a promiscuous women whose imprudent frankness has started certain ears ringing?"

"Why, you insolent fool," Ladoux said, sneering. "You want the truth? Then I'll give it to you—gladly. Madame Zelle has been with *too many men*. Too many men of influence, here and in Berlin and in Madrid and God only knows where else. And God only knows what information she has overheard from one and passed along to another in the privacy of her many beds. Do you understand now? She is an embarrassment, Corporal, a liability to France."

So that was it, Indy thought. Ladoux wasn't really interested in proof of M'Greet's spying. He was simply looking for an excuse to get rid of her.

"I've had about enough of you, Jones," the captain said. He opened the door and beckoned to someone in the corridor. A moment later Indy was saluting a captain of the military police.

"Corporal Henry Jones, alias Henri Defense," the tall, broad-shouldered officer began. "As of this day, your leave has been canceled. Be advised that you have twenty-four hours to report back to Captain Gautier in Verdun."

Indy's mouth dropped. "B-but . . . you can't!"

"We have," the officer told him. He handed Indy a sealed envelope. "Your rail pass and travel permit for the war zone."

Ladoux smirked. "You are dismissed, Corporal. Good luck in the trenches."

*   *   *

Indy searched for Remy at the Restaurant Chodu, then at the Baboon's Place in Montmartre. A Belgian lieutenant he met at the latter told him that Remy had been booted out of the *maison close*—for ''conduct unbecoming a client''—and suggested that Indy ask at a certain bar in Pigalle.

It was close to four in the morning when Indy finally located the place. No password was required at the entrance, but this time, when he told the doorman that he wasn't carrying a weapon, he was advised how judicious it would be if he were.

A hangout for two-bit *apaches*, cocaine addicts, and street-weary *clochards* and their tricks, the bar was as seedy a barrel house as Indy had ever visited. Dreary French ballads wafted from a poorly functioning gramophone, and the smoky air stank of spilled wine, cigarettes, and urine. But at a back table sat Remy, looking dead to the world. With him were two prostitutes, one of whom was Genevieve from the Baboon's *salon de choix*. The other was painfully slim and had mounds of ragdoll-red hair.

''Ah, Indy,'' Remy said drunkenly, making a valiant effort to rise. Bruises underscored both eyes now, and the rest of his face was puffy from drink and brawling.

''Been making the most of your moment, Don Juan?'' Genevieve asked in the same slurred tone.

Indy ignored her and spoke to Remy. ''I have to talk to you.''

Remy seemed to note Indy's agitation. ''What's made you go up in the air, *mon ami*?''

''They've canceled my leave.''

''What?'' Remy came fully out of the chair this time. ''Mine, too?''

Indy shook his head.

''But why? What happened?''

Indy worked his jaw. ''Because . . . because of a big misunderstanding.''

''Misunderstanding?'' Remy said. ''Between you and what general?''

"I can't go into it," Indy told him. "I just wanted to tell you, so you didn't have to wonder where I was."

Remy showed him a mournful look. "I am so sorry for you, Indy. And this was going to be our great time together."

Indy gulped back a groan of anger, frustration, and more. "I have to go, Remy. I'm expected to be on the early train out of the Gare de l'Est."

Remy kissed him on both cheeks. "I'll miss you."

"Yes, me, too," Genevieve said as Indy was heading for the door.

"But one thing, Indy!" Remy yelled. "You never told me about the woman who stole your heart this time. At least give me her name, *mon ami*, just her name!"

Indy swung around to face him. "*Mata Hari*," he snarled.

Remy, Genevieve, and the other woman exchanged perplexed looks. "Mata Hari, the exotic dancer?" Remy said. Then he guffawed. "Good joke, Indy, good joke indeed!"

27

Indy took it for granted that Captain Ladoux had ordered surveillance on him. He planned his actions carefully, going first by carriage taxi to the Gare de l'Est, then—after losing himself in the early morning crowd—by métro to the place de l'Opéra. He assumed, too, that M'Greet's activities were still being monitored by the two police detectives, Tapier and Boucher, as well as by select members of the Grand staff. So instead of marching past the front desk, he entered the hotel by way of the service entrance he had been forced to use the previous day, and he took the stairway to the third floor.

Up until that point he could always maintain that he had returned for his duffel, which was indeed in the room adjacent to M'Greet's suite. Only when he finally knocked at the door to the apartment did he contradict Ladoux's injunction, even then trusting that Twinbury or some other gadget-crazed intelligence agent had yet to install a hidden listening device.

Indy was well aware of the risks involved, in any case. But in times of love and war, risk was something everyone had to learn to live with; and it was for each person to decide whether his or her actions were justified. In the present instance he needed to hear how M'Greet had justified hers. And, beyond that, he had to warn her about the danger she was in—Ladoux be damned. In no-man's-land he had risked a court martial by waylaying Nivelle's countermand order; now, in the City of Light, it was merely his heart at stake.

M'Greet opened the door after peering at him through the spy hole. She was wearing her silk robe and her blue leather

205

slippers. Her hair was matted, and her face had a drawn and haggard look.

"Henri," she said, putting her arms around him. "I was worried you wouldn't come."

Indy stood stiffly in her embrace, arms at his sides. "Were you worried I'd had enough of your games, or that I was with someone else?"

She pulled back to regard him. "Were you with somebody else, Henri?"

He stepped into the foyer, closing the door behind him. "In a manner of speaking, I was, since I spent most of the night at the Ministry of Defense."

M'Greet shook her head in puzzlement. "I don't understand. Was it a military matter?"

"Oh, absolutely. They had a lot of questions for me."

"Who had a lot of questions?"

"A certain Captain George Ladoux, for one." M'Greet tried to hide her surprise, but Indy saw in her brown eyes that the name had registered. "Ladoux seems to think that I am helping *you* pass aviation secrets to the Germans." He paused briefly. "You're surprised, huh?"

"*Les bras m'en tombent*," she said. "Of course I'm staggered. But it's ridiculous, your passing secrets to me. Where do they get these absurd ideas?"

Indy hardened his scowl. "Maybe they're just wondering why you're sleeping with Minister Lyautey."

"They told you that?"

"They didn't have to."

M'Greet studied him for a second, then frowned in angry revelation. "You followed me last night. How dare you!"

"Why should it bother you if one more person is following you around? You already have two policemen tailing you, and you don't seem to care about them."

"Neither of them is my *lover*, Henri." M'Greet turned on her heel and stormed into the sitting room.

Indy pursued her. "Neither of them is *fool* enough to be your lover."

She whirled on him. "How could you profess to love me and say something like that?"

"Because you've done nothing but lie to me since we've known each other. It's clear as day you have no feelings for me. You're just using me to satisfy your own vanity."

She was speechless for a moment; then she cursed. "Don't flatter yourself, Corporal Defense. When you said you loved me, was that the truth?" She jabbed him in the chest. "From the heart?"

Indy knew he had to hurt her if he was to gain any ground. "No," he said.

M'Greet flinched but rallied quickly. "Oh, so *you* have been lying to *me*, but that's quite all right. Only why did you say you did if it wasn't true?"

"I knew it was what you wanted to hear." He could see by her expression that he had scored—deeply—and it immediately troubled him. "I shouldn't have said that. I mean, it's not that I don't care about you, M'Greet, because I do. That's why I'm here."

She smiled wanly. "What you care about is the pleasure I give you. But aside from that, ask yourself, Henri, if you would have really wanted to hear the truth about me—about my many lovers, past and present? I knew you weren't in love with me. I'm twice your age. My son, had he lived, would be as old as you are now." She regarded him for a moment. "But I did want us to have something separate from my usual life, something special. Was that so terrible of me?"

Indy was growing confused; the lines were less clearly drawn than he'd thought. "But if you wanted us to have something separate and special, why couldn't you have held off sleeping with your other lovers until my leave was up? It was only going to be a week, M'Greet. Instead, you kept me waiting here while you were carrying on with a . . . with an *old man*. I mean, you'd have to be an enemy spy to sleep with him. Ladoux must be right about you."

M'Greet almost smiled. "I won't deny making love with him. But it was *à contrecoeur*, Henri—grudgingly."

"I don't buy it."

"I thought he could help me with the travel permit to Vittel."

"For us," Indy said, ready to go over the top again.

"Who else?"

"How about goddamned Vladimir 'Vadim' de Masloff, for one?"

M'Greet seemed to deflate. On trembling arms, she lowered herself to the sofa and put her face in her hands. "I wondered how you were going to disappoint me, Henri."

"Me, disappoint?"

"Following me, going through my personal belongings . . ." When she looked up at him, her eyes brimmed with acrimony. "*Eh bien, je m'en fiche*," she said, almost offhandedly. "I don't care. You've only helped strengthen my decision to marry Vadim, Henri."

He took one straight to the heart, and fired back. "The name's not 'Henri,' it's Indiana—Indiana Jones. And I'm not Belgian, I'm an American."

"My God," M'Greet said in genuine distress. "My God, you're working for them!"

Indy's brow furrowed. "For who? What are you talking about?"

She skittered to the opposite end of the sofa, as far from him as she could get. "For the police! For the Centralized Intelligence Section!"

"Hold on a minute, I'm not working for anyone!"

"Then why would you use a false name?"

"I—Look, it's a long story—"

"Why did you search my belongings?"

"Because I had to know if what I was hearing was true."

"About my being a spy? Or about my being a courtesan?"

He averted his eyes. "I just don't like being lied to."

M'Greet exhaled relievedly and laughed, more to herself. "You should have told me you were with me for the *dinners*, Indiana. Besides, didn't I make up for those missed meals—in bed?"

"That's not the point. You were with other men when you were supposed to be with me."

She aimed a pitying glance at him. "You're talking like a jealous lover from a true-crime story. I never promised you anything. You had no claim to my fidelity or my life when we weren't together. I have many friends, and they are all demanding of my time."

"Many rich, old friends," Indy said, full of sarcasm.

"Not that old, and unfortunately not that rich."

"Rich enough to pay the rent, I'll wager."

M'Greet looked around for something to throw at him. A vase caught her eye, and she hurled it. Indy ducked, and the thing shattered against the wall.

Artillery, Indy thought.

"You know, I didn't come here to fight with you," he said, straightening. "I don't care about your lovers—you can do what you want."

"I'll *do* what I want—with or without your 'permission,' Corporal."

Indy accepted the rebuke. "But, M'Greet, about Captain Ladoux. He warned me not to see you. He's going to make trouble for you."

She rolled her eyes in exasperation. "He's simply trying to remove you from the picture."

"Don't tell me you and Ladoux—"

"Of course not. But he has asked me to work for him—for the French."

Indy took a moment to consider it. "But—that doesn't make any sense. The British and the Belgians are certain that you're a German agent known as AF44. They're giving Ladoux everything he needs to build a case against you."

M'Greet threw her hands up. "Must *everyone* talk of this spy fever? I'm getting sick to death of it!"

"Were you in Berlin at the start of the war?" Indy pressed.

"What of it?"

"Did you and the chief of German intelligence parade around in an open carriage?"

"I don't even *know* the intelligence chief. I was in the company of a lowly police officer named Griebl on the day war broke out."

"What about the black man on the train from Madrid?"

M'Greet looked at him as though he'd taken leave of his senses. "He happens to be the husband of the Russian dancer Lupchova, who had the berth adjoining mine on the train. The three of us dined together. Wherever did you get these questions?"

"They're not my questions. They're the ones the police are asking. And I don't think your explanations are going to matter much. They've already decided what's true. You're in grave danger." Indy recalled M'Greet's tarot spread but thought better of mentioning it.

"Nothing will happen to me," she was saying. "I have too many willing Prince Charmings."

"It's because of those Prince Charmings that something *will* come of it, M'Greet. Don't you see, your . . . indiscretions have made you a liability."

She glared at him. "My *what*? I will not allow my actions to be judged by their standards—or by those of a jealous lover. I don't take small steps, Indiana, and I never have. I see big, and I act big. I'm not some *hommesse*, ruled by my irrational emotions. I make my own decisions. I am spontaneous, and I speak my mind. You, on the other hand, are a sad little boy masquerading as a man. You hide behind a false identity, you play at being a soldier, then a lover, and now a cuckholded husband!"

"And your entire *life* is a lie," Indy yelled back. "There is no Mata Hari, exotic Javanese dancer. There's only Marguerite Zelle, the Dutch prostitute."

The two of them stood staring at one another for a long moment, stunned, wounded, short of breath. The battle had been fought, and no one had emerged victorious.

"I've been ordered back to the trenches," Indy said at last. "I have to leave Paris this morning."

"I'm sorry," M'Greet told him.

"Yeah, me, too."

She looked at him with sudden, sad compassion. ''Why can't we simply allow ourselves our illusions, Indiana? Life is so much easier when we don't have to confront the hard truths. Life deceives us, and so we in return deceive ourselves and others. It is humanity's karma. And it makes for love as easy as it does war.''

M'Greet spread her arms. ''Come to me, darling. Please. If only for the illusion.''

Indy forced an exhale. *Truce*, he thought, going to her.

An hour later he climbed from the bed, careful not to disturb her sleep. He dressed quickly, gazed at her one last time, and slipped from the room.

On his way to the underground, the duffel over one shoulder, Indy stopped in the place de l'Opéra to turn and look back at the Grand Hôtel. She was there, on her balcony, clutching the silk robe to her throat. He waved, smiled, showed her a brave salute.

And Madame Mata Hari blew him a good-bye kiss.

Epilogue

On October 15, 1917, in the early hours of a cold and rainy Paris morning, Marguerite Zelle was escorted from cell number 12 in the Saint Lazare women's prison and taken via military sedan to the fourteenth-century castle palace of Vincennes, in the eastern suburbs. There, at Caponnière, a field normally reserved for cavalry demonstrations, she was shot to death by a twelve-man squad of Zouaves.

The charge was espionage.

M'Greet's hand-chosen outfit included a pearl gray dress with a wide skirt, silk stockings, a lace *cache-corset*, elegant shoes, a tricorn felt hat, a blue coat, and long gloves that buttoned at the elbow.

She refused the blindfold when it was offered to her. And she thanked the *aspirant* in charge of the Zouaves, smiled at the two nuns who had cared for her during her eight-month imprisonment, and blew a kiss to her dozen executioners. Someone was said to have remarked, "By blue, the lady knows how to die."

One member of the squad fainted before he could pull the trigger. Nevertheless, eleven bullets found their mark, one piercing M'Greet's heart. The *coup de grace* was scarcely necessary, but in keeping with protocol it was delivered.

News of her death reached Indy a month later, in the contested territory of the Middle East. The trial had been conducted in utmost secrecy. But Professor Jacques Levi, whose ear was always to the ground, hinted in his letter that M'Greet was alleged to have sold French military secrets to a German major posted in Madrid. Proof of her crime was apparently obtained by the Eiffel Tower listening post, which intercepted a coded transmission between Madrid and Berlin requesting authorization for the payment to "H 12"—M'Greet.

Knowing how much M'Greet had needed money, Indy could almost believe that she had eventually offered information to the Germans. But surely she had sold them only stale *salon* rumors—that "intoxication" Ladoux had mentioned . . .

The professor likewise detailed some of the stories already in circulation: that M'Greet had enticed into bed the six inspectors who had served the arrest warrant; that the firing squad had been bribed to fire blanks, and M'Greet had been whisked away by her new lover, a man named Pierre de Morissac; that her lawyer had attempted to stay the execution by claiming that M'Greet was carrying his child; that dozens of prominent men had submitted requests for clemency, only to be turned down by Poincaré; that in addition to the alleged intrigue in Madrid, M'Greet had leaked plans for the British Mark I tank to the Germans . . .

New chapters in the growing legend of Mata Hari, Indy told himself. And he wondered what M'Greet might have thought of the veiled and black-garbed women of those desert realms, captive to traditions eons old.

M'Greet was as much a symbol of the mad contradictions of war as of the topsy-turvy spin of the social contract. A changed world was already emerging from the ashes of the former order, and M'Greet had found herself marooned at that perilous intersection of old and new. Captain Ladoux had said as much: there was no place in post-*belle-époque* France for a woman like Marguerite Zelle. She had been ahead of her time—dangerously so for many a small mind. M'Greet had taken big steps.

Indy was sorry he hadn't been her Prince Charming. There had been several women in his life since M'Greet, but he knew she would always remain one of his great loves—the woman who had introduced him to desire and sexuality, his *initiatrice*. And he hoped, should the truth of

her life ever rise to the surface, that history would one day
see her as the larger-than-life personality she was. Until
then, the world would have to content itself with the legend.

Regardless, he and M'Greet would always have Paris.
Indy thought he might even return there when the war
ended, perhaps to settle among the artists and bohemians of
the Latin Quarter and take classes at the Sorbonne.

The never-ending war was still in progress, but there was
some cause for optimism. The German forces had pulled
back from the Hindenburg Line, and Austria had made
peace overtures to the French government.

At the close of 1916, Joffre had been replaced as chief of
staff by Robert-Georges Nivelle, who in turn the following
May had been replaced by Philippe Pétain. It was now
widely believed that President Raymond Poincaré would
soon appoint Clemenceau as prime minister. America had
finally entered the war after the sinking of several merchant
vessels and the discovery of Germany's attempt to form a
secret alliance with Mexico. General Pershing, who had
once tangled with Pancho Villa's rebels, had been chosen to
command the American Expeditionary Force. China and
Cuba had also joined the allied cause.

Revolution had come to Russia in February, and the czar
had abdicated the throne.

And back at home, Buffalo Bill had died. Jass—or
"jazz"—was fast becoming the popular music form; Pro-
hibition had been amended to the Constitution; and 200,000
women had marched in New York City to protest the imprisonment of four suffragettes, arrested for picketing in
front of the White House.

There seemed to be no stopping women now; no stopping
the march for equal rights.

As for Indy, there had been a few changes in his life as
well. He had fought in East Africa and the Congo; worked
for the French embassy in Petrograd during the July riots;
become enmeshed in an intelligence operation in Barcelona
that had him dancing with the Ballet Russe . . .

His life had been filled with action and romance, just as

M'Greet's card reader had predicted—enough to fill pages and pages of the journal he carried. He had participated in upheavals, victories, love, and death on a grand scale. And throughout he had come to understand that amid the manifold uncertainties of the times, the conflicts between nations, the problems between men and women, fathers and sons, individual action could make a difference in the grand scheme of things; that one person could affect the whole, the way a single tipped domino could fell an entire life. There was no choice but to follow your heart, and accept that life itself was a grand adventure.

Setting the letter aside, Indy left the warmth of his tent for the dry coolness of a starry desert night and wept for her, down on his knees in the fine sand.

About the Author

Frequently on the road, James Luceno makes pit stops to write science fiction, action/adventure novels, and the occasional television or film adaptation. He drives a blue Toyota 4Runner and has a mustache.